Clare Atkins has worked as a scriptwriter for many successful television series, including *All Saints, Home and Away, Winners and Losers* and *Wonderland. Nona and Me,* which she wrote while living in Arnhem Land, is her first book.

www.clareatkins.com.au

Nona & Me

Nona & Me

Clare Atkins

Published by Black Inc.,
an imprint of Schwartz Publishing Pty Ltd
37–39 Langridge Street
Collingwood VIC 3066 Australia
email: enquiries@blackincbooks.com
http://www.blackincbooks.com

National Library of Australia Cataloguing-in-Publication entry:

Atkins, Clare, 1980– author.
Nona & me / Clare Atkins.
9781863956895 (paperback)
9781922231680 (ebook)
A823.4

Cover art and design by Astred Hicks, Design Cherry

Some sounds in Yolŋu languages do not conform exactly to English pronunciation. As it has become a written language, new letters have been included that symbolise these sounds.

ŋ	pronounced "ng" as in sung
ä	pronounced like the "a" in father
ḏ, ṯ, ḻ, ṉ	retroflex consonants formed with the bottom of the tip of the tongue curled up to the roof of the mouth

2007

I see her across the school yard. It's like a ghost passing. One second she's there and then she's gone, trailing Mrs Reid around the corner in the direction of the front office. Was it really her? I replay the moment. That glimpse of her determined, upright walk. The set of her face. Her quiet strength. A lot about her has changed, but that hasn't. It has to be her.

Something jabs me in the ribs.

"Hello, Miss Daydream!"

Make that someone. Selena is waving her hand in front of my face. "Rosie, you with us?"

"Sorry."

We are sitting in our usual spot, on the benches near the basketball court. Just close enough to see the boys playing, not so close that we seem desperate. It is May; the wet season has just ended, and everything glows green.

Selena sighs, as if having to repeat herself for a small child. "I was saying, do you want to get ready at my house?"

Anya chimes in. "For Libby's party."

"What time?"

"Whenever your mum can drop you into town."

I hate living out at Yirrkala. It's only a twenty-minute drive from town but it might as well be a different planet.

"I probably can't get there 'til after five. Mum will be working."

"Okay, but no later than that if we want to you-know-what."

Selena grins conspiratorially. She wants to go fridging before the party. She's tried to talk us into it before, but this time she's got an address: the house of some government guy who travels for work. He doesn't have a dog. She's insistent there's no way we'll get caught, but even the idea of it makes me nervous. I've never drunk alcohol before, let alone stolen it. I look away. My gaze drifts to the basketball court.

Selena's brother, Nick, is shooting hoops with his best mate, Benny. He jumps and grabs a rebound, pausing to brush his shaggy brown hair back from his face, before bouncing it back out to half-court. His long, lean body gleams with sweat.

There's a slight irritation in her voice as Selena says loudly, "Can you stop perving on my brother for one second?"

Nick is back at the hoop now. He pauses mid-shot, his blue eyes glinting with amusement. He's obviously heard. Anya giggles.

I turn back to Selena, embarrassed. "I'm listening!"

"What was I saying then?"

"Five at the latest if we want to you-know-what."

She senses my reluctance and says, "It's a Year 12 party. Everyone else will be drinking. Nick will be."

I sneak another glance. He's bouncing the ball in a lazy figure of eight now, laughing as Benny tries to swipe it away. I wonder if he's showing off for my benefit.

"So, are you in?"

Anya says, "I am." She looks smug. We used to be good friends, before Selena.

They're both looking at me now, waiting.

My stomach churns, but I say, "Yeah. Of course."

The bell goes. We pick up our bags and reluctantly meander to class.

Selena falls in beside me. "What are you going to wear, then? And please don't tell me your mum's making you something." She nudges me. "Well?"

"You said don't tell you."

"Oh no. What is it this time? Tie dye? Screen print?"

I mumble a response. Selena leans in closer. "What?"

"Tea towels."

"Tea towels?" Her voice rises to an incredulous shriek. "You can't be serious."

"She's sewing them together to make a dress." I have to smile. It is one of mum's crazier designs.

Selena shoots a look at Anya, who says, "Your mum is so out there."

She's sounding more like Selena every day.

Selena is laughing now. "You're not really going to wear it, are you?"

"I'll wear it as far as your house –"

"I can't wait to see that!"

"– then can I borrow something?"

"If you're nice to me."

Selena is always lending me clothes. She has a cupboard full of dresses by designers I've mostly never heard of. She buys them online or on her frequent family holidays to Darwin, Cairns or overseas. Her dad works at the mine: he's loaded.

Anya says, "Why don't you just tell your mum you want to buy a dress?"

I glare at her. She knows the answer; I can't bring myself

3

to tell Mum I don't want her to sew clothes for me anymore. She's been doing it since I was little. It's her way of convincing herself I'm not a "neglected single-parent child". I used to love her creations, but lately I've felt like it's a tradition I've outgrown.

We move into the History classroom and take our seats. It goes Anya, Selena, me.

Miss Fuller writes in big letters on the board, then turns to face us. "Federation."

Why do teachers always do that? It's up there in capital letters. We can read.

There's a knock at the door. And then Mrs Reid is showing her in. It is her. I knew it. It's Nona. I want to jump up and hug her but I stay glued to my seat. Nona raises her dark eyes and locates me in the sea of uniformed students. She gives me a shy smile. I feel Selena turn in the seat next to me. I don't need to look to see her disbelieving expression: *You know her?*

Nona is wearing a basketball singlet, stretchy purple shorts and worn white thongs. Her legs are tall, black and skinny. Her feet look tough. On her arms, I notice a few dark scars near her shoulders, and wonder what they're from. Her long wavy hair is freshly washed and tied back in a careful ponytail. She could be any Yolŋu girl in this school. But she's not.

There's only one desk empty so she sits up the front.

Mrs Reid smiles warmly at the class. "Everyone, this is Nona. She's joining 10B. She's just moved back here from Elcho Island. Please make her feel welcome."

She gives Nona a reassuring nod. "You need anything, just come and see me."

Nona nods back and Mrs Reid heads out.

Miss Fuller smiles at Nona then launches into a spiel about Federation. It's obvious she's practised this at home. Miss Fuller is young and enthusiastic, a fresh recruit from Melbourne.

Probably came straight from university to Nhulunbuy. She could've done worse than a remote mining town, I guess. She could've been posted to a community school like Yirrkala.

Miss Fuller hands out comprehension sheets, instructing us to pick out the key dates and put them on a timeline. She hesitates at Nona's desk, then squats down next to her, lowering her voice. "Do you want to do this? If you don't want to I can give you an exercise to do with Luke and Ali."

Ali has just arrived here. He's from Iraq. Until now, Luke has been the only Yolŋu kid in our class. Miss Fuller sets special tasks for them because their English isn't great. Half the time Luke's away. The rest he sits there, silent. Sometimes he just walks out. Miss Fuller never asks him where he's going or tells him to come back. She's out of her depth when it comes to Luke.

Ali smiles at Nona, but Luke just keeps staring out the window. I can see one of his skinny feet tapping to an unheard beat. I wonder if Nona and Luke are related and, if so, how.

Nona reaches out and takes the comprehension sheet.

Miss Fuller smiles nervously. "Okay, great."

She gives Nona a pen and paper.

Nona's voice used to be full of laughter, like even her insides were grinning. But now it comes out soft and flat. "You got a pencil?"

"Sorry?"

"Pencil."

"Oh. Yes. Sure."

Miss Fuller gets her one. Selena smirks. She writes on the side of her exercise book, nudging it over so I can read.

What are we – in primary school?

I force a smile. I tell myself the words are harmless, just a joke.

I watch Nona as she starts to work. She begins by colouring in the holes in the letters – the a's, the o's, the d's, the e's. By the end of the lesson they are all filled in. I lean forward and see she's also drawn in the left margin, decorating it with swirls and ... are they turtles? I can't quite make it out from my desk. It's beautiful, though. Shades of grey-lead ocean.

Selena catches me looking and underlines her previous words:

primary school

Miss Fuller passes Nona and sees what she's doing. I wait for a reaction but our teacher just nods and smiles and walks on.

Selena whispers, "Can you imagine if one of *us* did that?"

Selena always talks like that. Us and them. Ŋäpaki and Yolŋu.

She's right, though. If a Ŋäpaki kid – a non-Aboriginal kid – did that Miss Fuller would be telling them to start working or stay and do it in detention.

Selena articulates the question this time. "You know her?"

I want to say yes. I want to say, *She's my sister. She was my best friend*. But I know Selena would find that crazy and I don't want to explain. So I say, "She knows my mum."

"From the art centre?"

I nod, convincing myself it's easier this way.

The bell goes and we throw our timelines onto Miss Fuller's desk as we stream out to our next classes. Selena moves off.

She chose Cert One in Business as an elective, which is ridiculous. She hates anything to do with maths, and thinks the only function of the economy is to determine how much stuff from the US costs online. But her old man said she should do it, so she did. And Anya chose it because Selena did. I couldn't bring myself to study something I'd never use. I figured Hospitality at least might help me get a job in town once I get my P's.

I feel someone touch my arm. I look down and see a dark-brown hand. Long fingernails. A pale palm.

I hear her voice say, "*Yapa*." Sister. And suddenly I'm six years old again. We're in my bedroom holding hands.

I look up at Nona. "Mum said you were back."

"Got here last week."

"Are you living at your grandma's?"

Nona shakes her head. "In Birritjimi. My aunty's house. You remember Tina? She just had a baby, a little boy. We're living with them – me, my mum and the smalls."

I smile at the mention of her two little sisters; they're only a couple of years younger than us, but we always called them the smalls to make ourselves feel bigger. Nona smiles shyly back at me. There is so much to say. So much I want to know. But I can feel Selena and Anya watching us. They're standing outside their classroom, waiting to go in. Selena makes eye contact and frowns, as if to say, *What are you doing?* I remember what school was like before she came. Me and Anya, always on the periphery. Not a real group, just two loners clinging desperately together. It was years ago but it was yesterday. I feel sick.

I turn back to Nona. My words come out abruptly. "I'd better go. See you round."

I see Nona's face fall, a crumple of confusion. And then I'm walking away. I can hear a voice in my head. *Chicken-shit.* But I keep walking.

★

7

The school bus is a cool, air-conditioned bubble. Outside, trimmed green lawns blur into bush as we leave town. There's only a handful of us now. Most of the Ŋäpaki students get off in Nhulunbuy. For the drive to Yirrkala it's just a handful of kids from the primary school and me, Aiden, Mattie and Dhatam' from the high school.

Dhatam' and Mattie are in Year 7. The two girls sit in front of us, swinging their legs. Yolŋu and Ŋäpaki, side by side. They remind me of how things used to be with Nona. I'm almost jealous of their easy companionship.

Dhatam' listens attentively as Mattie discusses the virtues of various hairstyles. "I can do plaits on other people, but I can't do them on myself. I need Mum to do them. Or Dad. But he's not as good."

She swivels around to face her brother, who's sitting beside me. "Is Mum back from her bush trip today, Aiden?"

Aiden doesn't hear. He has headphones on. His hazel eyes are staring out the window. The volume is up so loud I can hear the music from where I'm sitting beside him. I peer at his iPod display. It says "When the War Is Over" by Cold Chisel.

Mattie waves a hand in front of his face. "Aiden!"

He removes one earbud.

"Is Mum getting home today?"

"Yeah."

Their parents are rangers. They moved here from some desert community five years ago. Aiden jams the earbud back in and returns to his window-gazing. Not the most talkative guy, Aiden. Still, I'm grateful for his company. It saves me from sitting alone. I hate being alone. I always feel so conspicuous, like I've got some huge sign on my head that says "loser for life". And even if Aiden's not super-popular, sitting next to him is almost cool because he's in the year above me.

There's only one road from town to Yirrkala. It is fairly

nondescript: almost imperceptible undulations of bitumen and curves of terracotta dirt. Eucalypts punctuated by cycads and the odd termite mound. Signs to the Nhulunbuy tip, the motorcross speedway and the gun club.

I must drive down it a thousand times a year, but today every patch of scrub is etched with memories. There's the turn-off to Rainbow Cliff, where we painted ourselves in *gapan*, smearing the white and orange clay on our bodies in made-up designs. And the airport road that took us to weekend swims at Goanna Lagoon. And the spot where I first tasted *guku*, sweet bush honey scooped straight from the tree into my waiting mouth. Like the road, all my memories lead in one direction. Nona.

There's a crest in the road, where it arcs over the cut red earth of the bauxite mine. From there the drive is straight and flat.

We're close to home now. The parade of signs begins.

Welcome to Yirrkala.

Don't drink and drive.

Kava licence area.

Go slow – kids around.

You are now on Aboriginal land – do you have your access permit?

The bus slows as we turn left into the community. I see that familiar glimpse of gleaming turquoise ocean, palm trees swaying in the breeze. We pass Nona's old house. It is low-slung, clad in blue corrugated iron. A concrete verandah stained with years of dirt and the sweat of living. Her grandmother, Rripipi, still lives there, with a crush of relatives I no longer know.

We turn right up Balnguma Road, drive up the hill past Teacher's Row, and lurch to a stop outside Yirrkala School. I stand and say bye to Aiden, but he hardly registers my farewell. He's off in another, more musical world. I walk up the aisle, thank Tony, the driver, and get off. The heat engulfs me. I walk home, over the crest of the hill, scanning the horizon as I walk. The ocean reaches far into the distance, as if trying to hold hands with the sky. I can't see any fishing trawlers out today.

Before I know it, I'm down the hill and I'm home. Our place is wedged in just behind the art centre, propped up on metal poles. I trudge up the wooden stairs, open the unlocked door, and swing my school bag onto the hallway floor. In the lounge room I turn the ceiling fan on to three, its highest setting, and sink into my favourite armchair. The soft, crumpled velour hugs my back and legs. I close my eyes. Nona's face appears again, her features etched with hurt.

"Hey, darling."

My eyes flick open to see Mum ducking in the back door. She's wearing a red batik bandana to hold her fly-away hair off her flushed face. She moves through the kitchen, to the lounge, and turns the fan down. "It's not that hot."

I sit up, guiltily. "Shouldn't you still be at work?"

"Forgot my lunch so I just popped home. Lucky we live next door, hey?"

I check the clock on the wall. "Mum, it's three o'clock."

"Yeah, it'll be a late lunch. Might just have an easy dinner. Fruit okay?"

"Fine by me."

Mum picks up her forgotten sandwich. "I've had the craziest day, driving all over looking for Waltjan. She was supposed to come in and sign these prints – it has to be done before I can send them off for framing – so, sure enough, she's nowhere to be found. I went out to Ski Beach and Birritjimi … oh, I saw Gulwirri there."

The mention of Nona's mum grabs my attention.

"She seems much better. Well, better than before they left. She said Nona's back at school. Did you see her there?"

"Yeah."

"It's great she's studying again."

I think of Nona's coloured-in letters and swirly margin. "Yeah, it is."

"Do you want to have her over one day? She could catch the bus home with you after school."

"Maybe."

I can feel Mum's eyes on me, questioning. She glances at the clock. "I'd better run. I finally found her in town, blowing money on the pokies at the Arnhem Club. Waltja<u>n</u>, that is. She's over at the art centre signing the things now. I'll be home around five. You want to make us that fruit salad?"

"Sure."

The screen door bangs shut behind her. I'm grateful she's gone.

I turn the fan back up to three again.

★

Will Nona be here today? I try to put her out of my mind, as I get off the school bus and make my way to our usual spot.

As soon as I see them, I know they've been talking about me. Selena and Anya are huddled, heads close together, knees touching, on our bench. They look up as I approach. Selena gives me an easy smile. She has perfect teeth. "Hey, you."

"Hey, yourself."

"We were thinking about going to the pool this arvo. You want to come?"

This is why I hate living in Yirrkala. I used to love it when I was little, when life was all about community. But now it's all about town.

Anya tilts her head, using a sing-song voice. "Nick will be there."

Their in-joke smiles decide me. I can't afford to be left out. "Could I borrow some swimmers?"

"We'll go past my place on the way there."

"Cool. Deal, then."

I smile, trying to look confident, but I'm already dreading the negotiations with Mum.

Selena looks past me, towards the front entrance. I turn to see Nona has just arrived. She's wearing a uniform today, but no shoes. We watch as she walks towards the cultural centre.

And then Selena comes out with it. "Anya said you were best friends with her in primary school."

She says it like she's testing me. I realise this must be what they were talking about. I look at Anya. She gives a small shrug, as if the information just happened to slip out.

"What happened?"

I take a deep breath. "She moved to Elcho. We lost touch."

It's the truth. Good intentions and weekly phone calls dwindled after Nona left for Elcho.

Selena's voice is a mixture of fascination and disgust. "Dad reckons they're totally primitive on Elcho. Did you ever go there?"

I wanted to. To visit Nona. But we never did. "No."

"He went on this massive week-long fishing trip. Moored off Elcho and saw a huge crowd of Aboriginals on the beach. The old ladies were beating their heads with rocks. Blood everywhere, he said."

Anya adopts the expected look of disbelief, which is ridiculous because she's been here since primary school. Her dad's a doctor at the hospital and her mum coordinates the Yolŋu apprenticeship program at the refinery. Anya knows about Yolŋu culture, but now she's not letting on.

"Must've been a funeral." It comes out so soft, I don't know if they hear me.

But they do. Selena nods. "Yeah, obviously. But still — as if you'd beat yourself with a rock. Crazy."

Anya nods in animated agreement. "Totally."

★

Nona has doodled her way through another lesson. This time it's English. I see our teacher, Mr Stephens, pretending not to watch her. He's probably wondering the same thing I am: can Nona write? Would she find it embarrassing if he asked her about it?

The bell rings for lunch. We all gather our books and exit the classroom. Selena passes Nona on her way out. She indicates her bare feet. "What happened to your shoes?"

From the tone of her voice I can't tell if she's making fun of her or innocently asking.

Nona keeps her eyes down and mumbles, "Grew legs."

"What?"

A bit louder now. "Grew legs."

"What does that mean? They got stolen?"

Nona stares at the ground. I can see she feels shame. I can guess what happened. An aunty probably asked to use her shoes that morning. She would've given them to her without blinking. I'd seen it happen heaps of times when we were kids. I think about explaining this to Selena, but by the time I open my mouth Nona has walked off.

Selena says, "Talk about rude."

She watches Nona's retreating back, her eyes narrowed. The last person who offended Selena was Anita White and she's practically a social outcast now. I close my mouth again.

★

"Please, Mum. Pleeeeease."

I hear her sigh through the phone. "I don't want to be driving in and out of town all the time, Rosie. Petrol's expensive."

"I'll earn it back somehow. I'll wash the car."

"We're printing again this afternoon. I can't leave just to pick you up."

"I already told them I'd go."

"Well, you should've asked me first."

"You want me to have no friends."

There's the sound of her smothering a laugh. "Oh, come on –"

I know I'm being melodramatic but I'm desperate. "You always say it doesn't matter that we don't live in town. That you'll drive me in when things are on –"

"This isn't a 'thing', you want to go swimming."

"Yeah – with my friends."

"With Selena."

Mum doesn't like Selena. So I quickly add, "And Anya."

Mum hesitates. She thinks Anya is a good influence, and maybe she was – Before Selena (BS).

"You'll have to catch the bus home."

Hardly anyone catches the public mini-bus. It only runs three times a day and I've never seen a Ŋäpaki person on there. I picture Selena watching in pity and horror as I climb on.

"Mum … come on …"

"If you don't want to do that then just come home. You can go swimming another day."

But I don't want to leave Selena and Anya alone. I already feel out of the loop. "Fine. I'll catch the bus."

I hang up on her before she can say bye.

★

It's a sunny twenty-four degrees at the pool. Some people think the water's getting too cold in May, but I swim all year round. I'm not a team-sports person. I value my underwater thinking time.

Selena and Anya have changed out of their uniforms into short skirts and singlet tops. They're sunbaking on plastic deck-chairs that they've pulled onto the grass near the fence, so they can chat to any boys of interest who pass.

I swim smooth laps, up and back. Reflected light dances like broken eggshells on the pool's pebblecrete floor. My mind tries to untangle the mess of Selena and Nona. What can I do? I don't want them to be enemies. But even if I could get Selena to be civil, what would they talk about? I mentally scroll through the list of things Selena and I usually discuss. Clothes, boys, parties, downloaded movies, other girls. Our favourite foods, teachers, parents, holidays. I can't see Nona relating to any of that stuff.

My thoughts hit pause each time I reach the shallow end. Nick is there, teaching a lone Thai lady to swim. She flounders, her arms slapping the water in clumsy freestyle. Nick's torso and legs stand patiently nearby. I can imagine his calm, level voice coaching her. "That's it. Long, slow strokes."

He's wearing boardies and a rash vest which keeps riding up. On lap ten, I catch a glimpse of something on his lower back. It must be a tattoo. I tell myself I'll swim ten extra laps if it's not the name of a girl. Please don't let it be the name of a girl.

By the time I next hit the shallow end, the Thai lady has disappeared. The lesson must have finished. I see Nick's legs walking towards my lane. I'm about to swim past him when he ducks under the surface and waves. I blush and stop, coming up for air. He's so close beside me I can feel his body heat through the water.

"Hey, Flipper."

That's what he calls me. Flipper. I can't tell if it's affection-ate in a you're-friends-with-my-little-sister way, or if it might mean something more.

"Hey, Nick."

I fumble to take my goggles off. He watches with that amused look in his eyes. I'm sure he knows I have a crush on him.

"You still hanging round with that white trash?"

He nods towards Selena and Anya, grinning at his own joke.

I smile back, forcing myself to stay calm. "Hey, they fol-lowed me here."

"And they won't even get in the water. La-zy. You want to race?"

"I've already done nineteen laps."

"So you're warmed up. I'm not. It'll be even.

I put my goggles back on. "Alright, then – go!"

I push off the wall, giving myself a cheeky head start. The water envelops me, muffling his exclamation. "Hey! Not fair!"

I power forward. He's gaining on me. I push harder and touch the end wall just ahead of him. I'm all gasping smiles.

He dunks me. "Cheat!"

I can feel his skin on my skin. I'm laughing. And gurgling.

Nick pulls away. "I'd better keep going. You're nineteen up on me."

He turns and pushes off. And then he's gone, swimming away. I watch his muscular arms plough through the water, then I turn and get out.

As I join the girls on their deckchairs, Selena shakes her head. She half-loves, half-hates that I've got the hots for her brother. "Flirt."

★

At the pool gates, Anya stops, looking up and down the road for my Mum's troopie. "What time did she say she'd pick you up?"

"She should be here any minute now."

"We'll wait then, yeah?"

Selena sits down on the footpath. Anya takes a seat beside her. I need them gone. The bus will be here any minute. I don't want them to see me catch it; I lied and told them Mum was coming.

"It's cool, guys. You go. She must be running late."

"We're not in a hurry."

"You just want to stay and flirt with Nick."

"Not true."

The bus comes into sight. It's turning the corner now. My stomach sinks.

"Seriously – just go."

"I'm comfy now."

Selena is sitting with her long, fake-tanned legs stretched in front of her in the sun. Her mini-skirt rides up, barely covering her undies. The bus pulls up opposite us. Two Yolŋu men climb out, both in shabby T-shirts, shorts and dusty thongs.

I should be walking over there. I should be getting on. The men cross the road and walk past us. One throws a disapproving glance at Selena's bare legs. The other man looks back, checking her out. I'm embarrassed, but Selena doesn't seem to care.

Three Yolŋu ladies get on the bus. The driver looks around. There's no-one else waiting. No-one except me and I'm on the wrong side of the road and I can't move. The door closes and the bus pulls out from the curb. I watch it drive away.

"Maybe you should call her," says Anya.

I can't think of a good excuse not to, so I dial Mum, hoping she won't answer. She does. I try to sound casual, off-hand.

"Mum, hi. I'm outside the pool. Where are you?"

I am grateful Selena and Anya can't hear what Mum says on the other end.

"What are you talking about? I'm screenprinting. You know that."

"Are you still picking me up?"

"We agreed you'd catch the bus."

My friends are watching. I grasp for words that fit my lie. "You said you'd be here at four."

"I did not. Rosie, have you got amnesia? I said catch the bus."

"Yeah, I think it's four now. I just saw the bus drive away. That comes at four, doesn't it?"

"You missed it?!"

I check to see if either of them heard Mum's screech. They didn't. I proceed calmly. "It's fine. If you come now you'll be here in twenty minutes."

"I'm busy! I thought I made that clear to you. I can't just drop everything to come and pick you up."

"I'll just wait here."

"Rosie!"

"See you soon. Thanks, Mum."

I hang up, knowing she'll come. That was the last bus: there's no other way to get home except pay fifty bucks to one of the Iraqi cab drivers or hitch.

I shrug at the girls. "She got caught up at work. She'll be here in twenty."

"Want to get something to eat?"

"Sure."

We cross the road and walk down the concrete path, through the town green, towards Woolworths. We debate whether to buy something from the supermarket or get greasy chips from the takeaway shop. The greasy chips win.

A few Yolŋu ladies are sitting nearby on the benches beneath the palm trees. Yolŋu often hang around here. I heard

Mrs Reid say once they wait to humbug family for food or money when they come out of the supermarket.

I'm trying not to look at them when I hear a deep raspy voice. "Mätjala."

The name hits me deep in my stomach. My Yolŋu name. I haven't heard it in so long. But I keep walking.

"Rosie."

Gulwirri is beside me now. I can't ignore her. Her eyes slide off mine, down to the ground. They are slightly bloodshot and her breath smells sour, like off grapes. She touches my arm. "You got a few dollars?"

"I don't have any on me. Sorry."

I keep walking, leaving Gulwirri behind me. Selena's eyes are round. "Who was that?"

I shrug.

"She knew your name." Selena gives Anya a look as if to say, *What's the big secret?*

Anya says, "Isn't that ...?"

I don't want to give her the satisfaction of saying it so I beat her to it. "It's Nona's mum."

Selena nods, mentally storing the information away for later. My gut is churning.

2.

—

1995

We are curled up by the campfire. Nona and me. I am almost asleep in my mother's arms. The smell of smoke and cooked fish lingers. Soft melodies wash through me, as my Dad and Bolu, Nona's dad, strum softly on their guitars.

My mum moves to stand. She gently eases my small body onto the mat, and lays my head on Gulwirri's lap, right beside Nona. I feel the tickle of her hair in my face and open my eyes. She is sleeping, hugged against her mum's legs.

I let my gaze wander. The embers glow dull orange, like crocodile eyes in the dark. Mum adds wood to the fire, stoking it until it transforms into a bright yellow frenzy. Dad looks up at her as he plays, his fingers tracing invisible patterns on the neck of his guitar. Their eyes meet and he smiles. It is a look of pure love.

I feel Gulwirri bend down towards me. She murmurs in my ear, "Sleep, *Waku*." Sleep, my child. I nestle into her and she strokes my hair, soft and rhythmic. She starts to hum. Her voice weaves in with the guitar. I close my eyes again.

3.

2007

Nona hasn't been at school for a week. But she's here today. She slides in the door as our Science teacher, Ms Bamkin, is setting up for the lesson. "Okay, class, today I thought we'd start with an experiment."

Whispered "yeses" around the room.

"We're going to cook an egg in ethanol. Ethanol is basically what?"

John Lane grins. "Piss."

"And its more socially acceptable name?"

"Alcohol."

"Thank you, Anya."

Charlie Mack mimes drinking from a bottle. *Glug, glug, glug.*

Ms Bamkin uses his joke to make a point. "Yes, I thought we'd do this one just in case any of you are thinking about drinking."

I freeze. Look down at my blank page. Does she know about Selena's plan to fridge? Is she talking to me?

"Of course, given that you're all fifteen or sixteen, it would be illegal, but on top of that it's not good for you. Your brains are still growing."

Charlie grins. "Well, some of ours are."

"Speak for yourself, Mack."

Everyone is laughing. Ms Bamkin tries to keep a straight face. "If you even think about drinking, remember this experiment – if alcohol can cook an egg, imagine what it does to your insides."

Selena nudges me, in mock seriousness. "Don't worry. We're superhuman."

I can't help but smile. She grins back, as Ms Bamkin continues. "Okay, everyone get a beaker out then come and get an egg. You'll also need to measure yourself 100ml of ethanol. It's up the front here."

Selena, Anya and I are lab partners. Anya is super-smart, not that you'd know it from the way she's been acting lately. She says she wants to be a doctor like her dad. I think I want to be an artist. Selena is typically dismissive of the whole what-do-you-want-to-do-when-you-leave-school question. She jokes that she's going to be one of those B-list celebrities who get invited to all the parties but don't actually have to do anything.

I get the egg and Anya pulls a beaker from the cupboard. Selena goes to measure the ethanol at Ms Bamkin's desk. There are only two bottles so people have to wait their turn. I see Nona hanging back as Selena dodges her way to the front.

John Lane fills his beaker and hands Selena the bottle. He winks. "Careful with that. It's pretty potent."

He's got a crush on Selena. He doesn't stand a chance. She lets him hope, though, and smiles back as she wafts the invisible fumes towards her nose. She inhales deeply, then raises her voice. "Maybe we should steal some and sell it to the drunks outside Woolworths. Make a fortune."

John looks uncomfortable but forces a laugh. It is Selena, after all. She pours a measure of ethanol then looks up, past John and the other students, to Nona.

Calmly, deliberately, she says, "What do you think, Nona? Reckon they'd buy it?"

Nona shrinks into herself, as if trying to disappear. I look around to see who else has heard. John catches my eye, in an uneasy plea for help. Behind him, Ali looks confused. Anya appears to be absorbed in her textbook. Ms Bamkin is busy helping Charlie; she hasn't heard.

Selena carries her ethanol back to our desk and sits on the lab stool beside me. I can't meet her eye. She nudges me. "What?"

I keep my gaze straight ahead. I crack the egg into the beaker.

"It was just a joke, Rosie. Geez, lighten up."

Most days I let her comments pass. I tell myself she isn't hurting anyone. But today is different. I can feel Nona's ache from across the room.

A few seconds later, Nona walks out. No one stops her.

★

Selena nudges me at lunchtime. "What's with you? You've been quiet all morning."

I look away. She persists. "You're not still mad about the ethanol thing, are you?"

My silence provides the answer.

Selena is disbelieving. "Why are you taking this so seriously?"

Anya says, "Because it's Nona, of course."

I'm quick to reply. "That's not it."

Selena says, "I don't get it. How could you guys possibly have been friends?"

"Not just friends. Besties," says Anya.

Selena's immaculate eyebrows arc up. "Besties?"

I shift. "I wouldn't put it exactly like that."

"Well, then – how would you put it?"

Her eyes are on me. I squirm. "You're changing the subject. What you said in Science was racist."

"How is it racist? There *are* drunks outside Woolworths. I didn't say they were any particular colour."

"You directed it at Nona."

"So this *is* about Nona."

"You say stuff like that all the time. It's always 'us' and 'them'."

"You've never said anything about it before."

Anya leans in. "Because it wasn't about Nona before."

I snap at her. "Can you shut up about Nona?"

Selena folds her arms across her chest. "I'm not racist."

Her voice is harder now. I start to waver. "You are sometimes."

"I'm friends with Jennifer and Lotu."

"You call Jennifer 'The Asian'."

"She calls herself that too!"

I try to downscale the accusation. "Anti-Yolŋu, then."

"I liked Wilson."

Wilson was in our class in Year 8. He got sent to boarding school in Darwin in Year 9.

"That doesn't count. He came every day, and he spoke perfect English."

"So Aborigines can't do that? Now who's being racist?"

"Don't be stupid."

"Give me another example, then."

"What about when Luke walks out of class? You always make comments."

"The double standard pisses me off. How come he's allowed to walk out and we're not? It's nothing to do with him being Aboriginal."

"Yolŋu."

"Whatever. I'm not racist."

"Okay. Can we drop the subject now?"

"Not until you take it back. I'm not racist."

Her face suddenly warps into a suppressed smile, like she's thought of something funny. "You want me to prove it? I like black guys."

I look at her sceptically.

She's grinning now. "I do! I would totally sleep with Snoop Dogg or Jay-Z."

She's winding me up and Anya snorts with laughter.

Selena is on a roll. "I'd be their white ho handbag any day. Just get them out here. Jay-Z in Nhulunbuy – can you imagine?"

I'm trying hard not to laugh, but she catches sight of the hint of a smile surfacing on my lips. "I saw that. You were laughing."

"No, I wasn't."

"You were!"

I shake my head. "You're an idiot, Selena."

She slings an arm around my shoulder and hugs me to her, grinning. "Lucky you love me."

★

Nona isn't in Maths. Or History.

As we're walking to English, I tell the girls I'm going to the loo. As a gesture of peace, Selena offers to come with me. I tell her not to worry about it. We're fine.

"Really?" she asks.

"Really."

I detour past the cultural centre and peer through one of the windows. There's a big Bob Marley poster on the wall, surrounded by photos of Yolŋu kids from our school. Mrs Reid is at her desk, marking papers or something. In the middle of the room, there's an island of desks surrounded by chairs. Luke is sitting there, with a few younger Yolŋu kids. He's playing the *yidaki*. That's what they call the didgeridoo up here. The sound comes out strong and full. Short bursts then sustained rhythms. The music takes me on a journey. He's good. Very good. But I'm not here for Luke. I scan the room.

And then I see her. She's standing by herself in the kitchen area, eating a piece of toast. Her face looks blank, withdrawn. Guilt overwhelms me. I step away from the window and look out at the playground. A single blue-winged kookaburra swoops across the cloudless sky and perches in the mango tree near the Science labs.

My mobile beeps in my pocket. I pull it out. It's a message from Selena.

You fallen in? ;-)

I am almost relieved as I turn and head back to my friends.

★

I sketch the outline carefully in pencil, then mix the perfect shade of blue-grey for the wings. The brush glides across my paper, leaving a wash of colour. Paint bleeds and blurs, dark in places, light in others. The world narrows to what's in front of me. My kookaburra takes shape. My breath slows. Up and down. Around. It follows the rhythm of the paintbrush in my hand. I dab at the palette. I'm running out of black paint. I look up. The spell is broken.

Next to me, Anya and Selena are mucking around. Art is my favourite subject, but they only chose it because they thought it'd be a bludge.

Selena pretends to slip and dabs paint on Anya's page. "Oops. Sorry."

"You ruined my artwork!"

"You call that art?"

"Shut up."

"What's it meant to be anyway?"

"A crocodile. Can't you tell?"

"I thought it was a giant green poo."

Giggles and shoves. Our Art teacher glares, and is about to reprimand them when there's a knock at the door. It's Mrs Reid. She leans into the room. "Ms Naylor, could I borrow Selena for a moment?"

"Sure."

Selena puts down her paintbrush and follows Mrs Reid out.

I frown over at Anya; what could that be about? She shrugs, but looks concerned.

I turn back to my kookaburra and try to lose myself in painting again. I fail.

★

Selena is waiting at my locker after school. Her face is blotchy red. Her eyes harden when she sees me coming. She gets straight to the point. "Was it you?"

"What?"

"Did you tell them?"

"What are you talking about? Are you okay?"

"Apparently someone in our Science class felt 'uncomfortable' about my 'racist comment'." Her fingers insert angry quotation marks in the air.

"I didn't say anything."

"Then who was it?"

"How would I know? What happened with Mrs Reid?"

"She took me to Mrs Seville's office."

My stomach sinks at the thought of the principal being involved.

"What did she say?"

"She's calling my parents. Big deal. Like they're going to care."

I know she's not just saying this to appear cool. When we studied Yolŋu Matha, the local Indigenous language, for a term in Year 8, Selena's dad, Mr Bell, sent a note in asking why we couldn't learn a "useful language". He's not going to care about some slur about alcohol.

I try to calm her down. "Then it doesn't matter, right? It's not like you're going to be in trouble."

"Was it you?"

"Selena, I wouldn't —"

"Not even for your bestie? Your so-called *sister*?"

She sees the surprise in my face. "Anya told me the full story. We were just waiting for you to 'fess up."

"There's nothing to confess to —"

"Then why didn't you tell me about it?"

"There was nothing to tell —"

"The whole thing's ridiculous anyway. How can you be sisters? She's black and you're white."

I avoid the question. "I didn't dob you in today."

Her eyes search out mine. "How do I know you're not lying?"

"I wouldn't."

"You lied about Nona —"

"I didn't lie. I omitted."

"I thought I could trust you." Her voice wavers.

"You can."

A bead of perspiration drips down my temple. I need her to believe me. I don't want to lose her. I can't lose her. "You're my best friend, Selena."

"Am I?"

She fiddles with her skirt, staring out at the sky. She looks vulnerable. I've only seen her like this once before. It was in Year 8, not long after she arrived. She'd sat with a group of girls who call themselves the Elites. After two weeks their leader, Stephanie, voted her out. Selena claimed it was because she was threatened, scared of the competition, and maybe she was right. Selena was pretty and confident, with all the imported cool of Sydney. Whatever the reason, Anya and I were secretly glad. Selena came and sat with us. We became a real group. We became someones.

Selena's eyes are teary. "What about Nona?"

I hurry to reassure her. "Yolŋu families adopt people. That's just what they do. The whole sister thing, it doesn't mean anything. We were kids. I don't even know her anymore."

I see Selena's shoulders relax slightly. "That's what I figured. Anya was just saying …"

"Forget Anya."

I realise I've been holding my breath. I breathe out. "Are we okay?"

"Yeah."

She pulls me into a hug. I hold her tight. She holds me tighter.

As we turn to go, I see Nona waiting on a chair outside Mrs Reid's office. She couldn't be more than three metres away. She stands, avoiding my gaze, and walks off in the opposite direction. My heart sinks. I can tell she's heard it all.

4.

1996

We are following Rripipi up a small stream. Bony fingers of mangrove reach towards us, grasping for the water's edge. We walk slowly, feeling the ooze of sticky mud envelop our feet as we walk.

Nona stops just in front of me, and calls out, *"Momo, dhän'pala!"*

Rripipi looks back at us, holding out a thin piece of wood she's been carrying. "You want the stick?"

Nona says, *"Yaka."*

She's already twisting her feet deeper into the mud. She pokes her bum out and wiggles it from side to side. I giggle and she grins at me and sticks her bum out even further and twists, twists, twists. "Look! It's the *dhän'pala* dance!"

I laugh out loud. Rripipi and the other old ladies look over and smile. Nona's cousins point and grin. Some start to copy.

The dark brown sand at Nona's feet has cracked into small faultlines now, like a miniature earthquake has taken place. She kicks some to one side, then reaches down and pulls up a fist of mud. She rinses it in the stream, then holds her open palm out towards me. On it is a large golden shell, covered in ridges that darken as they orbit down and out, ending in closed lips.

Rripipi claps her hands, and beams at Nona. *"Manymak, gaminyarr!"*

It is the biggest mud mussel I've ever seen.

Rripipi gestures me towards her. "Mätjala, one for you there."

She uses her bottom lip to point to the side of the stream. "See that?"

She makes the shape of a curved mound with her hand, but I can't see anything except sand, pointy new mangrove shoots and scattered longbum shells.

I take a step. Ripples rush forward, as if fleeing from my legs. And then I see it. The smallest bend in the water. A tiny liquid wrinkle, shimmering in the sun.

I leap eagerly towards it and twist my feet in. I want to copy Nona. I do her *dhän'pala* dance. I wiggle my bum just like she did. Nona starts laughing. And then I'm laughing too and she's slapping her leg and hooting and I can't concentrate at all. She's doubled over now, almost rolling in the mud, and Rripipi is telling her to get up, don't be so silly, she's covered in mud, but she's not listening, she can hardly hear her, we're both in hysterics and we're laughing, laughing, laughing.

5.

2007

"Go!"

We bolt from our hiding place in the bushes and run towards the darkened house. My heart is pounding. There's a street light behind us. I see my faint shadow cross the perfectly cut grass. Selena is in front, Anya just behind her. I'm last. We race towards the carport, desperate to conceal ourselves, and bang. A sensor light flicks on. *Shit.* Why did I let Selena talk me into this? I'm panicking. "Selena."

She waves me back. "Shhh."

She puts a hand over the gate and feels for the latch. *Come on, come on, come on.* Click. She finds it and pushes the gate open. We hurry through, relieved to blend back into darkness.

Selena says, "It's cool. No-one saw us."

I'm not so sure. I stand still, listening. A sprinkler shoots repetitive jets of spray next door. A dog barks somewhere in the distance. After ten long seconds, the sensor light clicks off.

I move back to the gate and look out at the street. The neighbours' houses are silent. I can see a TV flickering through a window across the road. They're watching *Home and Away.*

There are no yells of "Stop!" or "Who's there?" No-one has seen us. Phew.

I hear Selena whisper – "Guys" – and realise Anya is beside me, looking out. She looks as terrified as I feel. I feel a pang of sympathy for her before I remember her smug smile this afternoon.

Anya seems to be recalling the same thing. "If Rosie's too scared, we can go just the two of us, Selena." She straightens her back, shrugging off nerves, as she makes her way through the carport to the back of the house. I follow her. We round the corner and see Selena, illuminated in the glow of a fridge light.

She grins at us. "Hallelujah."

In front of her are rows of beer, a few casks of wine and a doorful of Coke Zero. She pulls out one of the beers. It has a foreign label. Maybe German? Selena smiles. "Benny said this guy had good taste."

Benny fridged this place a month ago. He's the one who gave Selena the idea. The man who lives here obviously hasn't learned because – lucky for us – he hasn't put a lock on the fridge.

Anya pulls her backpack off and hands it to Selena. She loads it with as many beers as she can fit, then zips it shut and gives it back to Anya. She tosses me a cask of wine to carry and grabs three cans of Coke Zero. Then we get the hell out of there.

★

The beer is warm and bitter. I have to stop myself from spitting it out. I think of that egg, scrambled in ethanol. Ms Bamkin's experiment worked.

Libby's house is packed, bursting with bodies and beats. I am standing with Selena, Anya, Nick and Benny. The boys have their own entourage. Two Year 11 girls hover next to them, trying to catch their attention. Benny hardly notices them. His eyes are on Selena. They've been flirting for months now. Tonight, she has dressed to impress. She's wearing a bright red strapless dress she ordered online. It clings to her curves, and ends elegantly mid-calf. Anya's is the same style, in aqua, probably a size or two smaller. She's petite; her hem touches the ground when she walks. She looks good, though. Confident in colour. I feel like the odd one out in a simple black dress borrowed from Selena before we went fridging. Still, at least I'm not wearing Mum's tea-towel creation.

Nick raises his voice above the music, leaning in towards Selena. "Where'd you get the beers from?"

"Magic. Found them outside our house."

"Yeah, right. Did you fridge them?"

He looks annoyed.

Selena meets Benny's eyes and grins. They say it at the same time, "4 Cassia Close." Then they burst out laughing.

Nick isn't impressed. "What if you'd been caught?"

"No-one was home. Don't pretend you've never done it," says Selena.

"That's not the point."

"Oh, come on, Nick. You can't seriously be mad about me taking a few beers. You did heaps worse than that in Sydney."

The Year 11s giggle flirtatiously. "Really? Like what?"

I'm curious, waiting to hear his answer, but he ignores them and turns to his mate. "Benny, don't corrupt my sister."

Benny can't stop smiling at Selena. "I haven't been able to – until now."

Selena smiles back at him. "Maybe tonight's your lucky night."

Benny takes a swig of his beer, probably trying to swallow his drool before it drips down his chin. Nick looks at me. "Did you all go?"

Before I can answer, Anya jumps in, laughing. "Rosie was shitting herself. You should've seen her."

Nick frowns. "I didn't take you for the break-and-enter type, Flipper."

"Trust me. She's not."

Anya's interjections are annoying me. I manage to find my voice. "Maybe you don't know me that well."

It has just the right dose of challenge. I've surprised myself. I've surprised Nick. I can't tell if that's good or bad.

Beyoncé's "Single Ladies (Put a Ring on It)" comes on, and Selena squeals. "I love this song! Let's dance!"

She drags Anya and me away from the boys, out onto the dance floor. Well, she drags me. Anya goes willingly. She and Selena are incredible dancers. They both do classes at the Arafura Dance Association after school. Another thing I can't do because I don't live in town. The training shows in the way their bodies move. They absorb the rhythms and translate them into sexy movement. Sometimes they even do short semi-choreographed routines. I silently curse Mum for making us live in Yirrkala, as I tap my feet from side to side. I am careful to keep a smile plastered on my face, as if I'm having fun.

I sneak a glance back at Nick and Benny. The Year 11s have drifted away, and the boys are now having a heated discussion about something – probably Selena. After a minute, Nick turns and storms off. Benny joins us on the dance floor. He looks willing to put a ring on it. He looks like, right now, he'd do anything for Selena.

★

Selena and Benny are pashing on a couch inside. His hands keep rubbing her ass like he's expecting a genie to emerge and grant him three wishes. I'm in the kitchen with Anya. She's found some orange juice in Libby's fridge and is sloshing it into a cup along with some of our stolen cask wine.

She slurs a little as she says, "This'll make it taste better."

She slams the bottle down, spilling juice onto the bench. She picks up the plastic cup and takes a sip. "Yeah, better. Way better. Try it."

It looks like piss. I reluctantly take a sip. It's sickly sweet.

She's looking at me expectantly. "Better, yeah?"

"A little bit."

We lean against the bench together. Anya takes another swig and nods out towards the party. "This is cool, huh?"

"I feel a bit sick."

She ignores me, off on her own drunk tangent. "Two years ago, did you ever think that we'd be here?"

I know she's talking about BS. I try to joke it off. "You mean, like, right here? Drinking piss in Libby Davidson's kitchen?"

Anya hardly hears me. "This is a cool party."

Her voice has a tone of wonder. It makes me suddenly sad. I lean over the kitchen bench to check if Selena and Benny have come up for air. They haven't. I see tongues.

I nod towards them, a bit embarrassed. "What are we going to do with them?"

Anya giggles. "Find them a room."

She's swaying slightly ... or is that me?

Nick enters the kitchen, discards an empty bottle and grabs another beer from the fridge. I attempt conversation. "You having a good night?"

"Not really. Thinking of heading off soon."

I'm about to ask him why, when Selena drags Benny over by the hand. "So Benny and I were talking –"

This strikes Anya as hilarious. "Really? When?"

She cacks herself. Selena continues, unperturbed. "Should we all go back to our house?"

Selena's parents are away for the weekend, fishing on their boat. We all got ready at her house earlier. The plan was always for us girls to stay there overnight. But now it looks like Benny's coming. And Nick will be home too. My heart starts beating faster, harder, louder. I try to sound relaxed. "You want to go now?"

Nick sculls most of his beer, then says, "May as well."

Selena and Benny start to stagger towards the front door. Anya follows them out. I'm frozen to the spot. Nick looks at me. "You coming?"

I manage to nod.

And then it happens. Nick Bell takes my hand. He holds it firmly, warm in his, and starts to lead me out of the party. I see the two Year 11 girls watching us go. I know there'll be gossip, but I don't care. I'm holding hands with Nick Bell. The guy every girl at school wants. I'm invincible. Superhuman.

★

The air outside the house is warm and still. The night sky glows deep blue-black. Nick drops my hand and fishes keys out of his back pocket. His ute is parked straight in front of the house.

Benny sees this and yells, "Rockstar park!"

Nick's expression remains stony. I haven't seen him like this before and it makes me uneasy. I try to joke him out of it. "Since when do rockstars have green P's?"

If Nick hears me he doesn't respond. He presses the button on his key and the Hilux doors click open. I'm suddenly nervous. "You sure you're okay to drive?"

"It's not far."

I can hear Mum's voice saying, *Do not get in that car!*

I ignore it.

Selena and Benny are arm in arm, propping each other up as they walk. I check in with Selena.

"You okay?"

"I'm good. Great. Fan-fucking-tastic." She dissolves into giggles. We ease her and Benny into the back seat and they start pashing again. Anya reluctantly climbs in after them, giving me a look that says, *You owe me.*

I get into the front seat. Nick slams the driver's door shut behind him and crunches the gears into first. He sees me watching, and mutters an irritated "I'm fine!"

The Hilux lurches forward. Nick and Selena's house is only a few blocks away. I watch the neighbourhood slide by my window. The identical low concrete houses and carefully watered lawns. Boats parked in driveways. Trampolines, their netting faded, destroyed by the intense sun.

My head is throbbing now. I'm relieved when we pull up outside Nick's house. The front wheel grates on the curb as he comes to a stop.

Selena slurs, "Home sweet home."

I let Anya deal with her and Benny, and follow Nick to the front door. He's fumbling with the keys in the lock. I'm starting to think he's drunker than he's letting on.

I say, "Want me to try?"

He hands me the keys and I aim them for the lock. But the slot keeps moving, swaying from side to side. It ripples, as if underwater. The key hits metal again and I realise Nick is watching me, amused. "Lucky you're here to help."

"Shut up." But I'm smiling.

And so is Nick. He takes the key from me and after two more tries he gets it. The key slots into the hole and he turns it, pushing the door open. I enter behind him, leaving the door open for the others.

I have been here heaps of times with Selena, but every time

I enter I feel a strange kind of awe. It is like visiting a city department store; the house is filled with expensive, oversized items. A massive leather sofa fills most of the lounge room. A flatscreen TV takes up a whole wall. There's a fridge with three doors and a built-in icemaker.

It makes our place look like a half-empty shack.

Nick starts to walk down the corridor. I ask, "Where are you going?"

"My room."

I hesitate, unsure what that means. Does he want to be alone? It doesn't sound like an invitation.

Benny and Selena stagger into the lounge room and collapse onto the massive couch, their bodies coiled together like a twist of rope. Anya closes the front door behind her.

Nick is about to disappear into his room, when he looks back at me. "You coming?"

I know Anya will kill me for leaving her with the lovebirds but I can't say no. I've waited years for this. Nick Bell. Inviting me into his bedroom. I have to see what's going to happen.

I start down the hallway. Out of habit, I almost veer into Selena's room, but I stop myself and keep walking, telling myself this is real. It's really happening. It is.

Nick's is the next room along. I find him sitting on the bed, his back against the wall, knees angled up in front of him. I've only been in here once before. About a year ago, I snuck in one night when I was staying at Selena's. I wasn't taking any risks – I knew Nick was out – but it felt daring, like I was breaking in. I remember just standing there, looking around me. The room was illuminated by a street light outside. I felt like I was getting a glimpse into Nick's soul. The music he liked: The White Stripes, The Killers, Red Hot Chili Peppers. His interests: street art, skating, snowboarding, surfing. I already knew he liked some of these things, but seeing them plastered on a wall in front of you is different. It's like a declaration. A manifesto: *These are the things I care about.*

Looking around me now, I notice he's added a few more posters. The crashing waves are still there, but next to them is a corner dedicated to busty blonde girls in bikinis. I hope they're not his type because I don't look like any of them. I have dark hair, pale freckly skin and green eyes. Dad's parents were Dutch missionaries and Mum's family came from Ireland. I think they came to Australia during the potato famine. I'm lean, but my boobs would barely be a quarter of the size of those of any of the girls on the posters. And I don't wear bikinis: they're not good for swimming laps and I'm always paranoid the top will fall off.

Nick is looking at me. I realise I'm hovering in the doorway. I take a step into the room. Should I sit on his bed? Would that make me seem more relaxed? Or would he just think I'm being easy? I stay standing and make awkward conversation. "You didn't mind leaving the party early?"

"Had a crap day anyway."

"Something happen?"

He shrugs, not wanting to talk about it. "You coming in or what?" He pats the bed next to him.

I sit down. I can feel him watching me. I'm radiating nerves.

"You okay?"

"Yeah."

"Ever drunk before?"

"First time."

Saying it out loud makes me feel young, immature. He's in Year 12. He's probably done this hundreds of times. In fact, I know he has. I've seen him drunk at heaps of parties, hanging out with his mates and senior girls. He's never paid me much attention at parties … until now.

Our eyes meet. He leans in slowly and kisses me lightly on

the lips. It's perfectly romantic. I can hardly believe I'm here. He reaches out and pulls me closer. This time he kisses harder. His tongue presses my lips apart. I try to hide my surprise. I've only ever kissed one boy before (Xavier Martin) and it wasn't anything like this. I try to keep up. Our tongues play hide-and-seek and Twister. His body presses me back. I feel his hands at my shoulders, pulling my dress straps down, touching my bra. My head is spinning. What the hell is happening? It's too much, too fast.

Then Nick's on top of me, grinding into my pelvis. I can feel him hard against me. I am pinned to his mattress. I can hardly breathe. My thoughts are a blur. What did I expect? He's in Year 12. He probably does this all the time. Does he really like me? *Oh my God. He's taking my bra off.* He knows how to undo the back. He's definitely done this before. "Stop."

"Rosie, come on."

"Nick."

"You like me, don't you?"

I edge my body back from his, trying to get my thoughts straight. "Of course I do but – stop."

I push him back. He groans. "I thought this was what you wanted."

I can't bring myself to reply. I feel like crying. Our flirting at the pool. The banter when I've seen him at his house. Is that what he thought it was about? Just sex?

He rolls onto his back, frustrated. I pull the top of my dress up again and lie beside him, uneasy.

Nick rubs his eyes. "I'm wasted. We started drinking early at Skate Park."

Is this his version of a disclaimer? An excuse to get rid of me?

"Do you want me to go?" My voice comes out as a half-whisper. I wonder what Selena, Benny and Anya are doing out in the lounge room right now.

Nick exhales loudly. "No, stay."

"I can see what the others are doing –"

"It's fine, Rosie."

"Or if you want to go back to the party –"

"I don't. Told you – I didn't feel like being there anyway."

He sits up, seeming to come to a decision. "Let's watch something."

Nick has some old *Simpsons* episodes downloaded on his laptop. We watch them, side by side on his bed. I can feel the alcohol swirling through my body. The cartoons seem hilarious. I relax. We laugh. We laugh at the same things. We pay each other out. I give as good as I get. I am gutsy, emboldened. This time *I* kiss *him*. This time it feels real. This time he doesn't push me.

Somewhere, in between episodes, I say, "*This* is what I wanted."

Nick looks surprised. "Yeah?"

"Yeah."

He puts his arm around me and pulls me closer. We keep watching. We watch five episodes.

Eventually Nick passes out. He rolls over, curling his body away from me. His shorts ride down just a little and I can see the full tattoo in the middle of his back, just above his bum crack. It's five small stars. The Southern Cross.

6.

1996

We are standing at the ocean's edge, holding plastic bags. It is a dark, moonless night, but the stars are bright. We watch as the men wade into the shallows to fish. I can just make out their silhouettes, spears in hand, phosphoresence trails in their wake.

I try to pick out the shapes of the men I know best. Bolu is in front, solid and tall. Then Dad, lean and wiry, holding an unlit torch. Then Nona's older brothers, Jimmy, cocky and upright, and behind him Lomu, gentle and quiet.

Dad clicks his torch on. A bright white beam splits the dark. He shines it on the water then quickly turns it off again. They are looking for *wäkun*, mullet.

The group veer away from us, moving further up the beach. I hear Nona "hmmph" beside me. She wanted to go with them. Jimmy had teased her. "Girls can't come. Anyway, you too baby. Too small."

Lomu was kinder. He gave us a shy smile as they departed. "I'll catch us a big one, *neh?*"

I feel warm lips of water kissing my toes, then a rough hand on my shoulder. Rripipi is behind us, one arm around Nona, one around me. She gently squeezes us together, looking up at the dark blue sky. Her voice is a deep, gravelly whisper. "See those stars there? They're *Yirritja*, just like this land. Just like Bawaka. And you know that place over there? Yalangbara? That's *Dhuwa*. Everything is either *Yirritja* or *Dhuwa*. Two sides of the one thing. Like *yothu-yindi*. Mother and child. It's what holds everyone and everything together. The stars, the water, you, me …"

Nona says, "I'm *Yirritja*."

I ask, "What am I?"

Rripipi says, "You're *Yirritja* too. Same as Nona. Same as this land and those stars."

I feel Nona's warm arm pressed flat against mine.

I stare up at the stars. They glow a little bit brighter.

<u>7</u>.

2007

I wake up, groggy and hot. Nick isn't there and for a moment I wonder if he's done a runner. Then I remember this is his house. And his bed. You can't run from your own place ... can you?

I get up slowly, my head already throbbing. In the glare of morning I notice things I didn't see last night. A pile of clothes shoved into the base of his built-in wardrobe. A surfboard tucked away in the corner. A UAC guide, lying open on his desk. There's something circled there. I look closer. Business. Sydney Uni. He doesn't strike me as a business type at all.

I make my way up the corridor, past Selena's closed bedroom door, and into the lounge room, where Anya is passed out on the sofa, snoring. She's alone, which means the lovers must be in the bedroom. Process of deduction.

I tiptoe past Anya to the kitchen. I can hear someone banging around. Nick is at the stove burning something that smells like bacon. He has headphones on and is quietly chanting words under his breath. I recognise the lyrics to "Stronger" by Kanye West.

I approach slowly, unsure where I now stand. Are we going out or was it just a one-off fling? How drunk was he? Does he remember? Does he really like me?

He looks up and sees me watching. He removes his headphones. Sheepish. Caught out. "Didn't want to wake you."

My whole body seizes up. Panic.

"What time is it?"

"Ten."

"Oh no. Mum's picking me up at ten thirty."

"It's cool. Don't freak out."

I touch my hair. It's messy and tangled. I hate to think what I look like. Nick reads my mind and says, "Have a quick shower. I'll make this bacon and egg roll to go."

Even in my stressed state, I notice the surly Nick from last night is gone.

I say, "You're in a better mood this morning."

Nick grins. "Am I?"

My gut unclenches. Things seem to be okay between us. I'm smiling as I turn to go to the bathroom, then I notice the state of the lounge. Anya is surrounded by beer bottles. The whole place stinks. Nick follows my gaze. "I'll hide the evidence too. Just go and shower."

I've never been more grateful.

I grab a towel from the hallway cupboard as I head to the bathroom. I lock the door behind me and jump in the shower, letting the hot water run over me. Steam fills the room. I draw a heart on the glass shower screen and try it out, just to see what it looks like.

R.G. 4 N.B.

Then I rub it out.

★

I emerge from the bathroom, showered and changed. Nick has tidied up the lounge room and opened the windows. The smell is gone, and so is Anya. I grin. "Where'd you hide Anya?"

"Mum and Dad's room."

He hands me a chargrilled bacon and egg roll. I take an enormous bite and BBQ sauce dribbles down my arm. I lick it off and we both laugh. He holds out a glass of fizzy red stuff. "Berocca. Trust me. It's the best. How's your head?"

"Feels like … scrambled egg."

"Let me guess – you're in Ms Bamkin's Science class?"

I nod, smiling. It's easy between us. None of the awkwardness I was worried about. But I still don't know – are we just friends now? Or more?

Through the front window, we see Mum's battered old troopie pull up outside the house. We hear it too. The crunch of gears, screech of brakes. I'm suddenly aware of how shabby our car must look to Nick. The scratched paint, the red dirt sprayed up its dented sides. I give Nick a small, embarrassed smile. Nick looks almost amused. "Your mum's here."

I take another quick bite of bacon and grab my things together. My head starts pounding all over again. I stop and hold my forehead. Nick says, "Slow down! What's the rush?"

But I don't want him to meet her. I don't want her to meet him. And I can't explain why, maybe not even to myself.

I move quickly down the corridor and open Selena's door, quiet as can be. Benny is sprawled out, taking up most of the double bed, wearing just boxers. Selena is … is she naked under that sheet? I try to keep my eyes averted while I sneak in and extract my bag. As I'm emerging I hear Mum slam the troopie door outside. Nick comes out of the kitchen, holding something up. I squint a little then realise what it is. Mum's tea-towel dress.

47

He's grinning. "Is this yours?"

"Where'd you find it?"

"In the laundry. I was looking for a tea towel and I think I found ten."

I grab it off him and stuff it in my bag.

Nick can't contain his laughter now. "Is that a dress?"

"No."

"It looked like a dress. Did you make that?"

"No! Shut up!"

He's laughing hysterically.

I can see Mum walking up the driveway. I start for the door, desperate to head her off.

"I'd better run."

Nick is still grinning. "No kiss goodbye?"

I turn to face him, unsure. Is he joking? I don't want to run back and kiss him if he is. But I don't want to snub him if he's not. I can hear Mum's footsteps approaching the front door.

Nick makes the decision for me. He walks straight up to me and kisses me on the lips. "See you soon, yeah?"

My heart is singing as I step out the door, quickly shutting it behind me. Mum is one step away from knocking. She stops, surprised to see me appear.

I say, "Hello."

She looks confused. I quickly make up an excuse. "The other girls are still sleeping."

"Ah."

We walk to the car and get in. I sneak a look back at the house, hoping for another glimpse of Nick, but I can't see him.

Mum starts the rattly engine, and asks, "How was the party?"

"Good."

She glances over at me. "You look tired."

I don't usually lie to my mum. I never need to. But today I do. "We stayed up talking."

She wrinkles her nose. "What's that smell?"

"What smell?"

"Your breath."

I freeze. I didn't get to brush my teeth. I can't tell – do I smell of beer? Or Anya's wine and orange concoction?

She takes another sniff. "BBQ sauce."

I'm so relieved I laugh. "I had a bacon and egg roll for breakfast."

"I thought you said the girls were still sleeping?"

I swear, mothers have a sixth sense. She never asks me this many questions. It's like she smells my lies along with the BBQ sauce. I cover quickly, "They are. I just made one for myself. I was starving."

She notices the tea-towel dress poking out the top of my bag. "Did people like the dress?"

I try to keep a straight face as I say, "Loved it. Total hit."

★

It's Monday morning and I'm walking into the school yard. I feel like everyone is watching, talking about me behind cupped hands. *Did you hear what happened at Libby's party? Nick Bell and Rosie Grains hooked up. She's had a crush on him forever.*

Then I remind myself that no-one else knows what happened, beyond us leaving together. Just me and Nick. And Benny and the girls. Both Selena and Anya called for the goss on Sunday. I told Anya the basics; Selena got the full story. She was a bit grossed out at the thought of her brother jumping on me, but decided her sisterly disgust was a small price to pay if Nick and I become a real couple and can double-date with her and Benny.

I head towards our spot on the benches. Even from a distance I can see that Nick and Benny are already there, playing basketball. My stomach somersaults. Nick shoots a hoop and announces his victory with a loud holler. I'm almost holding my breath as he looks up at me and, yes, winks. Acknowledgement. Encouragement? Is it possible that we might become an actual couple? I've never had a real boyfriend before. Xavier Martin hardly counts – we only kissed once last year, just before he moved to Perth.

Selena and Anya are grinning as I sit down next to them. I have a sudden flashback to how things were when Nona arrived. The girls huddled here, talking about me in whispers. Things couldn't be more different now. Selena hugs me like we haven't seen each other in years. Anya moves back to make room for me in the middle, forcing a smile. I can tell she's feeling on the outer. I know because, until lately, that's been me. Three isn't a good number for a group of girls. Someone's always left out.

Nick comes over and sits on the bench parallel to ours, slinging one leg either side. He grins at me, "Morning."

Benny sits down right behind Selena and wraps her in a hug. She squeals and shoves him away. "Gross! You're all sweaty!"

But they're laughing.

Benny leans in and kisses Selena. Anya pretends to throw up. "No PDAs, please."

"You're just jealous."

It's a standard retort from Selena; she uses it all the time. But today Anya pulls back a little. "Yeah, I'm really jealous. Why couldn't someone dry-hump me in front of everyone at the party?"

She means it as a joke, but doesn't manage to hide the bite in her voice.

Nick says, "Oooooo."

Benny says, "Please. We were a little classier than that."

Selena is not impressed. "Benny, you'd better start asking your friends who wants to hook up with Anya."

It's a classic Selena put-down. Backhanded. Slightly ambiguous.

Anya tries to pretend it's all still just jokes. "Not necessary."

"Oh no. I insist."

I look from Selena to Anya and back again, wondering what will happen next. The bell goes.

Benny kisses Selena goodbye, teasing Anya with a "No tongues this time. That okay with the PDA police?"

Selena shoots Anya a look, daring her to answer.

Nick falls in next to me. He lets his fingers graze mine. "See you at recess?"

I inhale delight. "Yes. Here?"

"Where else?"

He reaches out, tucks a strand of hair behind my ear, and he's gone.

Recess. Here. Today they are two of the sweetest words in the English language.

8.

1997

We're standing outside the transition classroom of Nhulunbuy Primary. Me, Nona, our mums and the smalls. The sky is an ominous dark grey, heavy with rain. I am dressed in a brand-new school uniform; the tag scratches at the back of my neck. Shiny black shoes pinch my toes. I eye Nona's bare feet enviously.

Other kids and their parents hurry past, and disappear inside. Mum holds her hand out towards me. "Come on. Let's go in."

Nona's voice is small. "Bye, Rosie."

Tears well in my eyes. Panic floods my chest. "I don't want to ... Mummy ... please don't make me go ..."

Mum crouches down and folds me in her arms. "Rosie, everyone's gotta go to school. Nona will be starting tomorrow."

"I want to go with Nona."

She tucks my hair back behind my ears. "Oh, darling. You know you going to Top School wouldn't work ..."

Top School is in Yirrkala. It's bilingual. They teach in

Yolŋu Matha and English.

I look at Mum with pleading eyes. "Then why can't Nona come here?"

Gulwirri's voice is gentle but firm. "Nona has to learn in her own language. It's important for her. To be strong."

I know she won't relent. Gulwirri works at Top School as an assistant teacher. There's no way that Nona won't go there.

My cheeks are wet with tears.

Nona says, "Don't cry, *yapa*. I can see you after school."

Gulwirri nods. "*Yo*. Every day."

I look out at the playground. The smalls have run off and are playing on the slide. Yumalil laughs as she helps Lilaba up the steps. They slide down together, one in front of the other. I feel a deep yearning in my chest.

A few spits of rain hit my cheeks.

I look back at Mum and take her hand.

I follow her, slowly, inside.

9.

2007

I text Nick. Nick texts me. Just stuff like:

Wot R U doing now?

Science :-(

BLTs 4 lunch @ canteen. Want me 2 get U 1 2?

YES. YUM.

But these silly little things make my day. Every time I feel my phone vibrate with a message, my heart starts dancing. It's been a twenty-four-seven disco lately.

At home, Mum starts to get suspicious.

Beep beep. I quick-draw my phone.

"Is that Selena again?"

"Um, Anya."

She is less likely to get annoyed if she thinks it's Anya. I'm not ready to tell her about Nick. Not until I know we're a definite, steady couple. We've sat together at school both days this week, but he hasn't mentioned the weekend, let alone the

D word (date). Still, it's only Tuesday. There's still hope.

Over dinner with Mum and Graham, I feel my mobile vibrate. I try to sneak my phone out of my pocket and Mum finally snaps.

"For God's sake, put that thing away! We're eating dinner here."

She glances at Graham for backup, but he just looks amused. Graham's her boyfriend. There have been a couple since Dad. It's hard in a community like this; people pass through. I get that. None of my primary-school friends stuck around more than a few years. Lily moved to Perth, and Evie to Karratha. Dana went to boarding school in Queensland. That's how we ended up, floating and lost, just me and Anya, in Year 7.

Graham's been working as a doctor at the clinic for almost six months now. I know Mum is hoping he'll renew his contract and stay. I have to admit, he's a catch for an old guy – smart, with a dry sense of humour and twinkly eyes.

He's teasing now. "Teenagers, huh?"

Graham can always get a smile out of Mum. She shakes her head. "Well, honestly."

Graham says, "We had a staff dinner down in Melbourne before I left. One of the younger nurses just sat on her phone the whole time, laughing at messages that came in and replying. At a staff dinner! As we were eating the meal, and during the toasts. She didn't seem to think it was rude at all."

"That's the thing, isn't it? They don't even know," says Mum.

I roll my eyes. "I know, okay?"

Mum finishes her mouthful of steak. "Then why do you do it?"

"Because … what if it's something important?"

"That Anya forgot to tell you in the last ten texts?"

Graham is laughing as he says, "Give her a break, Jen. Go on, check your phone."

They're both looking at me now. I open the message and read it. It says:

Slo cooked lamb 4 dinner. My fave. Wot R U having?

Mum prompts, "Well? Is it important?"

I tuck the phone back into my pocket. "No."

"There you go. No phones at the dinner table," says Mum. "Put your phone where I can see it, please."

I reluctantly place it next to me on the table.

Mum says, "Not there. Put it away somewhere."

"Geez, fussy!"

As I move it to the kitchen bench, the phone vibrates again. I sneak a glance at the screen. It's another message from Nick.

The rest of dinner is torture. I shovel it down, as fast as I can, listening to Mum and Graham rave on about the pros and cons of technology and how all teenagers are tech-addicts. Then I put my empty plate on the sink, grab my phone from the bench and sprint back to my room. I open Nick's message. Please, please, please let it be about the weekend. It's not. It's a reference to *The Simpsons*. It just says:

Flanders!!

This is something we've started doing, texting quotes from stuff we watched on Saturday night. I smile and text back:

Doh!

We could go on like this all night. And we do.

★

Dad calls every Wednesday night at seven thirty, just after the news. It's one of the few things he and Mum still have in common – they both *love* the ABC. Which is lucky for them, because it's one of the only channels that gets reception in Yirrkala. I keep begging Mum to get Foxtel but she says it's "not in the budget", which really means "I like having a monopoly over the TV."

Tonight, she clicks off the news just as our landline starts to ring. I know it's him, so I pick up the phone and put on a horrified voice as I say, "Did you see that story about Christmas Island? More boat people jumping the queue."

I'm joking, of course. Dad hates that expression. He's a total lefty. I can hear the smile in his voice as he counters, "Coming in the back door."

"Taking the place of real refugees."

"Shame!"

His low, throaty chuckle reverberates through the phone. "What's happening in Yirrkala?"

He always asks this, and the truth is, I never know. After Nona left, I stopped spending real time in the community. Bush trips weren't the same, so I stopped going. Now I pretty much just go from home to the bus stop into town. I wave at local people, but I never stop to talk. I don't know what I'd say if I did.

Dad is waiting for an answer, so I say, "I'd have to consult the expert on that one."

I call out, "Mum, what's happening in Yirrkala?"

She calls back from the kitchen. "Actually, sad news today. That old lady died. You know the one in the red house? Ganiwu's grandma."

When someone dies here you're not allowed to say their name. Cultural reasons. I relay the news. Dad knows exactly who she's talking about anyway. "She's been sick for a while, hasn't she?"

I don't want to become stuck in the middle of a conversation about people I hardly know, so I say, "Do you want to talk to Mum about it?"

Dad is quick to answer. He and Mum generally avoid talking. "No, no. It's okay. How are you, anyway, blossom?"

"Good."

"How's school?"

"You know. Just the usual."

I take the cordless phone into my room and shut the door so Mum can't hear – hypothetically, anyway, since the walls in our house are thin fibro and stop thirty centimetres short of the ceiling. Mum reckons it's to allow ventilation, but I'm convinced it's to torture teenagers by eliminating any sense of privacy.

My voice is almost a whisper as I get to the juicy bit. "Except … I've kind of started seeing someone."

"You mean like a boyfriend?"

"I don't know yet."

"Who is he?"

"Selena's brother."

"Ah, the infamous Selena." Dad's never met Selena, but he's heard a lot about her. Unlike with Mum, I tell him almost everything.

"His name's Nick. He's in Year 12."

"Year 12?"

I can hear the concern in his voice, so I quickly add, "He's really nice, Dad. You'd like him."

I'm not entirely sure that's true, but it's a fair bet Dad will never meet Nick. Dad lives in an Aboriginal community that's even more remote than ours. It's called Yilpara and is about three hours south of here, AKA in the middle of nowhere. In the dry season, when the road's open, he drives up once a month to get supplies. We usually meet up for a coffee or a milkshake after school, but he's always keen to head off so he doesn't have to do the whole drive back in the dark. I can't imagine him hanging around just to meet my boyfriend.

Dad asks, "What's he into?"

I think of my dad's interests: music, culture, Indigenous politics, carpentry. I want him to like the idea of Nick, so I think of his posters and say, "He likes … nature (*surfing*) and people (*girls*) and art (*graffiti*)."

It's half-true.

"Does your mum like him?"

"Um, I haven't really told her about him yet."

"Rosie …"

"I don't know if it's serious."

"You called him your boyfriend."

"No, I didn't. I said I don't know yet."

"Semantics."

"You know what Mum's like. Remember when I told her I liked Andrew Miller in Year 6?"

"Not really."

Dad left us when I was in Year 2 so he's a bit vague on anything after that.

"She made this huge big deal about it and kept asking me every day if I'd talked to him yet and teasing me about having a crush and asking if I wanted her to invite him and his parents over for dinner. It was excruciating. And so uncool. She's not like you, Dad."

"Is that a compliment to me or an insult to your mother?"

"Both?"

"You should give her a chance, blossom. She wants to know about your life – that's no big crime."

"We just don't have that kind of relationship."

"What kind of relationship do you have, then?"

"She talks, I listen. Not the other way around." My words

have gradually dried up, between when Nona left for Elcho and now, while Mum's have expanded to fill the silence.

Dad sighs. "Well, at least you're talking to me, I guess."

"Exactly."

I change the subject, raising my voice to normal pitch again. "What's happening in Yilpara?"

His voice becomes animated. "It's crazy here at the moment, Rosie. There's so much positive stuff going on. We want to trial this tourism thing, kind of like what they do in Bawaka now. Having tourists and corporates come and visit and experience Yolŋu culture."

I'm only part listening as I say, "Sounds good."

"And the Blue Mud Bay case is progressing. It could be a real breakthough – if we win sea rights …"

A message beeps on my mobile. Nick.

Want 2 hang out on Sat?

Finally! I text back, grinning, as I "mmm" and "right" and "yeah" to Dad.

4 sure.

Dad talks on, not even noticing that I'm hardly listening now. Once you get him talking about Yilpara politics, he can go on forever.

By the time he says goodbye, I've confirmed the time and location of hanging out with Nick, and exchanged several *Simpsons* quotes. 10am. His place. Mmm … donuts. Lisa, it's your birthday.

★

A 10am date is safe. There's no obligation to get romantic if it doesn't work out. At least, that's what I figure Nick is thinking. Still, I'm glad he's invited me. I'm pretty sure this counts as a date. Maybe. Sort of.

When I arrive, it looks like my theory is right. Nick has gone for safety in numbers too. Selena and Benny are there, swimming in the Bells' backyard pool. Selena and I swap faux-casual greetings.

"Hey."

"Hey, yourself."

"I didn't know you were going to be here."

Selena laughs. "I do live here."

"Yeah, of course, but …" I let the sentence dwindle into silence. It's not that I'm unhappy to see Selena, I just wanted to be alone with Nick.

Selena splashes me. "Get in! You brought your swimmers, right?"

"No."

"Nick, why didn't you tell Rosie to bring her swimmers, you doofus?"

Nick throws the insult back at her. "Because I didn't know we were having a pool party, Barbie."

Selena is sarcastic. "Haha."

I look at Nick, hopeful. "You didn't know they were going to be here?"

"Benny just told me yesterday."

Nick invited me on Wednesday. Maybe it's not a safety-in-numbers conspiracy after all.

Benny says, "You could skinny-dip."

"Get out of here!" Selena dunks him. They go under, laughing, a tangle of tanned skin, bikini and boardshorts. Nick and I swap an awkward smile.

When Selena regains her breath she says, "Borrow some of mine. You know where they are."

I nod and head into the house. The kitchen is full of the waft of golden syrup. Mrs Bell smiles when she sees me enter. "I hope you like Anzac bikkies."

"Who doesn't? I'm just grabbing some swimmers."

"Of course, love. Go for it."

I've spent so much time here over the past two years that it's like a second home. I wonder if Mrs Bell knows today is different. Today I'm not here as Selena's best friend. Today I'm here as Nick's potential girlfriend.

In Selena's room, I dig through her drawer of swimmers. They are all bikinis: tiny triangles, strings and small plastic clips. Her black one-piece is nowhere in sight. I open the window and call out to her. "Where's your one-piece?"

"Think I left it at school."

I can hear her laughing as I shut the window again. She's probably explaining my bikini-phobia now. I'm blushing as I turn back to the drawer and pick out the one that looks like it will give the most coverage.

I put it on and study my body in Selena's full-length mirror. The aqua halter-neck makes my boobs look bigger than they are. My stomach is so pale it is almost transparent. The flesh of my hips bulges slightly over the top of the skimpy bottoms. I grab a beach towel from the hallway cupboard and wrap it tightly around my waist as I head back out to the pool.

Selena lets out a low whistle as I emerge. I dump the towel and make a quick dash for the pool. As I slip in, Nick ducks under the surface and swims towards me. His body is submarine, fragmented by the light. His hands grab at my waist as he surfaces beside me. I push him away, self-conscious, but before I know what's happening, his wet lips are on mine.

Selena is squealing, "No BDAs, no BDAs!"

I try to ignore her and focus on the kiss. It is warm and a little slobbery. His tongue licks my lips. This is the kiss right here. The one I need to remember. The one that makes us a couple. It's broad daylight. There's no alcohol involved. He must mean it ... right?

We pull apart to see Mrs Bell standing there with a plate of warm Anzacs in her hand. She looks taken aback. "Well ..."

Selena swims over to her mum's side. She takes two biscuits and passes one to Benny. She doesn't notice Mrs Bell's frown, as she says, "Yum, thanks, Mum."

Nick says, "What the hell is a BDA?"

Selena grins. "Brotherly display of affection."

"You're a dork." Nick reaches over and grabs a cookie.

Mrs Bell holds the plate out to me. "Rosie?"

I catch her eye and feel suddenly, inexplicably, nervous. "I'm right, thanks."

She leaves the plate on the outdoor table and makes her way back inside.

Nick moves in beside me. "No cookie? You're crazy."

I glance towards the house and see Mrs Bell watching us from the kitchen window. I wonder what she is thinking.

★

I'm walking hand in hand with Nick, down the breezeway near the English rooms. It's official now. Everyone knows we're together. Selena and Benny walk behind us, arms around each other's waists. Anya is next to me, but she doesn't fit on the narrow path. She has to walk with one shoe on the grass. I can tell this annoys her by the way she bangs each pole with her hand as she passes, as if she wants us to be aware that she is sacrificing her walking pleasure for the benefit of the group.

Mrs Reid approaches, taking a short cut across the lawn to catch us up. "Rosie, can I have a word?"

We all stop. Five heads swivel towards her.

I move to one side, as the others wait nearby.

She says, "I was just wondering … you know your friend Nona?"

Her name hits me like a blow to the stomach. "Sorry?"

"The girl from Elcho Island. She started here in May?"

I'm silent.

She continues prompting, trying to jog my memory. "She only came for a few days."

I can tell Selena is eavesdropping, so I act vague. "Uh, yeah?"

"I was just wondering if you'd heard from her?"

She looks hopeful. I don't know how Mrs Reid manages to stay so positive. She's the cultural liaison person. It's her job to keep Yolŋu enrolments up, but everyone knows they're falling. It's not her fault, though. I want to help her, but I can feel my friends looking at me so I shake my head as she continues. "I've tried to contact her mum but I haven't had any luck. I'm still hoping Nona will come back to school. I wanted to make sure she didn't drop out because of … things that happened."

Her voice is hard. She throws a glance towards Selena, who quickly pretends to be engrossed in her fingernails.

I say, "I don't know, Miss. Sorry."

Mrs Reid hesitates. "Okay. I just thought … doesn't matter."

She gives me a tight smile and turns to go.

I rejoin the group.

"What was that about?" asks Nick.

I opt to feign ignorance. "I don't know."

★

Mum is cleaning the bathroom, which is never a good sign. Cleaning isn't a practicality for Mum, it's therapy. She's wearing rubber gloves and her hair is tied back in a matted mess. She calls out as I enter the front door. "Hey, you. How was school today?"

"Fine."

"Just fine?"

"Uh, yeah ... You're home early."

"Gave myself an early mark."

"Everything okay?"

I wait for her to spill all. I'm expecting some disaster at work, or an update about Graham deciding whether to stay or go. She finishes scrubbing the ring around the bath and stands, looking straight at me. "I got a call from your *momu*, actually."

I'm suddenly nervous. "Rripipi?"

Mum nods. "She's just back from doing some translating for the courts in Darwin. And she noticed Nona hanging around, not going to school. When she asked her about it Nona said she heard you say something upsetting to your Ŋäpaki friends. Do you know what that might be?"

There is no good answer. Either she already knows and is testing me, or she's genuinely asking. I take the cop-out option: silence. Mum peels off her rubber gloves. "Something about Nona not really being our family? That she doesn't mean anything to you?"

I'm sure guilt is scrawled across my face.

"I've never been so ashamed, Rosie. They're our family. They adopted us. That means something to them. Hell, it means something to me. It's not a plaything. Family is family. They don't deny each other. As Rripipi put it – they don't *raki-gulkthun*, break that string, that bond."

I know she's right. There's no excuse. She looks at me, disappointed. "Have you got anything to say?"

65

"I ... I didn't know ... I didn't mean ... maybe she heard it out of context ..."

"What possible context could justify disowning your sister, Rosie?"

I turn and stare out the window, refusing to meet her accusing glare. My eyes are flooded with shame.

"I don't care if you find something embarrassing or uncool ... or even if a family member approaches you and they're drunk or out of control ... I never want to hear about you denying our family again. Is that clear?"

I nod.

"I want to hear you say it."

"I promise. It won't happen again."

10.

1997

We are in the bath, surrounded by clouds of bubbles. We scoop them up, piling them on our shoulders, our heads, our noses. Nona looks hilarious. We giggle and grin. She takes a deep breath and blows at the bubbles on my head. A blob dribbles onto my back, while the rest explode into the air like dandelion spores.

Nona grins. "Let's do washing."

I don't know what she's talking about but I say, "Okay."

She reaches out of the bath, grabs her T-shirt and shorts, and pulls them into the water. I watch with wide eyes. This will get us into trouble, for sure. But Nona doesn't seem to care. She grabs the bar of soap and starts to scrub. Her T-shirt becomes a foamy lather. Her eyes sparkle with fun. "Get your dress."

I can hear Mum and Guḻwirri talking in the lounge, and the smalls laughing as they jump on Mum and Dad's bed. Dad's away, teaching in Garrthalala. He only comes home on weekends.

I make a decision and grab my dress. Nona hands me the soap and I get to work. I'm concentrating so hard that I don't hear Mum come in. Suddenly she's above us. "Time to get out, girls. It's Yumalil and Lilaba's turn."

We look up, guiltily. She frowns at our wet, soapy clothes. Then her face softens. "Oh good. You did the washing for us."

She's smiling. I breathe a sigh of relief.

"Come on, then. Hop out."

We stand up. I see Nona's gleaming dark body next to mine. I say, "Wait. Nona's still dirty."

Mum looks at Nona, confused. "She looks fine to me."

"But her skin. It's black."

Mum seems to hold her breath. She glances around, like she's checking if anyone else has heard. I can hear Gulwirri humming from the kitchen now, as she does the washing up. Someone turns the TV on, probably one of Nona's big brothers.

Mum looks back at me. "Rosie … just because someone has dark skin doesn't mean they're dirty." She hesitates, then asks, "Did someone tell you that?"

"Jessica. From school. She said black people smell 'cause they're dirty."

Nona scowls. "I'm not dirty. Tell her she's a *bäŋu bunydji*."

Despite Mum's serious expression, I smile. *Bäŋu bunydji* is Nona's latest favourite insult. It means you have no bum.

Mum gives me a warning look, and I quickly stop smiling. She lowers her voice. "Rosie. Don't ever say that again, okay? Okay?"

I know that tone. It means I've done something really wrong. I nod agreement.

Mum says, "We'll talk about this later."

I feel my face flood with shame. I can't bring myself to meet Nona's eyes. I know if I do, I'll start crying. We climb out of the bath, leaving our clothes in a sodden pile. Mum wraps us in soft purple towels, and I hurry to my room. Nona follows me in, and then I'm sobbing hot tears. I wipe my eyes, wishing they'd stop, or that Nona would stop looking at me, or that I could disappear.

Nona watches, then spits in the palm of her hand. She wipes the glob of saliva on her forearm, rubs it back and forth, then holds it out towards me.

Her voice is soft and kind. "It doesn't come off, see?"

2007

Nick and I are lying side by side on the grass. Our school uniforms are dappled by the sun peeking through the shade of the mango tree. We look up at the branches. There's no fruit yet. June is dry season – way too early in the year.

We let our extremities touch. Our ankles, fingers, arms. The feel of his skin sets my insides on fire.

Selena and Benny are sitting nearby, on our benches by the basketball court. We lazily listen to them talking.

Selena's voice is earnest. "Okay, but Benny. Be serious. You can't really rate Gaytimes above Magnums, can you?"

"It's the little tiny biscuit pieces. They get me every time."

"But the ice-cream quality …"

"Inferior, I admit."

"And the chocolate …"

"Yeah, that too. But –"

"Get over the biscuit pieces!"

"I can't!"

"Okay then, hypothetical. What if I take a slightly melted Magnum and roll it in biscuit pieces? Then which one's better?"

As Benny pauses to consider, Nick rolls to face me. "My sister is an idiot."

I smile. "In a good way."

"If you say so. Hey, you want to come over again this weekend?"

"With them?"

"Hopefully not. We could order in some pizza. You could stay over."

He must see the surprise in my face, because he hurries on. "I mean, if you want to. If your mum's cool with it."

I don't tell him my mum doesn't know anything about him. Instead, I say, "What about your parents?"

"They're cool. I've had girls stay over before."

I can't help frowning, and he quickly amends the statement. "I mean, just one. One ex-girlfriend. They didn't care."

I wonder who it was, and if he's lying about the number. I know who he's been out with. I've seen them around school together, last year, the year before. Tiffany. Rebecca. Jess. Melissa. Jane.

I pick a blade of grass and roll it between my fingers. "I don't know." I'm thinking of how it was with him, after Libby's party. Nick on top of me, grinding. Me freaking out.

Maybe he's thinking the same thing, because he reaches for my hand. "No pressure."

I look up and meet his eyes. "Really?"

"Really."

I take a deep breath and say, "I'll ask Mum."

★

I don't, of course. Mum would never let me. She'd say, *Who is he?* then, *I have to meet him first.* And then she'd say no anyway. She'd tell me I'm too young, that I don't know what I'm

71

getting myself into. *How long have you been together? Two weeks?! Why didn't you tell me straight away?* She wouldn't understand that I just want to lie with him, side by side. She'd say he has ulterior motives. And maybe she'd be right.

So I take the easy option and say, casually, over dinner, "I'm staying at Selena's this weekend, okay?"

I wait for Mum to object, to notice the guilt in my voice. But my staying at Selena's is nothing out of the usual, so she says, "Fine. Is Anya going to be there too?"

"Probably."

"Are you still hanging out with Anya?"

"Of course."

The truth is, Anya's drifting. Some days she doesn't sit with us at all. She says she's got assignments to work on. I think the couple thing bothers her.

"Why don't you invite her over one weekend?"

"Yeah, maybe."

"Selena too, if you like."

In the two years we've been friends, Selena has never come to my house. I always stay at hers. There's always the promise of the pool, or pizza, or a party to go to.

I try to explain. "There's nothing to do out here, Mum." I see the hurt in her face and add, "It's nothing personal. If we lived in town ..."

"We can't move into town, Rosie. You know that. This house comes with my job, and anyway ... I wouldn't want to. This is our community, remember? Our *family*. Our home."

I know she's hinting at what I said about Nona. I quickly backtrack before she can segue into a lecture. "Yeah, I know. Forget about it. I didn't mean it."

But I did.

★

I stay over at Nick's. To my relief, he keeps his word and it is all innocent kisses and cuddles. We snuggle up in his bed and watch *The Simpsons* again. In between episodes, I ask, "Why do you like this show so much?"

"You don't?"

"Yeah, I like it. But it's kind of old, isn't it? When was this made?"

"In the '90s. Or maybe the '80s."

"Exactly."

He's slightly defensive. "I just think it's funny." He hesitates, then adds, "The animation's clever. The drawings, you know? I used to draw cartoons when I was little. I mean, mine were crap compared to this, but ..."

I'm surprised. "Do you still draw?"

"Kind of ... it's not exactly drawing."

Nick leans over the side of the bed and digs into his bottom bedside drawer. He unearths an A4 scrapbook and holds it out towards me. The cover is blank. "Open it."

I do. The book is jammed full of photos of graffiti. There are tags, portraits, murals, stencils. The whole lot. I see his anticipation, the nervousness in his face. I put the pieces together. "You did these?"

"Some of them."

"When?"

"When we lived in Sydney. Before I got caught and banned for life."

"Is that what Selena was talking about when she said you did worse stuff than fridging?"

He looks kind of cagey. "In a way."

I leaf through the pages, stopping at a photo of an enormous tag. The letters are outlined in black. They take up an entire wall. Inside them, there's an explosion of colour. At the bottom of the wall, the artist has painted empty spray-paint tins, made to look like they're lying discarded on the footpath. I trace the letters with my finger, unable to decipher the stylised writing.

"What does it say?"

"Nicked." He's watching me closely. "Do you like it?"

"I do."

I keep looking, and stop again a few pages later. "This one is amazing." It's a photo of a black and white stencil, simple but clear. It shows a muscle-bound boxer standing over a guy he's knocked out. Nick grins. "You've got good taste. That's Muhammad Ali smashing Sonny Liston. But it's not mine."

"Oops."

"It's by an artist called El Chivo. Most of his stuff's in London, but there's a bit here."

"How do you know that?"

He shrugs, but doesn't answer.

I say, "You're full of surprises, Nicked. I never knew you were into art."

"I don't know if this qualifies as 'art'."

"Sure it does."

"You'd never see it in a gallery."

I look through the album again, more closely now. I find three more by Nicked. "This is a gallery."

I see pride in his face, but he shakes his head. "Yeah, but it's not real art, not like your stuff."

"What do you mean?"

"I saw that landscape you did in the school art show last year. The watercolour one. It was awesome. The colours were so bright. So real. I felt like I was there – but wearing polarised sunnies."

I'm amazed he noticed. I'm amazed he remembers it now.

"Where'd you paint that, anyway? It didn't say where it was."

"Rocky Bay."

"Where's that?"

"Out near Yirrkala. It had to be close to home so I could walk."

Nick nods. "You going to get your L's? When do you turn sixteen?"

"November twenty-fourth. Yeah, I'll get them, not that it'll do much good. Mum's only got the troopie and it's her work car so I'm not officially s'posed to drive it."

"Do you know how to drive?"

"Mum started teaching me when I was thirteen." He looks impressed. I add, "There have to be some advantages to growing up in the middle of nowhere."

He hesitates, then says, "Maybe you could drive my ute."

He sounds so unsure about it, I can't help teasing. "Maybe?"

"Once you've got your P's."

My heart does a flip. He's talking about us, in the future, together.

I poke him and grin. "I don't know if I'd dare! What if I crashed it? Your precious ute. Would that be the end of us?"

I've said it. Us, Rosie and Nick. Us, the couple. I hold my breath.

His answer comes soft and smiling. "Nah. You can't get rid of me that easy."

I fall asleep with his arms around me, his body warm against mine.

I fall asleep smiling.

12.

1998

We are lying in my single bed, side by side. I'm wearing a new Pocahontas nighty. Nona has a pink one I've grown out of. Her bony hip nudges me closer to the wall. "Move over."

There's a guest bed in my room, but she never sleeps there. "Too lonely," she says. I don't mind. I'm just happy to have her here. Happy not to be alone.

Outside, in the lounge room, I can hear my parents arguing. Again. I snuggle into Nona and try to block out their angry voices.

I whisper, "I hate it when they fight."

Nona shrugs, unruffled. I reach out and hold her hand. Her grasp is warm and strong. I say, "I wish you could stay here every night."

"The smalls would miss me."

"I'm your *yapa* too."

"Yeah. Course."

"Can you tell me how it goes again?"

Nona sighs. "Too tired."

"Pretty please?"

I've heard the story before, of course, but I want to hear it again.

Mum yells, "Bloody hell, Pete!"

There's a crash of something falling, or being thrown.

Nona relents. "Once upon a time, long, long time ago, my *momu* adopted your nan. It was back in the mission days, and your nan was a mission lady. She taught *Momu* English and *Momu* made her a sister. And when they had *yothu*, they were family too. So your dad and my dad was brothers ..."

I nod. *"Wäwas."*

"Yo. And those *wäwas* played together when they were little. In the bush, hunting and fishing, going on trips to Bawaka. And when your dad was big, he came back here with your mum. And my mum adopted your mum, so your mum and dad were right skin. *Momu* says there must be some good spirit, 'cause our mums got *yothu-mi* at the same time. Two *miyalk* too. Girls are lucky. Not trouble like boys."

"So we're *yapas*."

She nodded. "Yumalil and Lilaba too. And Jimmy and Lomu, your *wäwas*."

"All family."

"Yo."

I hold her hand a bit tighter.

"One big family. Together." I whisper the words like a prayer.

They hug me in the darkness.

13.

2007

Mrs Bell buzzes around the kitchen, making us French toast for breakfast. There's no sign of Selena. She must've slept in.

"What time's your mum picking you up today, Rosie?"

I check the clock on the microwave. It's 9.34am. "In about an hour."

Nick pours two enormous glasses of orange juice, and slides one across the bench to me. "I could drop you home later. I mean, if you want to stay longer."

Mrs Bell tenses. "Is that a good idea?"

"What do you mean, Mum?"

"I just … is it safe? I know you live out there, Rosie, but it's different, isn't it? For outsiders coming in? Is it dangerous?"

Something clicks in my head. Selena always saying, *Let's stay at mine*, bombarding me with reasons why being in town is better. Is this why?

I try to reassure Mrs Bell. "It's fine. Totally safe."

"So people are – more or less – friendly?"

I can't hide my surprise. "You've never been out there?"

"Well, I would've liked to come and see the art centre, but

I didn't know if it was allowed."

"Of course it is. You should come some time."

"Don't you need a special permit?"

"If you're doing something in the community, yeah. But not just to drop someone off or go to the art centre."

"Oh good. That's good ... Aborigines seem to like painting, don't they?"

Before I can stop myself, I correct her. "Yolŋu."

"Sorry, that's what they call them here, isn't it? I should get used to it. It's just so hard to pronounce. Yol-noo. Young-u." She laughs self-deprecatingly.

Nick rolls his eyes. "You sound like a try-hard, Mum."

She blushes and moves back to the stove. I feel for her and say, "Anyway, it's fine. Mum has to come into town to get groceries, so no need for Nick to drive me out there. Another time."

Mrs Bell gives me an appreciative smile. I can tell she's quietly relieved. "Yes, another time."

★

I'm in History. It's the last lesson of the day. I feel my phone vibrate in my pocket and sneak it out to have a look. It's a message from Nick.

Want 2 come 2 pool?

Miss Fuller is too busy raving on about women's changing rights and freedoms to notice I'm exercising mine by texting under the desk.

U teaching?

No. Thought we culd hang out.

Want 2 but prob can't.

Y not?

No pick up :-(

I'll drive U.

I hesitate. If I let him drive me, how will I explain to Mum how I got home? I think of the community bus. I could say I caught that. Mum won't be home until five. There's a good chance she'll never know. But I feel like my lies are compounding lately, building up like plaque on teeth. I can almost taste them and they taste bitter. I'm not a good liar.

My phone vibrates again.

So?

I stall for time.

Wot abt ur mum?

His reply is fast.

4get her.

I can hear Mrs Bell's voice in my head. *Is it dangerous? For outsiders coming in?* It occurs to me that maybe Nick's never been out there either. Before I can ask, another text comes in.

Will drive U sooner or l8tr. Might as well b 2day.

He's right, but I have a sinking feeling in my stomach. I tell myself it'll be fine. Over and over. *It'll be fine. It'll be fine. It'll be fine.*

★

The water is cool. There's a slight breeze blowing through the scrub from the beach. We have the entire pool to ourselves. We duck and dive. We kiss with cold, wet lips. We both swim twenty laps, matching each other's pace, stroke for stroke. I suspect he's going a bit slower than usual so I can keep up.

Afterwards, we sit on the grass in the sun. I run my fingers through my hair to help it dry. I remember doing exactly this in the smoke of campfires with Nona. I can almost hear the crackle of fire, feel the flames so hot they'd burn hairs off our legs.

"It's three thirty."

Nick looks from his watch to me. Any later and I'll be pushing it with Mum. I don't want to take any chances that she might see Nick and me arrive. When I talked to her this afternoon, she sounded slightly annoyed and said, "Whatever you do, don't miss the bus this time."

I stand, reluctant. Nervous. "We'd better go."

★

As we enter the community, Nick can't stop staring out the window. I see it all through his eyes. The run-down houses and abandoned cars. The clusters of Yolŋu families sitting in cross-legged circles on mats in their yards. The laughing kids barefoot, playing in the broken phone box. His face has a strange expression on it. I can't place it, but it makes me nervous.

We pass Rripipi's house. It appears empty today. Someone has put a tatty blue couch on the front verandah.

"Turn here."

Nick takes a right, as directed. We pass a few Yolŋu ladies – Milirrk and Gombu – who peer into the car, curious, as we pass. They recognise me and smile. Milirrk waves. Remembering my promise to Mum, I wave back.

I can feel Nick's eyes on me. "Who are they?"

"Oh, just some ladies … they live in that red house."

"Do you know everyone here?"

"Pretty much."

He looks far from impressed.

I shift in my seat, and try to make my voice sound light. "Can't believe you've never been to Yirrkala before."

He's defensive. "Why would I have?"

"I don't know – to go to Shady Beach?"

"Has it got surf?"

"Sometimes … not often, I guess …" I try again. "What about to watch a football game?"

"Don't like football. You know that."

It's a bit of a sore spot. His dad played AFL but, to his disappointment, Nick's only ever been a swimmer and a surfer.

He swerves to avoid a pothole. "These roads are crap. They really don't look after this place, do they?"

We pass the oval, the community store and the art centre. I indicate for him to stop in our driveway. He pulls over, peering up at our house.

I hesitate. "You want to come in?"

I'm hoping like crazy he says no. I've already taken too many risks. If he comes in he might stay, and if he stays Mum might come home, and if she comes home Nick will realise she doesn't know anything about him …

Nick says, "Nah, I'd better head."

Relief. I kiss him, quietly grateful, and climb out of the car, saying, "See you tomorrow."

I watch his Hilux drive up the street until it disappears around the corner.

Mum arrives home from work and says, "Who drove you home today?"

"What?"

"Your ŋamaḻa said she saw you in a ute. With a boy."

"Which ŋamaḻa?"

But I already know the answer. I remember Milirrk waving, peering into Nick's car.

I try to play it casual. "It was Nick – you know, Selena's brother? He came to pick Selena up and offered to drop me home too."

"To Yirrkala?"

I can hear the scepticism in her voice.

She gets straight to the point. "Are you seeing him, Rosie?"

"Um … I don't know yet."

"But you like him?"

"Yes."

The word lands like a thud between us. This is new territory. I've never had a boyfriend before. I have no idea what she'll say. She leans on the kitchen bench and taps her fingers nervously on the counter.

"How old is he?"

"Seventeen."

"So he's in, what – Year 11? Year 12?"

"Year 12."

I can see her putting a cross next to that fact on the suitable-boyfriend list in her head.

"Is he on his P's, then?"

"Yes."

Cross number two.

"I don't like you driving with someone on their P's."

"He's a safe driver."

"He's seventeen."

I grasp for pro-Nick arguments. "He's ... responsible. He teaches swimming at the pool. To little kids and everything."

"Have I seen him there?"

"Probably."

She thinks this over. "Hang on – messy hair, blue eyes, tall, kind of muscly?"

I nod. She pauses, probably thinking three strikes and he's out. "Why didn't you ask him in today?"

"I don't know."

Her fingers start up again. *Tap. Tap. Tap.*

"Would you have told me about him if Milirrk hadn't seen you?"

I shrug. She looks hurt. Or am I imagining it?

Finally, she says, "Well, I'd like to meet him."

"Okay."

I escape to my room, relieved the interrogation is over.

★

Dad gets more information, as always. He teases me. "How's the boyfriend? Does he qualify as a boyfriend now?"

"He does."

"Have you told your mum about him?"

I think of Mum's interrogation and say, "Yep. She's even going to meet him soon."

I don't tell him that in this equation, soon equals hopefully never. Mum keeps asking and I keep saying Nick's busy. I'm sure she knows I'm lying. There's not *that* much to do in Nhulunbuy.

Dad sounds genuinely pleased. "Well, that's great. She'll have to give me the low-down."

I'm suddenly nervous, thinking of what I've told Dad so far.

Or, more to the point, what I haven't told him. I've been careful to paint a cheery, domestic picture. Nick's dad's a real family man. He works driving trucks for the mine. He's good value, always joking around. And Nick's mum is an amazing cook. She works part-time, making meals for the childcare centre in town, and still finds time to bake at home. I haven't mentioned that she's scared of Nick coming out to Yirrkala, or that his dad's favourite brand of humour seems to be black jokes. I know this stuff wouldn't go down well, with either of my parents.

I hear Dad's voice again. "I'm glad you're giving your mum a chance, being open with her about things. I'm sure it means a lot to her."

Guilt swamps me.

14.

1999

I am sitting on the couch, in between Mum and Dad. The light is dull and grey, like the sky outside. Mum has her serious face on. Dad jiggles his leg, worried.

My stomach churns. "Am I in trouble?"

Dad hurries to reassure me. "No, blossom."

They swap a look above my head.

I try again. "Did someone die?"

"Nothing like that …" He shoots Mum another, more desperate, look. This one says *help*!

Mum takes control. "Rosie, your dad and I … we've decided to live separately for a while. He's been offered a job in Gapuwiyak."

My heart starts pounding. "Where's that?"

"About three hours through the bush."

I turn towards Dad, not comprehending. "But … you'll still come home on weekends, won't you?"

He shifts uncomfortably. "I think so … yeah, sometimes."

Mum shakes her head, frustrated. "Pete, we agreed –"

"She's seven years old."

"You promised – honest and open. Direct." Mum's voice is hard, leaving no room for argument.

Dad looks pained. Each word is an effort. "I won't be home on weekends. But I will come and visit you, at least once a month. And you can come and visit me. And I'll call you, all the time. And if you ever want to call me, I'm just on the other end of the phone."

My mind is reeling. I don't understand. Why is Dad leaving? Is it my fault? Is it Mum's?

She's getting teary as she says, "We're going to have to make some changes, Rosie. The art centre's asked me to work full-time. And I've said yes, which means they'll give us a house –"

"We've already got a house."

"I know ... but this one comes with your dad's job. He'll get a new one in Gapuwiyak ... and we'll have to move."

"I don't want to move."

"You'll like it, I promise. The new house is great. It's right behind the art centre – so close you can come and go, even if I'm working. You know, after school or in the holidays."

My insides are boiling. "I don't want to move to any stupid house!"

Dad reaches out to me. "Rosie ..."

I stand up, out of his reach. "Why can't we all go to Gapuwiyak?"

Dad says, "Blossom ... you can come and visit whenever you like."

Mum is emotional. "Your dad and I ... things haven't been good for a while. We've been fighting a lot –"

"So what? Nona's parents fight too and her dad doesn't leave. I mean, he leaves but he always comes back. But you're not coming back, are you?"

Dad looks heartbroken. "Rosie, I love you. This won't

change that, I promise. Nothing will ever change that."

Mum tries to pull me towards her. "Come here."

I push her away and start running. I can hear them calling after me, but I'm already out the door, up the driveway and onto the road. And I keep running.

I've got to get out of here.

I've got to find Nona.

15.

2007

We're eating a roast dinner with Graham when Mum finally snaps. "Rosie, I'm starting to think you don't want me to meet this boy, and if you don't want me to meet him, maybe you should ask yourself what you're doing together."

"It's not that –"

"He's continually busy."

"I told you, he teaches swimming and –"

"How many lessons could he possibly be teaching in June?"

"He –"

"What? Saves the world in his spare time?"

"You're being ridiculous."

Mum looks to Graham for backup. She always does this. Until recently, he's been a reliable right-hand man. But now it's like he's mentally checking out of our family dramas in anticipation of leaving. He gives me a small smile and says lamely, "I'd like to meet him."

Mum seizes on this shred of support. "Exactly – and Graham is leaving in four weeks if he doesn't extend his contract."

It's said pointedly. She doesn't want him to go. It's been the source of many heated late-night discussions. Graham says, "I still might be able to."

But his voice lacks conviction. I see the pain in Mum's eyes and it hurts me too. I don't know why he won't stay. Mum turns on me with renewed intensity. "Do you think we can do this before Graham goes?"

"I'm sure we can," I say.

"When?"

"I'll ask Nick –"

She stands and smacks an angry finger on a random calendar square.

"Twenty-first of June. Either Nick comes then, or you don't see him again 'til Graham and I have met him."

Graham nods. Apparently, they're still able to maintain a united front on some decisions.

★

"So ... my Mum wants to meet you."

Nick glances up at me, surprised. We're lying under our mango tree again. Today, it's just us. Selena is off supporting Benny in some football game, and we hardly see Anya anymore. She's stopped making excuses for not sitting with us at lunchtimes: now, it would be weird if she did.

Nick says, "That'd be great to meet her."

I'm not convinced. "Yeah?"

"You've met *my* mum."

"Yeah – your mum's normal."

"Define normal."

"She bakes, makes chitchat, volunteers at the canteen. She's ... domestic."

Nick says, "Your mum sews."

We both grin. I say, "Yeah – tea-towel dresses!" at the same time as Nick says, "Remember that tea-towel dress?"

When we finally stop laughing, Nick says, "She can't be that bad."

I feel suddenly guilty. "I never said she was *bad*. Just different. It's hard, you know, she's a single mum, working full-time. She doesn't always have time to do things ... like cook elaborate dinners like your mum does ... or drive me places ... or eat ..."

"How can anyone not find time to eat?" He's incredulous.

I laugh. "Sometimes she just forgets. Her mind's somewhere else."

"Where?"

"In work, politics, her relationship, the community."

"So I should expect her to be a bit vague?"

"No, I don't mean that. I mean ... I don't know. Just come and meet her."

"When?"

"The twenty-first of June."

Nick gets out his phone and consults the calendar, confused. "Next Thursday? Why is it a Thursday?"

"Because that's where her finger landed on the calendar."

Nick looks at me as if to say, *Are you for real?*

I nod. "See? That's what I'm talking about."

★

Nick arrives at six on the dot on the twenty-first of June, bright red hibiscus flowers from his mum's garden in hand. I raise an eyebrow as he hands them to Mum. He shrugs, giving me a mock-innocent grin. I wonder if he's done this before with other girlfriends' mums. We avoid talking about his exes.

Mum takes the flowers with a smile. "Thank you."

"No worries, Mrs Grains."

"Call me Jen. And this is my partner, Graham."

Nick and Graham shake hands with blokey vigour.

Graham says, "Nice to meet you. Can I get you a drink, mate?"

Mum is suddenly flustered. "Oh, I was going to do that! Sorry, Nick. What would you like?"

"What have you got?"

She opens the fridge and scans its contents. "Iced tea, milk, water ... prune juice?"

I lean forward. "Didn't you see I put Coke on the shopping list, Mum?"

"You know I don't buy that stuff, Rosie."

Nick says, "Water's fine, thanks, Mrs – Jen."

He stands stiffly by the kitchen bench as Mum pours him some cold filtered water. I make a mental note to ask Mum if we can get some bar stools like they have at the Bells'.

Graham says, "So ... it's good you could make it."

Nick nods. "I was happy to be invited."

I hold my breath. Nick smiles, oblivious to the fact there were tens of invitations I never passed on. Mum, luckily, is on her best behaviour. She swallows any sarcastic comments she could make about him being "busy" and hands him the glass of water. Nick takes a polite sip. His gaze drifts to our lounge room walls. They are a shrine to local art. There are lino-cut prints, bark paintings and carvings. Many of them are presents to Mum from Nona's family or people at the art centre.

Mum sees him looking and asks, "Do you like Aboriginal art?"

Nick shifts uncomfortably. "Ah ... it's not really my thing, to be honest. Mum likes it, though."

"Fair enough. It's not to everyone's taste."

There's an awkward pause. Is this what it's going to be like all night?

Nick makes another effort. "Dinner smells great."

"It's lentil soup."

"Is that like tofu?"

"It's a legume."

I can see this means nothing to Nick, but he nods. "Right. Smells good."

Another gap in conversation.

Mum tries to sound casual. "So ... Rosie tells me you're in Year 12. What are you thinking of doing next year?"

Nick shifts feet, uneasy. It's something we haven't discussed.

He says, "I'm not sure yet. Dad's keen on me doing Business, but I don't know."

Graham puts his two cents in. "Whatever you do, don't choose a course just to please your parents."

Mum gives him a wry look. "I'm sure your parents were devastated when you chose Medicine."

"I only studied Medicine postgrad."

Mum's surprised. "I didn't know that."

"Because I don't generally tell people about my shameful other life doing Actuarial Studies."

Nick asks, "What's that?"

Graham grimaces. "Maths. Boring, horrible, endless maths."

He's smiling now, and Nick grins back at him. "Sounds like a shocker."

"It was."

"Whose idea was it – your mum's or your dad's?"

"Both. They thought it would be a 'solid career'."

Nick sounds almost grateful. "That's exactly what Dad says about Business."

"There you go."

The men swap another smile. Mum ladles out her lentil soup.

★

Over dinner, Mum raves about the virtues of organic food and her attempts to start a vegetable garden. She's constantly "preparing the soil" or buying seedlings from Ian at the community nursery. But while our neighbours are harvesting baby tomatoes and pawpaws and rocket, we're yet to get anything more than a clump of spring onions.

"It could be something to do with the fact you always forget to water it, Mum."

She's indignant. "Well, you could help me."

"If I didn't have to catch the school bus at seven twenty I would."

Nick sounds amazed. "I'm not even out of bed by then."

"Exactly."

"What time do you get up?"

"Six thirty."

"Ouch."

I turn back to Mum. "If we move to town, I'll help you water your garden."

Mum's retort comes quickly, her irritation hidden behind a smile. "If you find me a new job in town, one that comes with a house, we'll move. How's that for a deal?"

Nick is completely innocent as he says, "Dad reckons the mine's always looking. They're expanding, you know. A guy from school started there this year. Straight out of Year 12, says he's earning two grand a week just for holding a sign."

I brace myself for a lecture about how the mine has insidiously destroyed Yolŋu culture and knowledge and poisoned the land. But Mum holds back and gives Nick a polite smile. "I'll keep that in mind."

I give Mum a grateful look and she smiles back, as if to say, *See? I can act normal.*

Graham is looking distractedly towards the kitchen. "Is there something in the oven?"

I can smell it too now. The smell of burning. Mum jumps up from her seat. "Oh no. The dessert."

She hurries to the oven and opens it. Grey clouds of smoke billow out. She grabs a tea towel and pulls out a black and brown lump of sizzling something. "Ouch."

The smoke alarm goes off: a high-pitched beeping. Mum flaps the tea towel at it, ineffectually, as Graham opens the window wider and tries to wave the smoke outside.

I glance over at Nick, who is trying hard not to laugh. I'm sure his mum never burns anything. I shake my head, embarrassed.

The alarm finally stops.

Graham indicates the ex-dessert. "What was it going to be?"

Mum whacks him, smothering a smile. "Shut up. It's apple pie. Can't you tell?"

I can't help myself. "Did you use organic apples in that, Mum? Smells delicious."

Mum is grinning as she says, "You can all go to hell."

Graham is quick to joke back. "Is this what they serve there? Charcoal pie?"

Mum laughs. Nick finally lets himself laugh too. And then we're all laughing. It feels good to laugh together. And for a brief moment I think maybe this dinner could go okay.

★

We finish our plain vanilla ice-cream, and relocate to the lounge room to watch the ABC news. I'm appalled that Mum insists on watching it even though we have a guest over, but Nick tells her it's cool, he doesn't mind. He's in the home stretch now, on his way to gaining full parental approval.

Graham settles into a velour armchair and puts the footrest out. Mum perches in the matching armchair. Nick sits on the couch and I awkwardly take a seat next to him. I don't know how close to sit. What says "together" but "innocent"? I don't want to freak Mum out. Should I hold his hand? Put my hand on his knee? No, too intimate. Nick solves the problem by slinging a casual arm around my shoulders. I glance at Mum to see if she's noticed, but I needn't have worried. Her eyes are firmly on the TV.

The newsreader is talking about something called the "NT Intervention". I've never heard of it before. The Prime Minister, John Howard, comes on screen, his round glasses glinting in the flash of cameras. "It is interventionist. It does push aside the role of the Territory to some degree, I accept that. But what matters more? The constitutional niceties or the care and protection of young children?"

"What's he talking about, Mum?"

"Shhh."

She listens intently. The newsreader's words wash over me. Federal emergency. Child abuse. Paedophilia. Sacred. Alcohol. Permits.

I wait for the story to end. "What does it mean, Mum? What are they doing?"

Her voice is dark with sarcasm. "They're finally addressing 'the Aboriginal problem'."

Graham says, more to Mum than us, "It's a political stunt. It's got to be. Another 'children overboard'."

Mum nods. "Howard has to know he'll get the boot when there's an election."

Nick misreads their tone and scoffs his agreement. "Did they say there are paedos here?"

Mum's head snaps to look at him.

I try to catch Nick's eye, as I say, "Well, not *here* exactly, in Aboriginal communities in general —"

"Like that's some big surprise."

Disbelief and outrage well in Mum's eyes. I jump in again. Rosie to the rescue. "It's getting late …"

Nick senses the mood has shifted, and tries to clarify. "Hey, at least they're doing something about it. I mean, sending in the army. That's good, right? They're taking it seriously."

But Nick has already dug a hole so deep he may as well buy a coffin. I can tell Mum is about to explode, so I pull him to his feet. "We should go."

"What? Oh. Okay. Night, Jen. Nice to meet you, Graham."

"You too, Nick."

I drag my boyfriend out the door.

Outside, there's a cool breeze. A raft of stars floats in the inky sky.

I can hear Mum starting to rant inside, so I walk Nick quickly down the stairs to his Hilux, hoping he doesn't hear.

He can tell he's stuffed up. "I said something wrong, didn't I?" He's genuinely oblivious as to what that could be.

I shrug. "Let's just forget about it."

But he can hear Mum's raised voice floating out to us now. We don't catch the words, just the tone. Nick is kicking himself. "I thought that's what she'd think too. That it's good they're doing something. My Dad would say it's a waste of money. I mean, places like this … they're screwed up, right?"

I don't know what to say. I constantly put Yirrkala down, but now part of me wants to defend it. To say there are good things here too. Good people. Community. Not that I'm really part of it anymore.

Nick scuffs his feet in the gravel. "Sorry. It was going really well 'til then, wasn't it?"

I nod. He gives me a light kiss on the lips. "Think I can win her back over?"

"I don't know."

But I do. There's no way Mum will approve of Nick now.

"Is that really the type of boy you want to go out with?"

Mum is outraged, in full flight. I shoot an arrow, trying to bring her down. "He's a nice guy, Mum. Just because he has a different opinion to yours —"

"*Mine*? What's *your* opinion, then?"

"I don't know. They only just announced this thing. I don't know what it means. Nick probably doesn't either."

"It's going to be a disaster."

"Well, don't blame Nick! He didn't order this stupid policy, or whatever they're calling it."

"I don't like him, Rosie."

"You thought he was fine before the news came on!"

Mum hmmphs.

I grasp at excuses on Nick's behalf. "He's never spent time in a community."

"Well, I could tell that."

"Just give him a chance."

"I gave him one tonight and what did he come out with? Paedophiles and the army."

"That was the news, not him."

"Did Nick have anything to do with what happened at school?"

"What?"

"You saying Nona wasn't your sister?"

"What? No."

She looks disbelieving, so I persist. "He didn't, Mum. Come on. Be fair. He made one comment. He's not some … evil person."

Graham watches the argument fly between us like he's observing a ping-pong match. He stays quiet, careful not to get involved.

Mum tries to calm herself. She takes a deep breath, then says, "I'm just ... worried, Rosie. I see you hanging out with a boy like that. I can see the appeal. I really can. He's good-looking, friendly, probably considered very cool. But those attitudes ..."

"Mum –"

She stays her course. "... those attitudes run deep. And I don't want you starting to believe them."

"I won't. I don't."

"It would break my heart, Rosie. After raising you in this community ..." Her voice breaks.

I want to reassure her. "You don't have to worry, Mum."

But her concern hangs between us, so real and present it is almost visible.

16.

1999

We are bumping along a dirt track, in the back of Gulwirri's ute. It's got an open tray with a grubby double mattress jammed inside. Nona and I are sitting on top of the mattress, along with a tumble of family members. The only person missing is my mum.

She chose to stay home today, saying she "needs to get things done". She wants to unpack, set up our new place. It makes me sad to think of her back there, in that big empty house, alone. I offered to stay, but she said no, she needs some space, she needs time to think. She needs a lot of things lately, and nothing I do seems to help.

Nona knows I'm sad. She tries to cheer me up. She grins and points to her long orange cotton pants. "Need new ones. Got holes." She pokes her fingers through the holes and wiggles them at me. I barely raise a smile. The pants make me think of Mum all over again. She's been sewing us matching pants for as long as I can remember; I used to complain about the scratchy grass when we went on bush trips, and when Nona saw my pants, of course she wanted some too.

Through the ute's back window, I see Rripipi slip an Elvis CD into the stereo. "Nothing but a Hound Dog" booms out at us. Nona starts miming the words, the wind whipping her hair as we drive along.

We pass a beat-up grey Land Cruiser parked on the side of the track. Gulwirri pulls over in front of it and cuts the engine. The music stops. Nona and her brothers jump off the back like excited dogs let off the leash for a walk. I climb out more slowly. Gulwirri gives a long, low call. A male voice echoes back. Nona's uncle, Larry, came out looking for *yidaki* earlier. We start off in his direction.

Rripipi walks with us and the smalls, her eyes scanning the tree trunks for bees or signs of a hive. Gulwirri darts ahead, weaving through the stringybarks, as if playing some strange combination of tip and hide-and-seek. For a moment I think we've lost her, but then she reappears. A slither of purple top. A flash of long leopard-print skirt.

Jimmy and Lomu orbit around us, scampering through the bush with bare feet. Jimmy, at twelve years old, is the clear leader. Lomu is practically leaping, trying to match his brother's long-legged pace.

We reach a section of burnt-off scrub and the trees thin out. The ground is hot and black, and shade is scarce. I'm grateful for my hat and sneakers. Nona only has a pair of worn rubber thongs, but she hasn't complained once. I'm full of admiration.

I hear Gulwirri call out, *"Guku!"* then the thwack of her axe cutting into hard wood. Nona gestures for me to follow her. *"Go!"*

We run, stumble, trip towards the sound. The smalls start whimpering at being left behind. Nona doubles back to pick up Lilaba, and Rripipi hoists Yumalil onto her hip.

I can see Gulwirri now, resting by a fallen tree. She calls out, *"Gapu."*

Jimmy brings her a bottle of cold water. She gulps it down.

Rripipi deposits Yumalil and picks up the axe. She brings it down on the tree trunk in loud, echoing thunks. The sagging skin on her arms shudders with each chop. After five swings, she's had enough. Gulwirri takes over again and cleaves the top side of the trunk clean away, exposing a well of sweet liquid gold. Jimmy dives straight in.

I feel a tap on my shoulder. It's Lomu, holding out a stick. He's beaten one end into soft, fibrous bristles, like a paintbrush. His smile is kind. "Here, *Yapa*. Bush lollipop."

I take it gratefully, and use it to scoop the dark runny honey out of the trunk. I suck on it like a Chupa Chup. It is golden syrup heaven. I just wish Mum was here to share it.

Nona and the smalls use their fingers, slurping and licking in contented silence. Jimmy and Lomu take chunks of thick brown honeycomb and suck them happily, off to one side. Gulwirri scoops out the *mapu*, the eggs.

Rripipi levers out the pollen, piling the powdery pieces of yellow into an empty yoghurt container, and gestures to it. "For your mum."

Mum likes to drink it mixed with water, just like the old people do. I think it tastes gross, but she says it makes her healthy and strong.

I know it will take more than pollen to make her better, but I feel so grateful I could burst.

"Thank you, *Momo*."

17.

2007

It is the last day of school before a month of holidays.
I see Mrs Reid near the library. I hesitate, then make my way
towards her. "Mrs Reid … I wanted to talk to you. About
Nona?"

She looks at me, distracted, like she doesn't know what I'm
talking about.

I try again. "You know, you asked me about her a few
weeks back?"

"Oh, yes, yes, of course. Sorry, Rosie, my mind's all over
the place today. This Intervention thing –"

Her phone starts ringing. She checks the caller ID then
silences it, giving me her full attention. "It must be crazy out
at Yirrkala. Is it?"

She doesn't wait for my answer, which is lucky as I have no
idea how to reply. The streets in Yirrkala seemed empty this
morning, but I didn't see anything that would qualify as
"crazy".

Mrs Reid continues. "I've been trying to call parents to tell
them not to worry. But there are no Yolŋu students here today

and apparently the airport is full of people trying to get flights out to the homelands. They think it's going to be the Stolen Generation mark two. Not that that affected people here much, but you can understand why they're worried."

My confusion must show because she adds, "Sorry. You wanted to talk to me about Nona."

I say, "I just wanted to tell you that her mum – Gulwirri? Judy? She's a drinker. You should try calling her grandmother instead. Her name's Rripipi. She lives in Yirrkala."

She smiles, grateful for the information. "I don't suppose you have her number?"

"No, but my mum would."

"I'll ask her. Thank you, Rosie. Nona did say you two were friends. If you see her, it'd be great if you could encourage her to come back. It's not easy when you've missed a lot of school. As I'm sure you know, she missed a lot in Elcho, looking after her sisters."

I nod, but the truth is I don't know much about Nona's life now at all. Mrs Reid's words hurt my heart.

"If I see her, I'll tell her, Miss."

"I appreciate it."

★

It's the school holidays and we hang out as a foursome. Me, Nick, Selena, Benny. No-one suggests inviting Anya.

We go to the pool, spend time at Skate Park and at each other's houses. Well, at their houses, not mine. Yirrkala is too far away and too boring.

Mum is far from thrilled. "I think we need a few ground rules."

I groan. "Come on, Mum. It's the holidays."

"You're in town or at Nick's house every day."

"What am I supposed to do? You're working."

"Not in the evenings, I'm not."

"So I have to be home when you are? That's fair."

She hears my sarcasm and sighs. "I'm not trying to kill your social life, Rosie. I just want you to be safe."

That's Mum's favourite rationalisation. It's hard to argue with "safe".

"No more coming home late. If Nick's driving, I want you home by dark. Otherwise I'll come in and pick you up any time before eleven. I think that's pretty reasonable."

"You hate driving into town."

"I'm willing to make the sacrifice." There's a wry note to her voice.

I try again. "Nick's a safe driver."

"I'm sure he is, but he's on his P's and I don't want him driving home alone in the dark either."

She manages to make it sound like she's concerned for his welfare too. She's clever like that.

I ask, "What if there's a party?"

"Eleven's your normal curfew anyway."

"But I can just stay at Selena's like I usually do."

"Oh sure. I know what that means now you're going out with Nick."

"Their parents would be there."

"Hmm."

Mum doesn't think much of Nick and Selena's parents, not that she's really given them a chance. She's polite when she picks me up, but never says yes to Mrs Bell's offers of coffee or tea. I'm secretly glad about that. You don't have to be a genius to know they wouldn't have much in common. Even the bumper stickers on their cars declare it: Mum's says *Stop Jabiluka mine* and the Bells' says *Why work when you can go fishing?*

Mum puts her foot down. "No more sleepovers at Selena's. Home by dark or picked up by eleven. Those are the rules, Rosie. Stick to them."

★

"Man, the water is cold this morning. Aren't you guys freezing?"

Selena climbs the ladder and perches on the top rung of her backyard pool. It's twenty-five degrees but she's shivering and her skin is a mottled grey-blue. She's only lived here a couple of years; she's acclimatised quickly.

Nick grins at her. "We're okay."

I'm lying next to him on a blow-up li-lo, soaking up the sun.

Selena says, "You two are totally hogging that thing."

Nick smirks. "Eat me."

She makes a face. "I'm getting out."

Benny grins as he hurries to follow. "I'd better help her warm up."

They head inside to the sound of Selena's giggles.

I snuggle into Nick and close my eyes.

Deep male voices float over to us from the carport. Nick's dad, Roger, has a mate over. He's showing off a bar he's just bought. It's made of timber, with a serving area and high counter, just like you'd find in a pub. He's set it up with barstools, and draped an old fishing net on the carport wall.

His friend says, "This is a find, mate. Where'd you get it?"

"The wife found it on the Gove noticeboard."

"Who was dumb enough to sell this?"

"Some guy who worked for the government. Was leaving town."

"Thought they were trying to get extra people up here, not lose them."

"You mean for that Intervention thing?"

Their voices are louder now. I peek over at them as they make their way towards us. They take a seat by the pool and sip cold beers, fresh from the bar. Roger is about fifty, balding but fit. Roger's friend looks a bit younger, with warm brown eyes. He's wearing board shorts and a Bonds singlet that leaves too much body hair exposed.

Roger continues. "Place'll probably be swarming with bureaucrats before we know it. Bloody paper shufflers. Don't know how they think throwing money at the problem will help. What they need to do is get people working."

His friend nods. "No more sit-down money."

"Like the guys who work at the mine. They're okay. They're putting in a hard day's work. Like that guy VJ."

"You mean BJ?"

"No, VJ. Or DJ, was it?"

Both men laugh.

Nick grins over at his dad, trying to catch his eye. Nick's weird like that – he swings between saying his dad is a money-focused moron and craving his approval.

His dad's friend asks, "What happened to him, anyway? Haven't seen him around lately."

"They gave him an apprenticeship. Trained him up. Next thing you know he's shot through to Darwin. Couldn't handle the pressure."

Roger catches sight of me listening and nods towards our li-lo. "This is my son, Nick, by the way. And his girlfriend, Rosie. This is Tim. He's fly-in fly-out at the mine. I used to work with his dad in Sydney. You remember Stuart, Nick?"

Nick nods politely, but I'm fairly sure he doesn't.

Roger asks, "Where are you staying then, Tim? Out at the G3?"

Tim nods. The G3 is mining accommodation that was built last year. It houses three thousand workers. A huge expansion.

Mum and Dad were both against it. Lots of people were. They thought it would change the "family atmosphere" of Nhulunbuy, and maybe it has.

Roger says, "Rosie's mum works out at Yirrkala."

Tim asks, "Where's that?"

"Bit out of town. It's an Aboriginal community."

"Yeah? What's it like?"

"We could always drive out there and have a look. They just got rid of the permit system, didn't they?"

I nod, uneasy. Nick jumps in. "I wouldn't bother. There's not much to see. Bombed-out cars and crappy houses."

I'm quietly annoyed by his response.

Roger says, "What do you reckon, Rosie? What percentage of people out there'd be on the dole?"

"I wouldn't know —"

"Take a guess."

I can tell what he wants to hear, but I say, "Oh, there are people working. Like the old man who drives the bus. And the artists who paint with Mum. There's a team that collects garbage. And Yolŋu people working at the school and the clinic."

"Huh."

I feel a small pang of satisfaction, but it dissipates quickly as Roger says, "Hey, I heard a good one the other day. You know Miwatj Health? The Aboriginal Medical Service? Me watch. You work."

He's always telling jokes like that when I'm around, like it's something we'll both relate to. I squirm, as Tim laughs and Nick says, "Or what about YBE? Yolŋu Break Everything."

He looks to his dad for approval and is rewarded with a husky chuckle.

Roger explains for Tim's sake. "YBE does maintenance in town." He holds up his empty bottle. "Might grab another beer. You want one, mate?"

The men head back to the carport.

I must look uncomfortable, because Nick squeezes me lightly. "They're just jokes, Flipper."

"I know."

"It's not like it's hurting anyone."

But there's an ache deep in my gut.

I twist out of his embrace, slip off the li-lo and escape underwater.

★

I sit beside Mum, sullen in the front seat of the troopie.

I mutter, "Nick was happy to drive me home."

"I was coming into town anyway. I had to get groceries."

"At seven o'clock?"

"Why not? It's after work."

Gove FM is playing softly on the radio. Some cheesy pop song. Mum turns it off.

"What they call music today – half of it's just noise."

We lapse into a silence broken only by the soft growl of the troopie's engine. I stare out the window. It's just getting dark.

Mum attempts conversation. "Work is crazy at the moment. I'm trying to get all the prints done in time for the Gapan Gallery. At least it keeps my mind off Graham. I don't think he's going to stay, Rosie."

She waits for a response, but I remain quiet. I don't want to talk about Graham: it makes me worry about Nick. We've only been together a few months, but I can't help my mind racing ahead. He's in Year 12. All the Year 12s leave to study or travel. Will I be like Mum then? Pining and grieving?

She's still talking. "They're expecting over a thousand people at the Garma Festival this year. I honestly don't know how I'm going to get everything ready. I've got Wäkwak helping, of course, but I could use an extra hand. If you wanted to help me with the printing I could pay you."

I see through her immediately. "Are you asking because you need me? Or so I don't spend so much time with Nick?"

She smiles sheepishly. "A bit of both?"

I roll my eyes. She never gives up.

We're almost at Yirrkala now. Mum's headlights glance off a large light-blue sign on the side of the road. I haven't seen this one before. It's new. I try to read the words, but the white writing is lost in reflected glare.

"What could they possibly need another sign for?"

"It's about the Intervention. They put it up today. *This is a prescribed area. No alcohol. No pornography.* Blah, blah, blah. If that's what they're looking for, they should go and check the G3."

"What are they really going to do about it, anyway?"

"Not much that I can see. Although they are giving us sensor lights and fences, I found out this morning. That'll keep all those pesky paedophiles at bay, the ones lurking out there in the dark."

I hide my smile, pretending to gaze out at the dimly lit street, as we drive into the community. I wouldn't want Mum to think she is amusing.

★

Mum's face is set in a contorted smile. I can tell she's trying not to cry. Her words are short and sharp. "It's fine. I understand."

She dumps a packet of raw pasta into a saucepan, then moves to the sink to add water. Graham hovers near the back door, like he wants to be able to make a quick escape. "Please don't be like this —"

She shrugs him off. "It's your decision. If you've gotta go, you've gotta go."

I am doing my homework at the dining table. I can see and hear everything. Not that I want to. I've seen Mum's heart break before and it's not pretty.

Graham says, "I just don't want to be here when some huge team of doctors rolls in …"

Mum snaps, "We don't even know they're really coming. There's no sign of the army −"

"That's different. They're serious about the health checks −"

"They were 'serious' about Closing the Gap last year and nothing happened."

She starts chopping onion. *Thwack, thwack, thwack.*

Graham says, "Jen, trust me. I can see how this going to go. They're going to get paid three times what we do, to do health checks we've already done. I don't want to be any part of that."

"You wouldn't be 'part of it', you're already here."

Mum's chopping becomes more furious, as if she's visualising killing those doctors. Or Graham. Then the thwacking stops. I don't have to look to know she's crying.

She says, "Bloody onions. I should wear goggles while I chop them. You know some people do that? Sadie swears by it."

Graham's voice is gentle. "Come here …"

Mum lets him hold her this time. She sags against his chest. I hear a sniffle, then a low sob. I can't bear it anymore. I pull my iPod from my school bag and stick the earbuds in.

As I scroll through the songs, I hear Graham murmur, "We both knew I'd have to leave some time …" and then "… this just seems like a natural time to go …"

Asshole.

I choose the John Butler Trio, and select the song "Good Excuse".

I turn it up loud to drown Mum and Graham out.

★

Nick comes to pick me up. Gravel crunches under his wheels, as the Hilux stops in the drive. I bound down the front steps and put my head in his open window.

I'm smiling. "Hey, you. Did you want to come in?"

He keeps his eyes on the gearstick. "Nah. Another time."

"Mum's at work, if that's what you're worried about."

"I'm not 'worried' about your mum."

He sounds irritated. I try to reassure him. "She likes you."

He scoffs, so I quickly add, "And even if she didn't, who cares? You've seen what she's like." He doesn't say anything so I keep going. "Dad's the sane one, which is probably why he left."

He looks up at me, interested. "You talk to him much? Your dad?"

"Every Wednesday."

"What's he like?"

I consider it for a moment. "He's … down to earth. Stable. And passionate about what he's doing. I admire him."

"You're lucky, then. Mine's a moron."

"What happened?"

I feel silly talking to him like this, through his car window. I pull the driver's door open. "Hey, come on. Get out. Sit with me for a moment. We're not in a rush, are we?"

He climbs out slowly, reluctant.

We sit on the bottom step, side by side.

"He's pissed off at me about uni."

"He still thinks you should study Business?"

"He thinks I should study something."

"I don't understand."

"I didn't submit the forms. The UAC ones – you know? Where you say your preferences for unis and courses?"

"What do you mean you didn't submit them?"

"I didn't hand them in. They were due before the holidays."

"Did you forget?"

He shakes his head. "I don't want to go to uni."

My heart does an involuntary leap at the news he might not go. Maybe he'll stay here. Maybe I won't be left alone. I know it's selfish, but I can't help hoping. I try not to smile, but maybe it looks more like a smirk because he says, "You too, then? Think I'm ruining my future?"

His expression is pained, vulnerable and raw. It catches me off guard. This isn't the boy I joke around with at the pool, or the popular guy from school.

I say, "Of course I don't."

"I bet you'll go to uni."

"What's that got to do with anything?"

"Will you?"

"I'm in Year 10."

"But when you graduate ... will you?"

"I don't know." I want to, but I can't imagine leaving Mum. How would she cope by herself?

Nick says, "Selena said you want to be an artist."

"I do."

"So don't you need to study for that? I mean, if you want to be really good?"

I've never talked to anyone about my uni dreams before. Not Selena, not Anya, not Dad. I sound hesitant, even to me. "Mum took me to this exhibition once, when we were down in Sydney to see my grandpa. It was at a school called COFA. College of Fine Arts. I took a brochure about it, which was stupid 'cause I was only in Year 8. But I've still got it. I look at it sometimes. I know. It's kinda lame."

"No, it's not."

"Really?"

"You're talented, Rosie. You're going places. Not like me."

"That's a stupid thing to say."

"I have no idea what I want to do."

"So take a gap year. You could always work at the mine. You were saying yourself –"

Nick snaps over me. "There's no way I'm going to work with Dad."

"Or stay here and teach swimming." Nick looks across at me. I take hold of his arm. "You're a brilliant teacher. And you can save money for whatever you do next … 'cause whatever you do is going to be awesome, I know it."

I can't tell if the look he gives me is gratitude or love. He jokes, "Can you tell my dad that?"

"Yeah, right, 'cause he looooves me."

A small smile surfaces on Nick's lips. He mimics me. "No, he likes you. He really does."

I roll my eyes as Nick adds, "He just thinks you're a freak for living out here. And your mum's a left-leaning hippy."

I open my mouth in mock outrage and shove him.

He tickles me. I tickle him back.

We're laughing now, and the world feels right again.

I have hope; Nick might stay.

★

Mum takes Graham to the airport for the morning flight to Cairns. I expect her to be gutted when she gets back, but her face is tense and angry. She stomps into the lounge room and picks up the phone. "I've got to call Sadie."

Sadie is her best friend. She's a nurse at the hospital in town. She's been here almost as long as we have. I watch Mum as she dials. She was a mess when her last boyfriend left, requiring endless cups of Earl Grey and whole packets of Tim Tams. But not today.

I eavesdrop shamelessly. Sadie answers and Mum launches in. "Guess who I saw at the airport?"

She pauses, irritated. "What? Yes, Graham's gone. But I saw Frank flying out and he said they're amalgamating the councils. No – what's the word they're using? Streamlining. Which basically means they're scrapping Dhanbul."

Dhanbul is our local Yolŋu-run council. It's probably one of the biggest employers in Yirrkala. Mum sounds outraged. "They were all given notice today. The guys at Yirrkala tip, the garbage collectors … it's all going to be done by people in town now. One white guy with a truck."

Mum listens, then says, "Well, no … I don't think it's officially part of the Intervention, but you can't say it isn't related."

She makes sympathetic noises before exploding. "Those were Yolŋu jobs! Who cares if they were CDEP?"

Another pause, then, "It's fine. I can hear them screaming in the background. I'll let you go. Bye."

She hangs up, shaking her head. "Talking to Sadie makes me glad I only had you. I swear those kids have scrambled her brain."

Sadie has three children under five. Her house is a permanent chaos of nappies and crappy plastic toys. Mum seems suddenly exhausted.

"Mum … do you want a cup of tea?"

"Thanks."

I fill the jug and turn it on, watching her out of the corner of my eye. I am waiting for the waterworks to start, but they don't come. I place the sweet, milky Earl Grey in front of her, finally venturing to ask, "So how'd it go … seeing Graham off?"

She snaps, "Why is everyone so bloody concerned about Graham? He had a choice. He left. Let's worry about the people who are still here – like Larry and Frank and Lomu …"

The last name catches my attention. "Lomu?"

Mum nods. "Didn't you hear what I said? The garbage run's been contracted out. All those guys are out of a job."

She sips her tea in tortured silence.

After a few minutes she says, almost to herself, "I just feel so gutted, Rosie. This whole thing is … devastating."

I wonder if she's talking about the council, the Intervention or Graham.

★

Mum nudges me from my sleep. "Hey, Rosie, get up."

I look over at my clock. Fluorescent green numbers glow in the darkness. It's 5.31am. I sit up, groggy and confused. "What's happening?"

"We're going for a walk to Shady Beach."

"Now?"

"Yep. Come on."

I groan. "Muuum. It's too early."

But she isn't taking no for an answer. "You can go back to bed later. You're on holidays."

When I still don't move, she drags my thin doona off me, determined. "Get up. Let's go."

I turn on my bedside lamp and dress in light pants and a T-shirt. As we stumble out the door I see stars. I grumble, "This is unnatural. Humans aren't nocturnal."

Mum is forcefully upbeat. "The sun will be up any minute. You'll see."

We walk up the hill, around the school, past the spot where I catch the bus. The rest of the community is happily sleeping. Which is what I should be doing.

For a while, all I register is the rasp of my sneakers, as tiny rocks of bauxite crunch underfoot. Gradually, my senses awaken.

I smell salt from the ocean, feel the damp cold of morning. I hear the trill of birds waking, and the gentle shush of the bush rustling in the breeze. The darkness dissolves into pale blue.

I realise Mum has been talking, soft and sad. "I must be an idiot. I really thought Graham was different. He seemed genuinely into this relationship. And he liked you. He liked us. I know that. So why did he leave?"

I know she doesn't need me to answer. I'm her sounding board, a silent companion.

We reach the rise in the road. We heave up and over it and the beach comes into view. A pale curve of sand, ending in deep red rocks. Sun pierces the sky, tingeing the low-lying cloud a milky orange. The little island just off the coast, Barrpira, appears to float on the horizon.

I look over at Mum. The sight of her tear-streaked cheeks breaks my heart. She wipes them away. "I don't want to be alone anymore, Rosie. I'm so tired of being alone."

I know it's not what she's talking about, but I say, "You've always got me."

She puts a grateful arm around me as we walk on together.

I squeeze her waist, wanting to reassure her. "Things will get better."

But I have no idea how.

18.

1999

We are in the back of Mum's troopie, with a bunch of old ladies yelling like crazy. "Bump him! Bump him!"

A wallaby has just bounded across the red dirt road into the bush. They point after him, calling out. They want him for dinner. Guḻwirri is at the wheel. She grins across at Mum, who is sitting in the front seat. "Want to?"

Mum shrugs. Her voice is flat. "Up to you."

She's been quiet the whole drive. Everyone else is in high spirits. We've been singing tunes from *Aladdin*, "Dr Jones" by Aqua, and songs in Yolŋu Matha like *guku marrkap'mi* and *dhum'thum*, the wallaby song. But Mum has just sat there, silent. She's been like this since Dad left, swinging between miserable and angry.

A few days ago, Guḻwirri came over. She took one look at the still-unpacked boxes and said, "You need to get away, *Yapa*. Just for a weekend. Let's go to Bawaka."

Mum had agreed, but without her usual enthusiasm. And now she can't even smile, while everyone else hollers and whoops.

Gulwirri looks at Mum again and seems to make a decision. She makes a sharp turn and the troopie lurches off the dirt road, into the bush. Scrub snaps under our wheels and stray branches scratch the car. Gulwirri swerves suddenly to avoid a tree, then a big termite mound. Nona and the smalls giggle with glee. Rripipi hoots. Everyone is yelling, pointing.

"*Wirrki, wirrki!*"

"Put your foot down!"

"*Bundjirr manu!*"

Mum is jolted to attention. She clutches the door handle and glances back to check I'm okay. I grin at her, my eyes wide with excitement.

We can see the back of the wallaby now. It's right in front of us. We're catching up. I watch the blur of his brown fur. The white underside of his tail. His frantic, jerky jumps. Then bang. We've mowed him down.

Gulwirri screeches to a stop. The aunties jump out the back of the troopie to claim their prize. A hint of a smile flickers across Mum's face. She shakes her head at Gulwirri. "You're a maniac."

Gulwirri just grins. "*Go.*" Come on.

Mum helps the other ladies drag the wallaby back towards the troopie. He's a big one. They struggle to haul his dead weight onto the roof racks. I stare at his black eyes, frozen open, glazed with fear. His back, where we hit him, is a mess of mangled fur and blood.

They finally finish loading him on. We all pile back in, ready to go. Gulwirri turns the vehicle around and starts driving, more calmly this time, following the path of flattened grass and bush back to the road.

I see something on the front windscreen, like a dark red crack appearing in our vision. I realise it's wallaby blood.

Gulwirri presses a button. There's a spray of water. The windscreen wipers flick on. But instead of cleaning the blood away, they create a crimson wash. The trees are smeared pinky-red.

And suddenly I hear Mum laughing. It is a sound I haven't heard in months. It starts as a soft snort, then grows into giggles, and erupts in a hahahaha. Gulwirri joins in too, then me and Nona and Rripipi. Everyone is laughing. Amidst cackles Mum manages to say, "Anyone want to sing the *dhum'thum* song again?"

Peals of laughter ring out again.

I can't stop grinning.

19.

2007

We walk home from Shady Beach along the corrugated dirt track. I can feel the first fingers of heat starting to grasp the morning air. The sun is up now, and the colours of day swim into focus. The lush greens of the banana farm. The crisp yellow of dry grass. Dusty terracotta hoof tracks and an enormous black turd. I keep a wary eye out for buffalo as we walk.

Mum is more upbeat. She takes a deep breath of fresh air. "See? Worth getting up for, isn't it?" A few steps later, she says, "Hey, want to spend the day together? There's a community meeting, kind of a protest –"

"I've got plans with Nick."

"Can you cancel them?"

"Mum ..."

"I feel like I've hardly seen you these holidays."

We cross the thin strip of bitumen marking Boundary Road. We're back in the community. I look around. The street is strewn with torn garbage bags and knocked-over bins. The camp dogs are having a field day.

I ask Mum, "What's with the rubbish?"

"What do you mean?"

"Why's the place so dirty?"

She looks annoyed. "It's been like that for weeks now."

"So? What's the story?"

"It's the garbage contractor from town. They pulled all the bin poles out. So now the bins get knocked over by dogs, there's crap everywhere and the new guy only comes here once a week."

I remember Mum's angry voice on the phone: *All the Dhanbul jobs gone. Garbage collectors fired. Lomu out of a job.*

I say the only thing I can say. "Oh."

There's disappointment in her face. "Honestly, Rosie. Does your mind still live here, or just your body?"

I'm about to defend myself when she adds, "At least you're coming today."

Mum one, Rosie nil.

There's no getting out of it now.

★

I trail Mum reluctantly down our driveway, and cross the road to Rika Park. It's not much of a park, just a flat expanse of grass with some weather-beaten play equipment and a sprinkling of trees. It's next to the ocean, though, which is nice.

I feel the breeze as we approach. I'm on my phone, texting Nick as we walk.

Mum's dragging me 2 sum protest. Wud rather B swimming with U!

He texts back within a few seconds.

Wot did I tell U? Raised by a hippy ;-)

I smile.

Mum waits for me to catch up. "Can you put that phone away for one second?"

I glare, feeling manipulated. "Well, if I was with Nick, like I planned to be, I wouldn't have to text him. Do I really have to come to this?"

"Yes, you do."

"You said spend the day with you, not you and half of Yirrkala."

"This is important, Rosie."

I look around the park. There are about a hundred people gathered, most of them Yolŋu. They sit clustered under the big banyan tree, or in the weak shade of palms. A few men are crouched in the sun, starting a small fire.

I ask, "What are they doing? It's not that cold."

"Larry said they're going to burn the Intervention documents."

There are only a few Ŋäpaki around. There's a guy I've never seen before, filming. Two nurses from the clinic wave at Mum but she keeps walking, probably to avoid talking about Graham.

I see Aiden across the lawn, sitting with two Yolŋu guys. I recognise one of them as Nona's brother, Lomu. He and the other guy are in a band with Aiden; it's called East Journey. They're really good. Lomu says something to Aiden, their heads momentarily close. Aiden smiles and answers. I wonder if he is speaking Yolŋu Matha. Does he know how to? I've never thought to ask.

A tall, skinny Yolŋu man taps the wireless microphone and starts to speak. It's in English, and I listen as I follow Mum. He's emotional. "We Yolŋu used to feel strong. We felt like we knew how to raise our kids. If they were doing the wrong thing, we felt we could give them a slap. But now we don't know what to do …"

We reach our Yolŋu family. They're sitting on a red plastic mat under the banyan tree.

White teeth and dark eyes greet us as we approach. Mum folds herself onto a corner of the mat, while I sit stiffly behind her. I expect Rripipi to tell me off for what I said about Nona at school, but she just smiles and says something in Yolŋu Matha. Years ago, I might've understood. Now all I recognise now are the words *gaminyarr*, grandchild, and Mätjala.

Mätjala is the Yolŋu name she gave me when I was born. It means driftwood. I've never liked it. Driftwood seems insignificant: debris swept around at the mercy of the tides. I remember whining to Mum, "How come Nona gets to be named after some magic spirit, like a fairy, and I get a boring old chunk of wood?"

I shift, feeling awkward. "Hello."

She holds out her arms, switching to English. "Give your *momu* a hug. Come on. Come here."

I lean in, and feel her bony arms around my shoulders. She pulls back, grinning, her face folded in a map of dusty creases. I notice her wiry black afro is now mostly grey. I try not to stare. How long has it been since I've seen her up close? A year? Maybe two? Is it possible she's aged so much in that time? I remember her as lean, graceful and strong. Now she sits stooped and tired. I do a quick calculation and guess she couldn't be more than fifty. She says something to Mum, which ends with "*marrkap'mi*". She's pleased about something, but what?

The tall, skinny man has finished talking. He hands the microphone to another Yolŋu man, this one average height and thicker set. It's Galarrwuy, one of the leaders of the Gumatj clan. Everyone knows who he is. He seems angry as he waves a thick wad of white A4 paper in the air.

I lean forward to Rripipi. "What's he saying?"

I know she'll be able to explain: she works as an interpreter in town and for the courts in Darwin. She speaks four Yolŋu languages and her English is perfect. She learned from Dad's parents, who were Methodist missionaries here in the '50s.

Rripipi translates softly, so only Mum and I can hear. "He's saying the federal Intervention is worrying and sickening, the lowest level of anybody's form of policy … we need to fight the sickness of this government setting out to simply take away what's ours … he refuses to sign the ninety-nine-year lease … he says our land has already been taken by mining, he won't let it be taken again."

A few minutes later, she says, "He's speaking about money now. Money for health and housing and education."

Her words remind me. I try not to let my guilt show, as I say, "There was a lady from school – Mrs Reid. She was trying to get in touch with Nona. I told her to call you – did she?"

"*Yo* … I think so … a while ago, *neh*?"

I nod. "Did you talk to Nona about it?"

"No point. She won't go back to school. I told her, the Intervention will get you. The army's coming."

There's a twinkle in her eye that tells me she's joking.

She continues. "Anyway, she's gone to her promised now."

I stare. Is this still part of the joke? "Her what?"

"Her promised. You know." Rripipi seems serious.

Mum leans forward, concerned. "Isn't she a bit young?"

"It was her choice. She wanted to go."

Mum asks, "What about school?"

Rripipi shrugs.

Mum frowns. "Who is he?"

"They call him Stretch. Tall guy."

"Is he *manymak*?" Good?

I'm relieved to hear her answer, "*Yo*. He's a nice one. Doesn't drink. He's the son of the Yolŋu minister – you know him?"

Mum nods. I look away, towards the centre of the park. A

line of Yolŋu are making their way up to the fire. It's only a small one, no more than a campfire, really. One after the other, they toss pages of the Intervention document in to burn.

Galarrwuy is still talking, but I hardly hear him now.

The paper crumbles into ashes, which dance above the flames. The black specks swoop left and right, twirling together in a dizzying spin, then float up into the clear blue sky.

20

2000

We are jammed together on the couch, between Rripipi and one of her sisters. The lounge room is full. The TV is on. We're waiting for the race to start.

At school today, it was the only thing anyone could talk about.

"Did you see her in the opening ceremony?"

"Man, she's fast."

"That French lady pulled out."

"Why does Cathy wear that funny suit?"

"Do you reckon it makes her faster?"

"She's Aboriginal, you know?"

"Well, derr."

I take a sip of green cordial. Nona is stuffing her face with popcorn. Jimmy and Lomu wrestle with their cousins for a spot right in front of the screen. The smalls are sitting on the floor holding someone's baby. Gulwirri arrives with two of Bolu's sisters and their kids. Mum invited the whole family. Rripipi's small box TV was broken during the opening ceremony. An uncle got so excited about seeing the group from Yirrkala perform that he knocked the set off its stool and onto the concrete floor.

The room quietens as the runners approach the starting line. The competitors are announced, one by one. The first five are ladies we don't know or care about in outfits that look like swimmers or crop tops and bike pants. And then there's Cathy in her signature green and white suit. Only her face and hands, a soft honey-brown, are visible.

The TV announcer says, "Lane six – Cathy Freeman," and the stadium crowd erupts in a roaring ecstasy of anticipation. In our lounge room, we are jubilant. She's going to do it for sure. She'll be the first Aboriginal person to win an individual Olympic gold medal. We can already taste victory.

A few extra bodies push into the room. It is Bolu and two men I don't recognise. One is older, short with greying hair. The other is tall and skinny. He looks about eighteen. The tall one winks at Nona and throws her a packet of jellybeans. She catches it, grinning, then turns back to the TV.

Cathy bends down low over the starting mark. Two triangles of yellow appear on her suit, just behind the arms.

Nona hands me a fistful of jellybeans. I can feel lolly man watching her. Why isn't he watching Cathy? I nudge Nona and whisper, "Who's that?"

"Who?"

"The guy who gave you the jellybeans."

"You know Stretch?"

Jimmy turns and whacks Nona on the legs. "Shut up!"

The starter's gun is in the air now. Bang. And she's off. A torpedo of white and green. I think she's coming third. The TV commentary is drowned in a cacophony of high-pitched shrieks and Yolŋu Matha.

"*Waḏitja!*"

"*Ma' wirrki wirrki!*"

"Djulk'maŋuna!"

Cathy powers around the corner and draws level with the front group. With just seconds to go she surges ahead, far ahead. She's done it!

My eyes remain glued to her face as she sits down, gasping for breath. Why isn't she smiling? Is she sick? Is she going to cry? She closes her eyes for a moment, then stands and walks off the track.

I can hear the announcer now. "What a legend. What a champion."

A female voice adds, "What a relief."

The crowd in our lounge room is laughing, shouting. Tears are streaming down Rripipi's face. Beside me, Nona starts dancing with pure joy. On screen, Cathy is doing the same. Victory has finally sunk in. She's smiling now, holding two flags. One Aboriginal, one Australian.

"Yo, manymak!"

"Look at the flags. *Märrma'* together."

Lolly man approaches us through the crowd, his eyes smiling from a round, friendly face. He towers over us. "Good race, eh?"

Nona says, "Good one – no, great one!"

Lolly man grins and pushes back his hair. It is thick and curly. He stands beside us a few seconds more, as if not knowing what to say, then turns and sidles away.

Nona yells at the TV. "Replay! Replay!"

I watch lolly man slide back in next to Bolu, then I ask, "Who is he?"

"I told you – Stretch."

"Why'd he give you lollies?"

"He's my promised husband."

I'm stunned. "What?"

"I'm gonna marry him. When I'm older."

She sees the shock in my face, and shoves me, playfully. "You look like Cathy." She contorts her face into a mirror of Cathy's shocked expression after she won. Nona's always been a good mimic. She grins, "Thought she was going to have a heart attack."

I ask, "Is he nice?"

"*Yo*, he's from Gikal. Plays for Baywarra."

She holds out the packet of jellybeans. "Lolly?"

"No thanks."

I look back at the TV. Cathy is on the podium now, victorious, elated.

I guess some things take a while to sink in.

21.

——

2007

Mum and I eat a late lunch of toasted ham, cheese and tomato sandwiches. Our silent munching is punctuated, every now and then, by a roar from the oval outside or the sound of a car horn tooting. I try to sound nonchalant as I ask, "Do you know who's playing today?"

Mum looks over at me, surprised. "You mean the football?"

"Yeah."

I haven't shown any interest since I was small. Bolu used to play, and sometimes Jimmy and Lomu too. Nona and I would hang out with the girls by the side of the field.

There are questions in Mum's voice as she says, "I'm not sure."

I chew the last bite of my sandwich and put the empty plate on the sink. "I might go down to the shop, get an ice-cream."

Mum can't help herself. She raises a curious eyebrow. We never buy anything from the Yirrkala store anymore. We used to; when I was little it was community-owned. But now that it's run privately it's a complete rip-off. I expect Mum to object but she just hands me a twenty-dollar note. "Get one for me too? That should hopefully cover it."

I smile back, grateful for the lack of questions.

I stuff the money in my pocket and slip out the door, clunking down our front stairs and turning left into the street. The football looks like it's drawn a decent crowd. The shop car park is almost full and there is a line of battered old four-wheel drives parked by the side of the oval. Groups of Yolŋu fill the small metal bleachers and huddle in the shade of nearby trees. A police paddy-wagon cruises past. They seem to be out here more often lately.

I walk towards the store, nodding polite hellos at three ladies who pass me with boxes of greasy chicken and chips.

I reach the front of the shop and push the thick plastic doors open. Inside, the light is dim and musty.

A few kids giggle as I pass. One of them says, "You Jen's daughter." Another asks, "Where's Jen?"

I say, "At home," and smile as I head towards the freezer. There are no prices marked. I grab two Magnums and carry them to the counter. The lady in front of me is buying two loaves of white bread and a jar of Nutella. The man at the counter rings up twenty-one dollars. She hands it over without blinking and sails towards the exit, the cheeky kids hurrying to follow her out.

The man scans my Magnums. "Sixteen dollars, thanks."

Outside, I hold Mum's ice-cream by the end of the packet, as I open mine. I fold back the crinkly packaging and take a cold, creamy bite.

I start to walk towards the oval. In just a few steps, I'm there. I check the scoreboard: 50−52. I'm guessing that means it's close. A thick metal pipe runs around the perimeter of the field. I sit down on it to watch, licking drips from my melting Magnum. In front of me, four boys chase a mini-football, wrestling it off each other in imitation of the main game. By my side, there's a group of Yolŋu ladies sitting on a dusty, old sheet. One of them smiles up at me, so I ask, "Who's playing?"

She says, "Ŋuykal *ga* Baywarra."

Anyone living here knows Ŋuykal is one of two teams from Yirrkala. They won the final last year; there were fights with the other Yirrkala team every night for a week.

I scan the field. Baywarra is all Yolŋu, but Ŋuykal is a mix. I spot Aiden up the back, near the goal, in a double blue Ŋuykal shirt. He watches the ball as it sails towards him, only to be out-jumped by a Baywarra player at the last minute. The ladies on the sheet next to me go crazy. The guy with the ball has thick, curly hair, but it couldn't be him: that player looks about my age. My eyes keep roving and, bingo, there's a tall guy with a round, open face. He soars over the other players, snatches the ball out of the air and kicks it. His movements are smooth, his body lean and muscly. Athletic. He must be in his mid twenties now. What would it be like to be married to him? Would he be gentle? Kind? Do they live together? Where? With his family or hers? Do they have their own room?

Baywarra must have scored, because the ladies on the sheet start whooping in unselfconscious celebration. A siren sounds and the players troop off the field. My new friend looks up and smiles again. "Half time."

The Baywarra team retreat to a small bleacher on the other side of the oval, beside a huddle of ladies on plastic mats. And then I see her. Nona.

She says something to one of the women beside her. I feel Mum's ice-cream melting in its packet, and reluctantly turn to go.

I wonder if Nona watched the football on Elcho Island.

Does she like the game, or does she just come to watch him?

★

School's back in, and we fall into a routine. Nick drives me home three days a week, on the days when he doesn't work at the pool.

Some days, like today, when we know Mum won't be here, he comes in.

"You want a drink?"

"Coke?"

"You know we don't have that."

"What hippy stuff have you got, then?"

"Iced rooibos tea."

"Hit me."

I pour us both a long, cold glass. Outside the kitchen window, I can see workmen putting up a fence around our house. It is low, only about a metre high, made of metal piping and wide loops of cyclone wire. I remember Mum's joke and smile.

Nick says, "What?"

"See that fence? It's to keep the paedophiles out."

He looks nonplussed. "What's that supposed to mean?"

"You know the Intervention?"

"Was that the thing with the army? Weren't they supposed to come?"

I can't believe he's forgotten so quickly. "Doesn't matter. It's not important."

He takes a sip of his iced tea, then puts the glass on the bench. He leans in and kisses me, slowly but deeply.

It gets passionate quickly. His hands begin exploring. I inch backwards. He follows. It's a dance we've started doing to a song with no words.

I angle away. "What if Mum comes home?"

"Didn't you say she's working 'til five?"

He's all hot breath, licks and fumbles. I think I love Nick. I think he loves me. But I'm just not ready yet. Not like this. Not here. Not now.

I push him back, this time more forceful. "Nick, there are guys working right out there. What if they come in?"

He leans back against the kitchen bench, frustrated. "Man, Rosie. There's always some excuse, isn't there?" He drinks his tea, staring off in the direction of the lounge room.

I look back out the window. I see a blue kingfisher swoop down to perch on a section of our newly built fence. It tilts its head, seeming to look at me, then flaps off towards the art centre, disappearing out of sight.

★

Dad is on the phone for his weekly Wednesday update.

"How are things in Yirrkala?"

"Fine. Are you coming up soon?"

There's a momentary pause, then he says, "Not sure. There's been a bit of a hiccup."

I can guess his excuse. He's used it a lot lately. "Something to do with the Blue Mud Bay case?"

"Actually, no. You know how I told you we're trialling a tourism thing down here?"

It rings a few vague bells. "Uh huh."

"Well, it's kind of stalled. I applied for grants and we got a few, so technically we're good to go. But now the old man isn't sure he wants to do it. He thinks with all this Intervention stuff, no-one will want to come. Anyway, I really need to be here, to try and sort it out. So I might shop in Gapuwiyak this month. It's a bit closer."

I know he can tell I'm disappointed, because he hurries on. "I heard there was a meeting in Rika Park on the weekend?"

I grunt, non-committal. I want him to ask about me, not the stupid Intervention.

He doesn't get the hint. "Did you go?"

"Mum dragged me down there."

"Good on her. How was it?"

"Rripipi said Nona's gone to her promised."

My words surprise both of us. I hadn't intended to bring this up. But it's too late to back out now, so I say, "Don't you think that's crazy? He's heaps older."

"Who is he?"

"Some guy who plays for Baywarra. He's got to be at least twenty-five."

"What family?"

"Does it matter? She's my age. Fifteen."

"It's different. You know that." Dad sounds uncomfortable.

"So it would be okay if I shacked up with Nick?"

"It definitely would not."

I'm trying to pick an argument, but I don't know why. Dad and I never fight. He's my confidant, a calm presence on the other end of the phone. He hasn't been here for the curfew arguments, or the pocket-money wars, or Mum's ongoing "I wish you'd go out with someone other than Nick" crusade. He doesn't know how to handle this. Mum's always said he's bad at dealing with conflict. Politics and community stuff is fine, but when it comes to personal issues, he avoids talking about them.

He says, "Look, I think fifteen is too young – for Nona, for you, for anybody. But it does happen and there are cultural considerations ... and even culture aside, I really don't feel comfortable judging ... I mean, I lost my virginity at fifteen ..."

I seize on this. "Who said anything about virginity?"

"I'm just assuming ... okay, this is awkward ... Do we need to have a talk about sex, Rosie? Is this something you're thinking about?"

"No."

It comes out sharp and embarrassed. I'm usually so open with Dad, but this is one topic we can't discuss. It's just too weird. There's a silence, then he says, "Do you want to put me on to your mum?"

I panic. "What for?"

I hear Dad's smile through the phone. "So I can ask her about the Intervention meeting, seeing as you're so full of information."

I want to ask him about sex and confusion and culture and Nona, but I don't.

I carry the cordless phone into the hallway, and call out, "Mum …?"

She's at the kitchen sink, washing up. "Yeah?"

"Dad wants to talk to you."

"Oh. Right. Okay."

I can tell she's surprised. We both are. She dries her soapy hands on a tea towel and takes the phone.

I watch as she answers, "Hi, Pete … Yeah, it was quite a good turnout … Galarrwuy spoke, and they burned the Intervention papers … Oh, you know, the usual faces …"

She starts reeling off a list of long, complicated Yolŋu names, some of them familiar, some not.

I loiter in the kitchen as Mum flops onto the lounge and continues to fill Dad in.

I've never heard them talk like this: casually, without fighting.

I wait to see if they talk about Nick or Nona or me.

They don't. It's all community and politics.

For the first time since Graham left, I see Mum smile.

★

I try not to think about it, but it's driving me crazy.

In Art, I whisper to Selena, "Hey … have you and Benny …?"

"What?"

"You know."

She feigns confusion. "What?" Her eyes twinkle with amusement. She's making this hard for me and loving every moment.

We're interrupted by Ms Naylor. "Hello, everyone. Quieten down."

Selena leans in towards me and smirks. "Are you talking about *sex*?" She says it in a scandalised tone, like she can't believe I'd bring it up.

Ms Naylor raises her voice. "A bit of quiet please, guys. Okay. I want to tell you about your next assignment."

Bodies sag into moans. Heads sink onto the art tables in mock despair.

"Come on. It's not that bad. I think it will be fun."

Charlie Mack calls out, "You have a warped sense of fun, Miss."

Titters as Ms Naylor continues. "For your end-of-year assignments, you'll each be creating a triptych."

There are a lot of blank expressions.

She says, "Does everyone know what a triptych is? Yes? No?"

I feel her eagle eyes scanning the class. I slouch lower in my chair, but she's onto me. "Rosie. Can you help us out?"

"It's a painting with three panels."

"You got it."

Selena mutters, "Suck."

I catch Anya watching us from the other side of the room. She sits with Anita White now. Anita's in one of those groups that don't really get invited to parties. Selena made sure of that in Year 9. Anita didn't invite her to a sleepover, so Selena spread a rumour about her being a stuck-up slut. She even wrote her number on the wall of the boys' toilets with the words "For a good time".

Ms Naylor is still talking. "So who can guess what the theme of the triptych is?"

A few voices ring out in a groaned chorus. "Identity."

It isn't a hard guess. We've been doing variations on the same theme all year. Self-portraits, collages, sculpture, all asking the same questions: Who are you? How do you portray that? What makes a person who they are?

Ms Naylor opens her supplies cupboard. "You can use any medium you like – oils, watercolours, pastels, acrylics, charcoal ..."

Selena pretends to think it over. "Hmm ... what medium do you think says 'me'?"

I shoot her an amused look. "Um ... fluoro highlighters?"

"'Cause they're bright?"

"I was going to say artificial."

"Bitch."

But we're both grinning.

"We're going to start our planning today," Ms Naylor says. "So feel free to sketch ideas, or cut and paste from magazines, or look through books for inspiration ..."

Selena has her *Girlfriend* magazine out in a shot. She scans the contents page. "Top ten Aussie bachelors of 2007. Sounds like inspiration to me."

"I thought you were taken."

"No harm in window shopping."

She turns to the relevant page as I sketch three rectangular panels in my book.

Selena gives me a coy smile. "So you were saying ... have Benny and I ...?"

"Forget it."

"If you're thinking about screwing my brother, I don't want to know."

"Selena!"

She loves shocking people by coming straight out with things other people would never say. I look around, checking no-one has heard. Luckily they're all too busy talking, sketching, trawling books for ideas.

"So are you?"

"I don't want to talk about it."

"You brought it up!"

I trace unnecessarily around the edges of my three panels, making them darker and darker. I'm buying time. I have no idea what I want to fill them with.

After a few moments, Selena inches her chair closer to mine, lowering her voice to a whisper. "The answer is yes. Benny and I have …"

She bobs her head to finish the sentence. She doesn't need to say the words.

I'm surprised and hurt. I knew they'd come close but … "What happened to telling me?"

"We only did it a few weeks ago. In the holidays."

"I can't believe you didn't say something."

She shrugs. There's not much she can do about it now.

I hesitate, then ask, "Did you like it?"

"You know …"

For a girl who loves making outrageous statements, she's strangely non-committal.

I probe again. "Why didn't you tell me straight away? We had a deal."

The deal was whoever sleeps with anyone first has to tell the other, with all the gory details. We made the deal after watching *She's the Man* one night. We both love trashy chick flicks.

Selena says, "I was going to tell you … it just didn't come up." She grins. "No pun intended."

I'm not letting her off that easy. "So?"

She pretends to be engrossed in her magazine, before saying softly, "So … maybe I wish I'd waited. Just a bit, you know … 'til I felt totally ready."

A rare look of vulnerability flickers across her face.

Then it's gone as she says, "So don't hurry to screw my brother, okay? God, even the thought of it is enough to make me want to vomit."

I shoot her a mock-disdainful look and say, "Haha."

I'm more confused than ever.

★

A car horn blares around the community. It comes closer, louder, fuller, rounding the corner of our street, then fades away in the direction of the oval. It means someone has died. Someone dies in Yirrkala every few weeks.

I keep getting dressed for school.

Mum comes to my door, leaning on the doorframe as she says, "You know what I hate? I hate that when I hear that horn now I think, 'Who died this time?' and then I think, 'How will that inconvenience me?' You know? Who's not going to be painting? Who won't come to work because of the funeral? That's terrible, isn't it?"

"You're just being honest."

"Sometimes I think I've been here too long."

Mum's words surprise me. I can't imagine her anywhere else.

For a moment, I dare to hope. "You don't mean that, do you?"

If she left, then I could too. Not now, but for uni. We could both move to Sydney.

She sighs. "Of course not. This is my home …"

The thin wisp of hope vanishes in the air.

Mum gives me a wry smile. "… not that it's been great for my love life."

Her mobile is ringing. She moves back into the lounge room to answer it.

I brush my hair and tie it back, checking my reflection in the mirror. Selena is always on at me to wear makeup, but I just can't bring myself to do it. For one, it's expensive. For two, I don't really know how to put it on.

Mum reappears at the door. Her face is ashen. "I feel even worse now. It was family of Rripipi's, a nephew or something. Young guy, died in a car crash. I told your *momu* we'd pick her up and go in to the morgue. Will you come?"

"I've got school."

"Rosie, this is family."

"I don't even know who you're talking about."

"You promised you'd make an effort –"

"If I knew him, if it was close family, I'd be there."

"Would you?"

"Of course."

Mum's shoulders sag. I know she hates dealing with these things alone, but I stand firm. "Come on, Mum. You'll have *Momu* with you."

I grab an apple from the fridge and head out the door.

As I close it behind me, the car horn wails past our house again.

22

2000

We are standing in front of Bolu's body, in the lounge room of Rripipi's house. I stare at his still face. He could be sleeping, but I know he's not. His eyes are closed and there's a red and gold fleecy blanket pulled carefully up to his neck. All around us there are people crying, wailing, mourning. I can hear the constant clap of *biḻma* and smell the waft of smoke.

Nona is sobbing. She sits next to the body and gently strokes her dad's face. She gestures me towards her but I'm frozen to the spot. I don't want to touch him. I've never seen a dead body before – well, not exposed and not this close up. I've been to funerals, of course, lots of them, but Mum always holds me back from the parts she thinks are too distressing. Today, she didn't have a choice. Dad drove in from Gapuwiyak as soon as he heard the news. He insisted I be here for all of it.

I feel something push against my leg and look down. Rripipi is tearing at her hair, doubled over on the concrete floor. Her grief is so raw I can hardly bare to look. Mum pulls me aside as two aunties bend to help her up. She throws herself down again. I hear the slap of skin on concrete. I cling to Mum's legs. She wraps her arms around me.

Gulwirri appears at our side.

Mum hugs her and kisses her cheek. "I'm so sorry, *Yapa*."

I hear Gulwirri murmur, "It was a heart attack. This morning. Eight o'clock this morning. We're waiting for the boys to come back from Bawaka."

The crowd shifts and jostles. A group of men approach the body, holding spears. I catch sight of my dad amongst them. A slither of white between black. He's the only Ŋäpaki there. He knows the dance, though. The motions, the ritual. He has taken part in this so many times – he has done it since childhood – but this time it's for his brother. His eyes look wild and angry and sad and lost.

Mum touches my arm. "Come on. Let's go outside."

I look back at Nona. I want her to come with us. I want us to be together. But she is bent over her dad's face now, kissing his forehead.

She doesn't see me at all.

She doesn't see anyone but her dad, lying there motionless. Dead.

I let Mum lead me out.

23.

2007

Art is cancelled so that all the senior classes, Years 10 to 12, can attend a "talk". We stroll in a haphazard line from the art room to the hall. Normally, I'd hate to miss Art, but today I'm relieved. My triptych is still three blank rectangles.

Ms Naylor slows to walk beside me. "How are you feeling, Rosie?"

"Okay."

Selena watches on, curious.

Our teacher tentatively asks, "Did you know him? The boy who died? He lived out at Yirrkala, didn't he?"

I shrug, embarrassed by her attention.

"Was he a friend of yours? Or family?"

I'm careful to be honest. "I didn't know him." I want to end the conversation.

She finally takes the hint. "Well, if you need extra time for your assignment ... you know ... if you have to attend ceremonies or anything like that."

"Thanks, Miss. I'll let you know."

She picks up speed, heading to the front of the line.

Selena grins. "Lucky you. Extra time. Why say no?"

★

Selena and I take a seat on the cool floorboards. Mrs Reid is up the front of the hall, calling for attention. Once we're quiet she says, "Good morning. We called this meeting this morning for a very sad reason. I'm sure some of you already know … a boy died last night. It's not culturally appropriate to say his name, but some of you may have known him, particularly the Yolŋu students. He came here a few years ago before transferring out to Yirrkala."

The students are silent. Death is common in Yirrkala, but in town it's still rare.

All faces are turned to the front, listening intently as Mrs Reid continues. "I know there are rumours flying around, so here are the facts. The boy was hanging out with his friends in Yirrkala. They were drinking. The boy decided he wanted cigarettes. He asked around and couldn't find any. He decided to drive into town and crashed into a tree."

She takes a deep breath. "There are a lot of issues wrapped up in this. He shouldn't have been drinking. Or driving, for that matter. But the fact he died is a tragedy. He was only fifteen years old."

There's a wave of mutters. I hear some kids near us trying to figure out who it was.

Mrs Reid waves her hands to indicate silence. "If you want to talk about this, there are people here for you. The school counsellor, Mr Martin. Myself. Mrs Roberts, your vice princi-pal. Any of your teachers. If this worries you, please talk to us. We're here."

She winds up the meeting, and students move to talk in

clusters. Some approach the teachers up the front. Selena takes my hand and starts to pull me across the hall. I can see her target; Nick and Benny are chatting to two of their basketball mates, Reggie and Matt. Matt is a lanky guy with acne. Reggie's short, nuggety and fast. I'm not huge fans of either of them, but apparently they're good players, perfect for two on two.

Nick laughs with them about something and they shove each other, pretending to scuffle. Benny forces a smile. Aiden walks past and glares. I wonder what that's about. We reach the boys. "Hey, what's going on?"

"Not much."

"Sad, huh?" says Selena.

Benny nods, "For sure."

The others are still sniggering.

Selena looks at them. "What's so funny?"

Nick says, "Nothing."

Reggie and Matt are smirking.

Nick takes my hand. "Early recess. Reckon the canteen'd be open?"

★

I walk to the car park to meet Nick for my regular ride home from school.

Aiden is slouching towards the bus stop, scrolling through his iPod. As he passes me, he mutters, "Don't you catch the bus home anymore?"

My step falters. I turn to look at him. "What?"

He blushes, embarrassed, but repeats it anyway. "Don't you catch the bus after school anymore?"

His tone is strange, like he's annoyed or something.

I try to keep things light. "Got a better offer."

"From Nick Dad-bought-me-a-brand-new-ute Bell?"

I'm taken aback by the bitterness in his voice. "Are you guys not friends?"

"Are you joking? The guy's a racist dickhead."

My eyes narrow in confusion.

"Did you hear him in there? After the meeting? He was singing 'Another One Bites the Dust'."

"He wouldn't do that."

"Well, he did. I heard him."

This whole conversation is surprising. I've never heard Aiden say more than a few words – and now he comes out with this?

He scowls. "You'd better run or you'll miss your ride."

He shoves his headphones in and keeps walking.

★

I sit quietly in the passenger seat as Nick starts the engine.

He looks over at me, sensing my mood. "You good to go?"

"Yep."

He turns the radio on. Triple J fills the space between us. We start to drive out of town. Aiden's words jostle and argue in my mind. Would Nick really sing "Another One Bites the Dust"? Sure, I've heard him make jokes before, but a fifteen-year-old boy just died. To laugh about it would be heartless. And Nick's not heartless; he's sensitive and kind. But why would Aiden make something like that up?

We're approaching Yirrkala now. The signs pass in a blur. I've noticed at the bottom of the new one someone has sten-cilled *No Intervention, no racism*. It's done in the exact same font as the rest of the sign so it blends in. I've thought about point-ing it out to Nick, not for the politics, but as clever graffiti. Graffiti for a reason, a cause. But now doesn't seem like the right time. We swing left into the community, and Rripipi's house comes into view. A line of bright-coloured skirts hang drying on the verandah. She's sitting out the front on the beat-up blue couch. I recognise her grey afro immediately. She raises a hand in greeting. I wave back as we zoom past, leaving a trail of light brown dust dancing on the road behind us.

Nick asks, "Who was that?"

"Who?"

"The old lady with the crazy hair. I've seen you wave to her before."

I take a deep breath. Here goes. "She's my adopted grand-mother."

I watch him carefully, gauging his reaction. He doesn't flinch or falter, just asks, "So she adopted you?"

I try to make it easy to understand. "Not me – my grand-mother. She was adopted here, ages ago, by that old lady. The whole thing trickles down, though, which means I'm adopted too."

"I've heard about this."

I'm surprised. "Yeah?"

"Why do they adopt people?"

I think before answering. "I guess it's their way of placing you in their world."

I am almost holding my breath, hoping he understands. He nods, like he's considering my answer. Then he says, "Yeah, but that doesn't really mean anything, does it?"

I flinch. "What do you mean?"

"Well, you know Jono from school? In my year? He was adopted. I remember him telling me about it. He said he'd see some guy at the beach and they'd say, 'You're my uncle.' And Jono was like, 'Sure, whatever, I don't know you.' Or a lady would see him in town and ask for money – you know, 'cause he's her 'brother'. It's a bit of a scam, isn't it?"

I try not to sound emotional. "I don't think so."

"No?"

"I guess it's like any extended family. With some people you're close, others you're not. You can see a lot of them, or a little. You can hang out with them, or never see them."

"Like you."

I'm about to protest, when I realise he's right. I say, "I used to do stuff with them … when I was a kid."

"Yeah? Like what?"

"Mum and the ladies went fishing almost every day. And we went on bush trips – looking for *munydjutj'* – these little berries – or wild honey, or *yidaki* – trees to make didgeridoos. Or camping at Nona's dad's homeland, Bawaka. It's amazing out there. We'd go hunting …"

"You mean serious hunting? Like, with a spear?"

I'm disappointed that out of all my precious memories this is what he's seized on, but I'm also relieved. I'm sure Aiden's got it wrong. Nick's not racist, he just doesn't know much about Yolŋu culture. A lot of people don't. It's hardly a crime.

As he pulls into my driveway, I manage a small smile. "Yeah. With a spear."

★

"Look who followed me home."

Mum smiles over at me from where she's buttering bread in the kitchen. I see the profile of a Yolŋu guy sitting in one of our armchairs, a small girl curled sleeping on his lap. He turns to look up at me. "Hi, *Yapa*."

I realise it's Lomu. I manage a surprised, "Hello."

I'm glad Nick didn't come in.

Mum explains, "I gave your *wäwa* and *gäthu* a lift back from the hospital. I wanted Lomu to come and see Bill about work."

I ask, "Any luck?"

Lomu shakes his head. *"Bäyŋu. Wasn't there."*

Mum says, "Maybe if you come tomorrow morning. I know he needs someone to prepare barks. I mean, if you're sure you want to work."

My *wäwa* nods. "I miss it, eh?"

Mum has the jaffle iron out now. "We're just having some toasted sandwiches – you want one?"

"No, thanks."

"We saw *dhaŋarra* driving back here," says Lomu.

I don't know what he's talking about. He says, "The flowers, you know? White ones. Stringybark."

I start to remember. "Does that mean it's *guku* season?"

"Yo." His face broadens into a grin. "Maybe we can go out looking some time. With *Momu*. We can take this one too. My daughter, Kaneisha."

He indicates the girl in his arms, so proud he could burst.

"How old is she?"

"Three."

Mum looks at me, reproachful. "You should've come today."

I force myself to ask, "Was Nona there?"

Lomu shakes his head. "She's staying at Gikal now. Stretch's homeland."

"Her ... husband?"

"Yo."

I ask, "Is it nice there?"

"Beautiful. Small beach. White sand – like Bawaka. You remember Bawaka?"

How could I forget? So many childhood trips. I feel like I have to say something. "I'm sorry about ... the guy who died. Mum said he was family?"

"He was my brother."

I must look confused, because he explains, "My birth mother's sister's son."

I remember Mum telling me Lomu and Jimmy aren't actually Gulwirri's sons. They are Bolu's children, born to another mother; she died just after Lomu was born. Gulwirri raised them as her own.

I say, "Heard it was a car crash."

"Black magic. No good."

"You mean *galka*?"

I know the word from when I was small. Rripipi told all the kids *galka* stories to make them come home by dark. Stories designed to frighten, about bad spirits and ghosts.

"Yeah, people thinking bad things. Making bad things happen for our family. *Momu's* sick …"

"What's wrong with her?"

"Don't know. Maybe flu. A lot of us lost our jobs. That one crashed his car."

Mum eases two toasties onto a plate. She rests it on the arm of Lomu's chair and he eats them one-handed, careful not to disturb Kaneisha. The toasties are gone in under a minute. He licks his fingers, then says, "My *bäpa* tried to kill himself last week. Extension cord. Tied himself to a streetlight."

He acts it out for us, ending with the sound of someone strangled. "Crrch."

My eyes widen. Mum looks shocked. Obviously no-one thought this was serious enough to mention today. "Did someone get him help? Was he okay?"

"Yeah, he's okay. He's in Darwin Hospital now."

He's so calm he could be talking about fishing. Or playing football. Or going to the shops.

24.

2000

I get off the school bus at Nona's house. Gul̲wirri and a group of ladies are sitting down the side of the house, playing cards.

I approach and ask, *"Ŋamal̲a, is Nona here?"*

She shakes her head. *"Bäyŋu."*

"Mum said she was back from Bawaka …"

"Yo … she's around …"

"Well, do you know where she is?"

Gul̲wirri shrugs. Her eyes don't move from her hand of cards. She's changed since Bolu died. She's quieter. More abrupt. Mum says she's stopped going to work.

I say, "If she comes home, can you tell her I'm looking for her?"

"Ma'." Okay.

I walk along the road and down the hill. I check our usual spots. The oval. The sport and rec shelter. The shop. No sign of Nona. I stop in at the art centre. Mum hasn't seen her either. I grab my bike from home and do a lap of the community. I see the smalls and Nona's friends from Top School outside the red house on Marrakulu Road. There's a small crowd gathered. I gesture Yumalil to my side. She tells me someone found a pair of boxing gloves and everyone's been taking turns for the last two days. It's the type of thing Nona would usually love. She's always been able to sniff out what's happening in the community. But today she's not here.

There's only one other place I can think of where she might be. I ride to the boat ramp, park my bike in a hibiscus bush and walk down to the shore. I leap from rock to rock, making my way around the small headland. There's a crocodile that lives here, so I keep well back from the water. I pass a few houses as I round the corner to a small, protected beach. We celebrated our joint eighth birthday here. The party had a pirate theme, and Mum hid chocolate coins in the rocks, like secret treasure. We slid on boogie boards down the sand dunes, and played pin the tail on the parrot.

I look up at the dunes. Sails of golden sand and blue sky. And then I see her, sitting on the highest peak, staring out at the ocean.

I call, "Nona …"

She sees me, but doesn't smile. I climb up towards her, my feet sinking into the warm sand with each step. I plop down beside her. "I was looking for you everywhere."

Nona shrugs. It's obvious she doesn't want to talk, so we sit there in silence. I scan the flat grey ocean, looking for dolphins. There aren't any today.

The sky turns pale and milky. Heat starts to leach from the day. I smell campfires and the waft of people cooking dinner. Mum will be wondering where I am.

I say, "We should head back."

She tucks her knees up to her chest. "Just a bit longer."

There's another long silence, then I hear her voice, barely a whisper. "What do you think happens when you die?"

I know she's thinking of her dad.

I say, "I don't know. What do you think?"

She picks up a small round rock and rolls it between her pale brown fingertips. "*Ŋamaḻa* says we sing for people and it guides them back to their homeland."

I want to comfort her, so I say, "I can imagine your dad in Bawaka. He'd be fishing. Walking along the beach with his spear. Watching the water."

She looks over at me, hopeful. "You think so?"

"Sure. Why not?"

Her eyes cloud over. "*Momu* says we go to heaven or hell."

"Maybe you can go to both?"

"Heaven and hell?"

"No, heaven and your homeland, I mean."

"But how?"

I struggle to find an answer, but come up blank.

Nona is close to tears. "I don't want him to get lost."

I reach out and put my arm around her shoulders. "He won't. He's your dad. He won't."

25.

2007

Someone has left a light on.

I slip out of bed, and walk towards the kitchen. I see Mum at the sink, staring out the window into the night. She's lost in thought.

I say softly, "Can't you sleep?"

She turns, startled. "Rosie ... come here ..."

I walk over and hug her. She holds me close.

I ask, "What are you doing?"

"Just thinking."

"What about?"

She shrugs, but her eyes look sad. I take a guess. "Are you missing Graham?"

"Sort of. I mean, yeah, of course I am. But that's not ..." She stops, then says, "I was thinking about Lomu and Kaneisha."

I look at her in confusion.

She continues. "What did you see this afternoon? I mean, when you looked at them together?"

I shake my head. I have no idea what she's getting at.

Her voice is raw as she says, "I saw a loving dad. But if

someone in mainstream Australia saw that, an Aboriginal man and a little girl, with what's going on politically …" She breaks off, getting teary. "Sorry, I'm just a bit emotional."

"It's okay."

"You should go to bed. You've got school tomorrow."

She walks me to my bedroom and watches as I climb into bed. Then, maybe by impulse or old habit, she sits beside me. She pulls the doona up to my chin and tucks it in around my shoulders. She kisses my forehead, like she used to when I was small.

She whispers, "Goodnight, Rosie."

"Goodnight, Mum."

I watch as she walks out of the room, closing my door behind her.

A small part of me wishes she'd left it open.

★

Nick drops me home at six thirty, just before dark. I enter a house of grey shadows. Mum is in the lounge room, on the phone. She's so engrossed in conversation that she's forgotten to turn the lights on. I flick the switch. She glances up at me in surprise, but keeps talking. "I wish I could've been there. Frank says the look on their faces was priceless."

My stomach is growling. I head to the kitchen. From the odd ingredients on the bench, it looks like Mum has made a start on dinner. There's a tray of semi-charred capsicum and a pot of stock left forgotten, boiling away to nothing on the stove. A recipe book I've never seen before is open at a page that says "Chicken and Roast Vegetable Risotto". Mum's laughing now. "I know. I know."

I scan the recipe and grab butter from the fridge, rice and more stock from the pantry. I turn the radio on. ABC Radio blares out at me. Mum indicates for me to turn it down. I do, changing the station to Gove FM. I'm starting to rescue dinner as Mum says goodbye. She hangs up and sees I've taken over cooking. "I wanted to make us something special. Is it salvageable?"

"I think so."

She starts peeling blackened skin off the capsicums, a playful smile on her lips. "So ... you'll never guess what happened today."

I humour her. "You bought a recipe book?"

She looks sheepish. "Actually, it's Sadie's."

"You decided to get us an air-conditioning unit?"

Mum laughs. It's an ongoing joke between us. At least, she always assumes I'm joking, but I'm actually not. We must be the only Ŋäpaki family in the community whose house only has ceiling fans.

She's beaming as she says, "We kicked the Intervention Task Force out of Yirrkala."

Not exactly what I was expecting. "Okay ... and that means what?"

"People from the government came here and the community asked them to leave. Told them not to come back 'til they send the head honcho. You know, the army guy, David Chalmers?"

She does a funny little jig towards the fridge. "I told your dad I'd have a celebratory wine for him, seeing as he can't drink in Yilpara."

She's got my attention now. "That was Dad?"

She nods and pours herself a generous glug of white. She grins. "Do you want a tiny glass? A first taste of alcohol?"

She's never offered before. She's in a very strange mood. On a high. Elated. But her offer just reminds me of warm beer and scrambled egg. I shake my head. I stir the buttery rice around the pan, check the recipe and add more stock. "Since when do you and Dad talk?"

"What do you mean? We never stopped talking."

"Yeah, but you don't talk much. And you never sounded friendly to him on the phone. You never *laughed*."

"Didn't I?"

"No."

Mum considers this before responding. "I guess we didn't have much to talk about, except you. And that was always a minefield because we never agreed about how you should be raised."

"I think you've done an okay job."

She smiles, amused. "Thank you, Rosie. Me too."

I'm still struggling to make sense of this new world order. "So now ... you and Dad ... you're what? Friends?"

"Comrades, I guess. Comrades, against the Intervention."

I can't tell if she's serious or joking.

★

We're at the Latram River, just a short drive through the bush from Yirrkala. You can swim here, as long as you check for crocs first. The water is shallow, fresh and crystal clear. We used to come here with Nona's family after long mornings looking for *guku*. We'd pile out of Mum's troopie, a squash of sticky bodies. There was lots of splashing and jumping, giggles and squeals.

Today, it's quiet. Just me and Nick and the soft hum of the bush. He is lying on a Quiksilver towel, dozing on his stomach in the dappled sun. His board shorts hang low and I can see all five stars of the Southern Cross. I trace them with my index finger, drawing a circle around each one and linking them up. He shivers at my touch. His skin prickles into goosebumps.

I ask, "When did you get this?"

"Ages ago."

"Like when?"

"You're not going to let me sleep, are you?"

A cheeky smile. "Nope."

He props himself up on his elbows, thinking. "A few years ago? We were in Bali. Mum let me get it. Just before we moved up here. 2005?"

"Why'd you choose the Southern Cross?"

"'Cause I'm a star?"

I hit him lightly. "In your dreams."

"Are you saying I'm not?"

"Be serious for once."

"I just thought it was cool."

I don't buy his flippant responses. "Come on. It's gotta mean something."

He uses his fingertip to draw stars in the damp riverbank sand. I'm reminded of an old story Nona told me about how the Milky Way is made up of the spirits of children, who fall down into the water when they're ready to be born. I can almost see one falling from the sky now. It floats like a feather, drifting side to side, then comes to rest on the river's surface, gliding downstream … to who?

Nick has found his voice again. "There's no big story behind it. I just like the symbol. And I love this country."

"So do I, but I wouldn't get it burnt into my bum crack."

"It's not in my bum crack."

"It's pretty low."

"What are you looking down there for, anyway?"

"I'm looking at the tattoo!"

"Sure you are!"

I shove him, grinning.

"Admit it. You think I'm hot." He pulls me closer, tickling my sides.

"Stop. Stop!"

"Admit it."

My laughter glances across the water, ricocheting off the bank on the other side.

"Okay! You're hot. Gorgeous. Can't get enough of you."

"That's more like it."

He holds me. Kisses my neck. A cockatoo rustles in the trees above us, foraging for food.

I hear Nick's voice, soft and low in my ear. "I love you, Rosie."

"I love you too."

And suddenly the place feels like it used to. Alive. Full. Bursting.

26.

2001

We are hugging and grinning, in the middle of the playground. I haven't seen Nona in weeks, then she shows up here, at my school. Her T-shirt and shorts are smeared with charcoal and dirt. I ask, "Where've you been, *Yapa*?"

"Gapuwiyak."

"With who?"

"Tina. Mum's sister. You know her?"

I nod. "Why didn't you tell me? I could've come with you, could've visited Dad."

She shrugs. "I was just at BP, and Tina and Sheree were there getting petrol. They said to get in, so I did."

"*Momo* was worried. She's been sick, you know."

"Mum could've told her."

"Don't think she's been home."

Nona scowls. Gulwirri's been drinking, disappearing into town for days at a time. I've heard Mum and *Momo* talking about it.

Nona says, "You got any food? I'm starving."

I start to lead her towards my school friends, Lily and Dana.

I notice she's limping. "What happened to your foot?"

"Hurt it."

"How?"

"Walked over a fire."

"A campfire?"

She nods. For someone with a burnt foot she's setting a cracking pace.

Miss Emmerton approaches. She's on playground duty. "Hi, Rosie. Who's your friend?"

"Um, this is Nona."

"Do you go to school here?"

I'm worried we'll get in trouble, so I say, "She goes to school in Yirrkala … but she's hurt her foot. I think she needs a bandage."

Miss Emmerton lifts Nona's bare left foot gently. I catch my breath. The sole is deep red and purple-black, oozing pus and something that looks like tree sap. Part of the flesh is almost falling off. Miss Emmerton's face pales. "Hooley dooley. You need more than a bandage. Is that painful? Sore?"

Nona shrugs.

"You should probably go to hospital. Is there someone I can call? Maybe your mum?"

Nona stares at the ground, silent.

"Or your dad? A grandparent?"

No response.

I speak for her. "You can call my mum."

27.

2007

I meet Mum in Woolworths to do our weekly shop. It is cool and air-conditioned inside. I'm guessing it must be pay day because the whole supermarket is crowded with Yolŋu.

Mum sees my hair, still wet from the pool. "Water warming up yet?"

"Yeah. It is."

"How's Nick?"

"He's good."

I never elaborate much more than that. I know she's not really interested in the answer. She only asks in the hope that one day I'll say things are rocky, that we might be breaking up. And that's not going to happen any time soon. We're in love. We've even said it. A few times now.

We make our way up and down the aisles. The barge is late this week; the meat fridges and the fruit and vege section are almost empty. There's only long-life milk. We fill our trolley as best we can, and wheel it towards the checkout.

I hear Mum's pleasantly surprised voice say, "*Yapa*. Hello.

And nice to see you, *Waku*."

I look up and see Guḻwirri and Nona in the line in front of us. They're unloading their trolley, stacking the conveyor belt with two-minute noodles, powdered milk, frozen bread. Chips and soft drink.

Mum smiles at Nona. "Ṟripipi said you're staying out at Gikal now."

She nods. "Had to do some shopping."

"How often do you come in?"

"Every two weeks. On payday."

Mum nudges me into politeness. I say, "Hi."

I expect Nona to ignore me, and she does. I haven't seen her since that day in school. She keeps her eyes down. I watch her as she finishes unloading. She looks tired and drawn. Her usual spark is missing.

Guḻwirri gives me a small smile. *"Nhämirri nhe, Waku?"* How are you, my child?

I respond automatically. *"Manymak."* Good.

The basic Yolṇu Matha rolls around in my mouth. A word I used to use all the time. It tastes familiar. It tastes like childhood.

The checkout lady finishes scanning their items and reads out the total: $248.60. Guḻwirri takes out her purse and hands over a green and white card.

The lady takes it. "You got enough money on here?"

Guḻwirri shrugs. "Hope so." She lowers her voice to Mum. *"Yapa*, you got *rrupiya* for petrol? Got these cards now. Money's stuck on there."

The checkout lady punches in numbers then hands the card back. I peer over. It says Basics Card. I've never heard of it.

Mum digs a twenty-dollar note out of her wallet and gives it to Guḻwirri, then gestures to Nona and says something in Yolṇu Matha. I make out the word *rirrikthuna*. Sick. Guḻwirri answers and Mum responds with a surprised "Wah …"

I hear Gulwirri say, "Trying to hide it."

Nona's eyes remain averted, her hands in her pockets. She seems embarrassed by our mums' conversation. The transaction goes through and she starts to push their bag-laden trolley towards the door. She gives Mum a small nod. *"Nhäma, Namala."*

I may as well not even be there.

Mum calls after her, "If you need anything …"

It's hard to tell if she hears as the automatic doors open and close around her and the trolley. She can't wait to get away and I don't blame her. Gulwirri says goodbye and follows Nona out. Mum watches them go, her face a mix of regret and disappointment.

I ask, "What was that about?"

Mum's surprised. "You didn't understand?"

I snap back, on edge. "Obviously not, or I wouldn't ask."

Mum ignores my tone and says, "Nona's pregnant."

★

"It's *my* eighteenth."

Nick folds his arms across his chest and leans back against the plastic deckchair. He's just finished teaching a lesson to a group of "squidlet" kids. Now that it's September, the pool is starting to get busy again.

Selena frowns. "Mum will be devastated."

Nick is adamant. "I'm not having it at our house. The whole cake and speeches thing? No way. Dad would use it as an excuse to start crapping on about my future and why I should go to uni."

Benny is propped up on his elbows, lying on a towel on the grass. There are flowers on the mango tree behind him. He looks over at Nick. "Where are you thinking of having it, then?"

"The lookout."

Benny gives Selena an apologetic shrug. "The lookout is a good place for a party."

Nick nods. "And we won't need parents to buy us alcohol. I'll be legal. So it doesn't matter if they like it or not."

Selena sighs. "They'll just be hurt, that's all. Eighteen is a big deal."

A trickle of water runs off Nick's hair and over his shoulder. He turns to me. "Think you could stay over?"

Selena gives me a cheeky wink and pulls Benny to his feet. "Let's swim."

Benny groans but allows himself to be dragged to the edge of the pool, then does a quick turn, grabs Selena and throws her in. She's squealing as she surfaces. He dives in after her.

Nick ignores them, his eyes still on me. "So? What do you say?"

I'm tempted. "You know I want to … but my Mum …"

"This is a special occasion."

"To her, that's all the more reason to say no. It's an eight-eenth. She'll know there'll be alcohol. And she's not going to love that it's at the lookout with no chaperones."

"So don't tell her."

I look back at the pool. Selena and Benny are holding each other in the water. They're close and whispering. They look so carefree. Loved up.

Nick persists. "Or don't tell her about the party at all. Just say you're staying at a friend's place. Someone she likes. Keep it inno-cent. You did that before, didn't you? When you stayed over?"

"I told her I was staying at Selena's. It wasn't exactly lying, she just didn't know about you then."

"Same diff. Come on, what does it matter? It's just a tiny white lie … and it's for a good cause." Nick puts on a puppy-dog face.

I shove him, laughing. "Stop it."

I stand up, pulling the bottom of my swimmers down to make sure they're covering my bum. "I'm going to swim some laps."

I can feel him watching me as I walk to the edge of the pool and climb in. The water is so tepid now I no longer flinch when I get in. I put my goggles on and wade over to the roped-off lanes. Then I'm pushing off the wall. The rush of water in my ears drowns out all sound. My world is once again defined by lane ropes and lines. It feels safe. Familiar. Contained. My arms propel me forward in that comforting rhythm.

One, two, three, breathe.

One, two, three, breathe.

Don't think about Nick. Or sex. Or the party. Just swim.

One, two, three, breathe.

One, two, three, breathe.

Don't think about Nick. Or sex. Or the party. Just swim.

★

Selena shows me the packet. I recognise it from sex-education classes in school.

I look at her in shock. "You're on the pill now? Since when?"

"Since yesterday. Mum took me to Endeavour."

The medical centre in town. I shake my head. "I can't believe she's being so cool about this."

Selena's mum walked in on her and Benny doing it last week. I squirm even thinking about it. It has to be every teenager's worst nightmare, but Selena insists it wasn't as bad as it sounds. Apparently her mum just excused herself and left. Later, she sat her down and said if Selena wanted to be sexually active that was her choice, but to make sure she used protection. She brought her home a packet of condoms the next day, and now this, the pill. I can't believe how understanding she's being.

I say, "My mum would freak out."

"Yeah, well, your mum's ... different."

I think about Mum's reaction to the news Nona is pregnant. The whole way home she was quiet. As we were unpacking the groceries, she said softly, "I really thought Nona would be different. She had that spark, you know, even as a little girl. She was so smart, she could've done anything. I remember her saying she wanted to be a nurse."

Selena nudges me back into the present. "So?"

"So what?"

"So ... are you going to stay over after Nick's party?"

I know what she's really asking. I answer honestly. "I don't know."

She grabs the box of condoms from her bedside drawer and pulls out a small river of blue plastic packets. She rips off a couple and hands them to me. "Well, take these. Just in case. I mean, no pressure or anything, you know even the thought of you and my brother makes me sick, but if you're going to do it ..."

I look at the shiny packages in my hand.

Selena shrugs, "Better than getting knocked up. At our age – can you imagine?"

28

2001

We are lying on our bellies, watching *Rage* on TV.
Nona's white bandaged foot taps the air behind us, in time
with the music. The smalls are on the couch, bowls of Weet-
Bix balanced precariously on their laps.

"I Wanna Be Sedated" by the Ramones comes on. We've
seen the clip before. The band are sitting at a table eating
cornflakes, while the room behind them is going crazy with
nuns and ballerinas and cheerleaders. A nurse with long dark
hair appears and gives the singers fake oversized needles in the
arm. She's wearing a short skirt and a headband with a huge
red cross on it.

I nudge Nona and joke, "Look! It's Nurse Nona!"

She's been talking about hospital ever since she got back
from Darwin. The beds with backs that go up and down. The
food delivered on a trolley. Having a TV in your room. But
what made the biggest impact on her were the nurses. I feel
like I know them, just from Nona's descriptions. Shelly, who
laughs at her own jokes. Lena with the cool tattoos. Nicole,
who showed Nona photos of her family in Scotland. And

Nona's favourite nurse, Jennifer, from Maningrida, who's related to Nona somehow – maybe a distant cousin? Nona's decided she's going to be a nurse when she grows up. We all tease her. Nurse Nona. It has a good ring to it.

I expect Nona to laugh or hit me, but she gestures at me to be quiet. I realise she's been listening to Mum and Rripipi talking in the kitchen. I tune in.

Rripipi's voice is low and earnest. "I went to the Arnhem Club and asked them to ban her. They didn't want to help me so I tried the Walkabout. I told the lady, 'Please, my daughter-in-law has young kids. She shouldn't be here drinking. If you see her, please send her home.'"

Rripipi notices that we're listening, but continues talking. "That Walkabout lady wanted to help but she didn't know how. She said I should try the police. So I stopped in and saw Tony. You know him? He really helped us last time Jimmy was in trouble. But even he said it's a family problem. I told him Gulwirri doesn't listen to me, but she'd listen to him, someone in uniform."

Mum asks, "What did he say?"

"Said he can't stop someone drinking if they're not causing trouble."

"*Ŋamala*, I'm sorry."

"I've bought her a ticket to Elcho. Her sisters said they'll help her dry out." Rripipi coughs. Her chest sounds wheezy.

Mum casts a look in our direction, indicating that we can hear. Rripipi waves her concern away. "They know. I haven't seen the boys, though. Jimmy's been sniffing again, and Lomu disappears for days. They only turn up to take money. I'm tired. And there's no-one to look after the girls."

I know Mum has heard these stories before. I hold my breath, hoping, praying … and finally she offers. "The girls can stay here for a while. You should rest."

I hear the relief in *Momu*'s voice, as she says, *"Ma'."*

Nona and I reach out and squeeze each other's hands in silent celebration. She starts singing gleefully along with the film clip, changing the words, but all the time grinning into my eyes. "Bam bam bam bam ba bam bam bam … I'm gonna stay at your house …"

29.

2007

"Mum, can I stay at Anya's on Saturday night?" I'm hovering by the lounge, nervous, in my pyjamas. It's late, but I've put off asking too long. Nick's party is this weekend. I don't know what I'll do if she says no.

Mum is staring at the TV, engrossed in *Lateline*. I wonder if she's heard me. "Mum? Can I stay …?"

"Shhh." She waves me into silence so she can hear the reporter.

"… backing up its Intervention in the Northern Territory Aboriginal communities with a massive funding boost. It's more than doubling its spending, taking the total outlay to more than $1.3 billion. This extra money will be spent on housing, health and education in remote communities …"

I'm getting impatient now. "Mum."

She finally turns to look at me. "What?"

"Can I stay at Anya's on Saturday night?" It wasn't meant to come out this way. I sound irritated and curt.

Luckily, Mum's too distracted to notice my tone. "You haven't talked about Anya for a while."

I opt for semi-truth. "We haven't been hanging out much. But I feel kind of bad about that and she asked me …"

Mum nods, still staring at the screen. She sounds vague, as she says, "I like Anya."

"So can I go?"

"I'll pick you up at eleven."

"Mum, it's a sleepover. That means all the other girls will be sleeping over?"

Mum forces herself to focus. She looks at me. "Who else is going?"

I try to think of who I've seen Anya with lately. "Um, Anita White and Jennifer Chu."

"I've never heard you mention them before."

"They're … new friends."

Mum actually looks pleased. "Oh, that's nice. I'll pick you up from Anya's at ten in the morning then."

"Can we make it the bakery? Anya wants us to go for coffee."

"Sure thing."

I feel both ashamed and proud of my cover story. I'm getting better at lying. They do say practice makes perfect.

I hear the *Lateline* reporter saying, "About eighty Wadeye children have been given check-ups by federal clinic doctors in the past two weeks …"

I hesitate, then try to sound nonchalant as I ask, "Have you heard from Graham lately?"

"No."

I consider asking more, but her eyes are fixed firmly on the screen again. She hardly notices me go, as I head to my room and text Nick.

All systems go.

He texts back within seconds.

Let's party.

★

I get dressed in a singlet top and knee-length denim skirt. Tie my hair in a ponytail. Check myself out in the mirror. Nothing suspicious there. I'd believe I was going to a sleepover.

It's been a logistical nightmare coordinating the lie, but it's worked. Mum's dropping me at the shops. I told her Anya and the girls were having pizza first. Then Nick's picking me up from there. In the morning, I'll meet her at the bakery as agreed.

I pack an overnight bag with clothes for Nick's party: a borrowed dress from Selena and some low-rise heels. A fresh outfit for tomorrow. I feel like I'm undercover. Toothbrush and facewash. A change of underwear.

In the back of my undies drawer I see the two blue plastic packets Selena gave me. I pull them out and look at them. The house is quiet, but for the rattle of the old ceiling fan wheezing breath into my stuffy room.

Am I making too big a deal of this? I love Nick. He loves me too. Should I just sleep with him and get it over with? Everyone else seems to be doing it. Except me.

I bury the condoms at the bottom of my bag.

★

Thud.

The bouncer's hand shoves up against a bony dark-brown chest. The old Yolŋu man staggers backwards but keeps talking, muttering in Yolŋu Matha. The bouncer takes a step forward, gesturing him away with his hands. The old man looks around

175

the Arnhem Club car park. His glazed eyes swing over Nick's Hilux.

I hunch a bit lower in my seat, willing Nick to hurry up. He's in the bottle shop buying alcohol for his party. An eighteen-year-old's rite of passage, apparently.

Smack.

This time the bouncer swings a closed fist. When I look again the old man is on the asphalt. He crawls backwards, still hurling abuse. There is blood on his face. He stands and staggers away as Nick emerges with a slab on his shoulder and a bag of bottles on his arm. He grins, triumphant, and tries to give me a thumbs up as he carries his precious haul towards me.

The bouncer moves back to the club entrance. He says something to his bouncer mate, who has just appeared from inside. They're in matching uniforms – black and official. Bouncer One looks proud. He demonstrates what happened, like he's replaying the highlights of a fight.

Nick loads the alcohol into the back of the ute, then climbs into the driver's seat. "I forgot, they brought in that permit thing. Wrote my name down 'cause I bought over a hundred bucks' worth. Not that it really matters."

I'm still reeling. "Did you see that?"

"What?"

"That bouncer. He went completely over the top."

"The guy was giving him lip."

"He was an old man!"

"Doesn't matter, Rosie. If you can't hold your liquor and you get aggro, you'll be booted out."

"He hit him. With his fist. In the face. There was blood."

I search Nick's face for compassion but see no trace of it.

He says, "He probably deserved it." His voice is hard. There's a look in his eyes. What is it? Dislike? Disgust? Hate? I hear

Aiden's voice. *The guy's a racist dickhead.* I try to block it out.

I put my seatbelt back on. "Let's go."

★

Nick turns off the main road at the sign to Roy Marika lookout. He's playing Silverchair, and I'm grateful for the conversational silence it imposes. I don't want to talk. I keep seeing the old man outside the bottle shop. *Thud. Smack. He probably deserved it.* The look in Nick's eyes.

We're heading up the hill now. It's steep; my body presses back into the chair. Nick hits stop on the stereo and "Straight Lines" ends, mid lyric. Other sounds come into focus. The chirp of cicadas. A tinny stereo blasting Chemical Brothers into the night. Laughter. Voices. We can see the lookout now. The area around it is full of parked cars and kids from school standing around, drinking, gossiping. There's no room to park, so we keep driving along the dirt track on the crest of the hill. We reach the last car and Nick pulls over behind it.

Benny and Matt have seen us arrive, and approach to help us carry the booze. Benny hoists the slab on to his shoulder. "Impressive haul, Nicko."

Matt slaps him on the back. "Happy birthday, mate."

He takes the plastic bag and they walk ahead of us, leading the way. Nick reaches out and holds my hand as we approach the mob.

"Hey, birthday boy!"

"Eighteen! Woo hoo!"

"Hey, Rosie."

Selena makes her way towards us, squeezing me in an over-enthusiastic hug. "I thought you guys were never going to get here! You want a drink?"

She holds up a bottle of Midori, answering the question before I can even ask. "And no, I didn't fridge it."

I force a smile, remembering the panic in my chest that night. I feel an echo of it surfacing now. A hot ache in my gut.

Selena continues. "Mum gave it to me for the party. She's still upset we're not having it at home, but she wanted us to have a good time. It tastes good with pineapple juice. You want some?"

"Okay."

She starts to pour the bright green liquid into two plastic cups. I look around. Something sails over our heads into Nick's hands.

"Good catch, mate."

I lean forward to see what it is. It's a can of spray-paint.

Benny grins at us. "For prosterity."

Nick laughs. "It's posterity, you goose."

"Whatever. Make your mark, man. Eighteen."

Nick shakes the can. Something small and metal clangs up and down inside it.

Selena is adding juice now. She indicates Benny and Nick with a nod of her head. "Boys, huh?" She smiles.

I watch as Nick takes the lid off and starts to spray the look-out sign with large letters. Nicked. His tag. The strokes of the N look like sharp red gashes. I can just make out some of the writing behind it.

> You are on Rirratjiŋu land
> … everything is divided into two moeities, Dhuwa and Yirritja.
> Yolŋu land owners hope you enjoy your visit to Nhulun.

I remember Dad bringing me here when I was little. I can almost hear his voice: *This is a very sacred place, blossom. It was damaged when the mine was first set up. The Yolŋu were so upset they brought their spears and performed a special* buŋgul, *right here where we're standing, to demand respect for their land ...*

As Nick finishes the "D", I say, "Do you have to do that?" But my voice sounds weak and unconvincing. I almost choke on the words.

He shrugs, grinning. "Reminds me of being fifteen."

Selena hands me one of the cups and I take a sip. It tastes acidic and sweet and like medicine all at once.

Selena is watching me, expectant. "Good? Better than beer, right?"

I nod, tip up the cup and swallow it all. It makes me feel warm and numb. It drowns the memory of Aiden's voice and fades the colour of blood.

Selena looks at me, laughing. "Whoa, Rosie. Easy."

I hold out my cup for a refill. She thinks it's hilarious.

She pours again. And again. And again.

★

Three quarters of a bottle later, the base of the lookout is covered in red, white and black tags. I sit, half-defeated, half-drunk, leaning on the trunk of a nearby tree. Selena dances next to me with a few other girls. Her movements are fluid and graceful. Beautiful, even.

Nick approaches through the tumble of dancers. He pulls me to my feet. "Let's go up."

The lookout is a small wooden platform perched four flights of metal stairs above the ground. He takes my hand and leads me towards it. I stumble, the earth uneven under my feet. I hardly notice. My body is liquid. Runny. Dissolving.

Still holding my hand, Nick guides me up the narrow stairway. We pass people coming back down and squeeze past them. Then we're at the top. Nhulunbuy is stretched out below us, just darkness and a few glinting lights. The oval is lit up. People must be training. To our far left the refinery glows a dull orange, its enormous bulk silhouetted by the night. I can smell the salt of the ocean.

There's another couple pashing in the opposite corner. Nick moves in behind me and kisses my neck. Tingles erupt on my skull and shoot down my spine. I turn into him and I don't hold back. I want to feel him. I don't want to think. I want to surrender.

We kiss long and deep. I forget where we are. I forget who he is and who I am and that we are separate. Different. I don't want this feeling to end.

I say, "I want to sleep with you."

"Rosie ... you sure?"

I nod. His back is on the metal railing. I press myself up against him. I can feel the whole length of our bodies crushed together. I kiss him again.

He tries not to sound too eager, but excitement thrills in his words. "Let's go down to the car."

"Okay."

I don't remember getting down the stairs.

I don't remember saying goodbyes.

I remember tripping and grazing my knee as we made our way back to Nick's Hilux.

I remember blackness.

30.

2001

I feel her push back the sheet. The two beds in my room are permanently shoved together now. Nona stands, quiet in the dark, then slides out our bedroom door. Her shadow crosses the pale yellow light from the bathroom. I hear the front door open and close.

I hurry to follow, tiptoeing across the hall. I shove my thongs on and slip out into the night. The air is still and muggy, the community quiet. Nona hears me on the stairs and waits for me to catch up.

"Where are you going?" I ask.

"The oval. You wanna come?"

Her smile glows in the dark. Mum will kill us if she finds out. It's not the first time Nona's nicked off in the middle of the night. Last time, Mum was so worried she called the night-patrol ladies to bring her home.

I whisper, "Mum said no going out after dark."

Nona gives a cheeky shrug. "She's sleeping. She won't know."

Against my better instincts, I follow her into the unlit street. The crunch of gravel is loud in my ears.

I'm already starting to feel guilty. I know Mum's found it hard, having Nona stay. The smalls left for Elcho after a few weeks; they missed their mum. But Nona's been with us three months. Three months of her racking up huge phone bills calling her mum and sisters. Three months of Mum feeling like a "twenty-four-hour taxi service". Three months of Nona disappearing and Mum calling around worried, only to learn she's playing cards somewhere or visiting family, and have her show up three days later, wanting to wash her clothes, eat and shower. Mum's tried to lay down some rules, but none of them have stuck.

We cross the shop car park and make our way onto the oval. It looks like a dark hollow in the ground. The lights are always broken.

I put my hand on Nona's warm arm. "We shouldn't go too far."

"You scared? Think *galka*'s gonna get you?"

"'Course not."

I hear murmurs from the other side of the oval, near the bush. I tighten my grip on Nona. "What's that?"

"Sheree and Minhala were gonna come down."

She moves fearlessly towards the voices. My eyes start to adjust. I can make out figures in the blue-black night. A cigarette lighter flares, briefly illuminating Sheree's face in its tiny orange glow.

A harsh voice cuts through the darkness. "Rosie! Nona!"

I jump. My heart is pounding. Nona screams. Her cousins clamber backwards. "Wah … *galka* …"

A body lurches out of the dark, tall and menacing.

"What do you think you're doing out here?"

It's my mum. Fine drops of her spittle land on me as she walks towards us, fuming. "How many times have I told you? No wandering at night. You should be in bed. It's not safe out here. And to bring Rosie with you …"

"Mum, it's okay. We're okay."

She barely hears me. "Get home. Now." Her voice is low and menacing. We stand there, stunned. She hollers, "Now, girls!"

We start walking. We are silent the whole way home. Back in our lounge room, I see that Mum is torn between anger and tears. She says, "I honestly don't know what to do, Nona. I want you to be happy here. But there have to be rules. All this coming and going, taking money, wandering at night … it's exhausting for me … and it's not good for you."

Nona doesn't say anything.

Mum looks exasperated. "Did you hear me?"

Nona says, "I want to go and live with Mum. On Elcho."

"You don't have to do that. I'm just saying –"

"I want to."

My insides are screaming, *Don't leave me! Don't go!*

There's a long silence, then Mum says, "I'll book a seat for you. When do you want to go?"

31.

2007

I wake up in Nick's bed. My head is pounding. I feel someone sit beside me. The mattress dips to accommodate the weight. I hear Nick's voice. "Here. Drink this."

He's holding out a cup of fizzing blood-orange Berocca. I sit up and the sheet slips to my waist. I realise I'm only wearing undies. I pull the sheet back up, feeling self-conscious. I drink the Berocca. My head is spinning. Did I? Did we? I don't remember. How can I not remember?

Nick reads my expression. "Don't worry. Nothing happened." He can see I'm relieved and laughs. "It wouldn't have been that much of a disaster, would it?"

I don't know how to answer that, so I say, "Where are my clothes?"

"In the wash. You spewed all over yourself – and my car."

"Oh no. Sorry."

Nick's ute is his pride and joy. "It's okay. You had a bit much. You passed out."

The night is coming back to me in pieces. Selena pouring

us drinks. Graffiti. Music. Stairs. An old man muttering. Stars. The hard look in Nick's eyes. But that Nick is not the Nick here with me now. This Nick is gentle. He tucks a knotty strand of hair back behind my ear. I feel like crying. "Thanks for not … you know …"

He looks at me, so loving. "What? Taking advantage? As if I would. You know me better than that."

Inside, a small voice asks, *Do I?* I try to ignore it.

He grins. "But if you want to now I won't say no …"

He kisses me. I squirm away. "I've got to meet Mum at the bakery."

"What time?"

"Ten."

Nick reaches over and turns his bedside clock to face us. It's 9.24am.

I try to hide my relief as I get up. "I'd better shower."

★

I wait in Mum's troopie as she ducks into the bakery to buy some bread. Even on a Sunday morning the place is busy with miners from the G3. They emerge with what I'm guessing is their staple breakfast: meat pies and half-litre iced coffees. Even the thought of eating makes me feel queasy. My head is throbbing. The Berocca didn't work this morning.

Mum appears with a loaf of wholemeal and *The Arafura Times*. She shoves both into my lap as she clambers into the driver's seat. "Managed to get a copy of the paper."

I try to sound interested, but only come up with a "Hmmph."

She indicates the cover photo. "Did Anya's parents say anything about this?"

I glance at the photo. It's three men standing side by side:

one Yolŋu, another Indigenous man, and a suited-up white guy. They're all smiling.

"Um, no …" I'm worried she'll ask about my sleepover, so I try to distract her by asking, "Who are they?"

Mum looks appalled that I don't know. "You recognise Galarrwuy, of course."

I look back at the photo and nod as she continues. "And that's Noel Pearson, the leader from Cape York. And Mal Brough, Minister for Indigenous Affairs."

I read the headline: *Indigenous leader signs 99-year land lease to government.* Mum mistakes my looking for interest, and says, "Galarrwuy's done a backflip on the Intervention. He signed a lease for the land. Can you believe it?" She looks over at me, expecting a response.

My brain is foggy. I manage to mumble, "Maybe he changed his mind."

Wrong answer.

"How can he change his mind? He's spent most of his life fighting for land rights. This goes against everything he said he believed in."

I close my eyes. I think of my lies to Mum. Nick at the Arnhem Club. Aiden's accusations. I say, "Sometimes things aren't black and white, Mum."

She stares. "Is this coming from Nick?"

I almost laugh. "He wouldn't even know who Galarrwuy is."

"I'm not talking about Galarrwuy. I'm talking about standing by your principles, no matter what."

I'm hungover and irritable, and I snap. "You think everything has an answer. It's so clear to you, right? What everyone else should do?"

She looks stunned. "You know that's not fair. I grapple with issues every day …"

"Oh, I know, and I have to hear about them all, don't I? I

have to listen to you rave on. *My boyfriend left me. Work's so draining. We don't have enough money for x.* I've got my own shit to deal with. I don't need to hear about yours."

I know I've crossed a line because she doesn't reply.

She drives in hurt silence for the rest of the trip home.

★

I'm in Nick's room. On his bed. After school. The curtains are drawn against the daylight trying to peek in from outside.

He moves in to kiss me, but I pull back. Away. "I don't feel like it."

"You wanted to on Saturday night."

His voice is gentle and coaxing, but I stand firm. "Nick, I need to ask you something ..."

"What?"

"What do think about Yolŋu people?"

He looks bemused. "I don't think about them at all."

"But when you see them –"

"I don't."

"Come on, be serious ..."

"I only see them around town." He's irritated now. Defensive.

I force myself to say it. "You don't like them, do you?"

He stares up at the ceiling, avoiding my gaze. But I've come too far to back down now. I need to know the answer. I need to understand. I push him. "Nick?"

"I don't 'not like them' ..."

"I see the way you look at them."

"I just ... there's history ..."

I don't say anything. I don't give him any excuse to stop talking.

After a long pause, he says, "There was a girl. Back in Sydney. She went to my school – on and off. We had a thing for each other, I guess. We'd meet up in the park after school and fool around. Her name was Shaniquwa."

Despite his serious tone, or perhaps because of it, I smile. He does too.

"Everyone just called her Shan. She was Aboriginal. Koori, they call it down there. At least, that's what she told me."

I try to hide my surprise. I keep my voice level as I ask, "How long did you go out with her for?"

"I wouldn't say we 'went out'. We hung around. She was into graffiti. Sometimes we'd walk the backstreets. It was like she took me on my own personal tours. She knew a few of the local artists."

"Is that how you got into tagging?"

"I was already interested, but yeah. What she showed me made me better at it."

"What happened?"

"I dumped her for a *Dolly* model in the year above me."

He sees my amused disbelief. Even he has to smile. "I was only fourteen."

"Shaniquwa must've hated you."

"She did. She hated me so much she told all her brothers and sisters and cousins. And they came after me, one afternoon after school. They found me at the station. One guy pulled a knife."

"Oh, Nick."

"I was lucky – other people saw it and they ran off. After that, I started carrying a knife too. For protection. Kept it hidden in my bag."

"Did you see them again?"

He shakes his head. "End of the year, we went to Bali, before coming here. Mum said yes to me getting a tatt, and I was looking through this book and … something about the Southern Cross seemed right. It said, *Fuck off, this is my country; you can't hurt me.*"

His eyes plead for understanding. My heart aches for that scared fourteen-year-old version of Nick. But I can't let him think that then is now, or there is here.

"Nick, they weren't Yolŋu."

"They were Aboriginal –"

"Even that's pretty irrelevant. They could've been from anywhere."

He shrugs. "It's proof, you know, that we should stick to our own kind."

"It was one bad experience."

"I lost it, Rosie ... I was so scared for so long ... like, nightmares and stuff ..."

His voice cracks. I've never seen a boy cry before. I don't know what to do.

I pull him towards me. "I'm sorry that happened."

He lets me hold him as the tears fall. "Me too."

★

I wake to the sound of our landline ringing. The whole house is dark. My gut clenches. Midnight calls are never good.

I hear Mum fumble her way out to the lounge room.

She answers the phone. "Hello?" Only a few seconds pass before she says, "I'll be right there. I'm coming now."

She sounds stunned and panicky. I stagger to my bedroom door and open it to see her hurrying back to her room. "Mum? What's happening?"

She looks up at me in shock, like I've caught her doing something she shouldn't.

"Um ... an accident. I've got to go and help. I don't know much. You sleep. I'll tell you about it in the morning."

Mum turns on her bedroom light. I squint at the sudden brightness. She pulls on a long cotton skirt and heads towards

the front door, grabbing her car keys and slipping on Birken-
stocks as she goes.

"Mum, who is it?"

But she just says, "Try to sleep. Do you think you can?"

There's a growing sense of dread in the pit of my stomach.

Mum tries to reassure me. "It'll be okay. I've got to go."

And she's out the door. I check the glowing clock on the
microwave. It's 2.34am.

★

I don't sleep, of course. I toss and turn. The build-up has just
started and the night air is warm and sticky. I turn the fan up
to three and lie on top of my sheets. I try not to let my imagi-
nation run wild.

Camp dogs start to bark on the other side of the community. Others join them in a cacophony of howling and yapping
that swells towards our house like a cresting wave. The dogs
next door start up too.

Then there's silence.

I watch two geckos scamper across my ceiling, weaving
sticky trails around each other.

There's the sound of raised voices somewhere up the hill,
yelling in Yolŋu Matha.

I doze. I'm tired. So tired. A confused bush turkey warbles
in the dark outside my window.

I open my eyes again. Daylight is creeping through my
green cotton curtains. I move into the corridor and peer into
Mum's room. Her bed is unmade and empty.

I pad towards the lounge. Mum is there, passed out on the
couch. I try to walk quietly into the kitchen, but she's a light
sleeper and wakes immediately.

I ask, "Mum, what happened?"

Her face is a mess of tired lines and dark eyes. She says, "It was your *wäwa*. The one who came here a few weeks ago."

Lomu.

"What happened, Mum?"

I can see her weighing up how much to tell me. She sighs, exhausted. Drained. "I guess you'll find out sooner or later. He hung himself, Rosie. Hung himself from the banyan tree near the *buŋgul* ground."

She starts to cry. "Why would he do that? Why didn't he come here? I told him our door was always open. He should've known that. Damn it. Nothing's ever so bad … there's never a reason to …"

Her words dissolve into heavy, chest-wrenching sobs.

She collapses into my arms and I hold her. Tight.

★

I don't go to school. I stay home with Mum.

She fields calls and makes arrangements. She goes out a few times, to see Rripipi and drop people places.

I stay behind. I want to be alone.

Nick texts:

U sick or just still hungover, U bludger? ;-)

And later:

Hey, U OK?

And later still:

Rosie, where R U? What's up? We good?

But I know now that I can't expect compassion from Nick. Not when it comes to Aboriginal people. I tell myself that's okay. Just got to compartmentalise. Keep the worlds separate.

I make myself reply. I keep it short.

Sum1 in community died. Got 2 B here 4 Mum.

I make a loaf-of-bread's worth of sandwiches and Mum takes them to *Momu*'s house.

I can't get the image out of my mind. A lone body, swinging in the shadows of the banyan tree. I know that tree. We used to play there as kids. Its arcing trunk forms a natural hollow in the middle. Its branches are grand and sweeping, with thick roots trailing towards the ground, like long, gnarled fingers reaching down for the earth. Perfect for climbing. For swinging. For hanging.

What was he thinking? Was he thinking at all?

He was sitting in our lounge room, his tiny daughter curled on his lap. He was smiling. Proud. Unperturbed by death. Was he thinking about it even then?

What was he thinking? Was he thinking at all?

Eighteen. Not much older than me. Not much older than Nona. The same age as Nick.

Lomu, with laughing eyes, handing me *guku*.

What was he thinking? Was he thinking at all?

★

It's late afternoon when Mum gets the call. I don't need to be asked. I'm ready and waiting by the door. The body has to be taken from the hospital to Darwin for an autopsy.

We stop at *Momu*'s house first. There's a large crowd already gathered, sitting on blankets in the dirt yard. It's like a morose picnic with no food.

Mum jumps out and helps *Momu* to the troopie. She seems even frailer than when I last saw her. I clamber over the front seat, to the back. A swarm of relatives piles in with me. I recognise some of their faces. They are my *ŋamaḻa*s, *ŋapipis*, *wäwa*s and *yapa*s. Some of them I haven't seen in years.

Last in is Nona. She slams the back door shut behind her. Mum starts to drive.

I try not to stare. Nona's belly has a distinct curve. She's wearing a loose singlet to hide the bump. Her floral skirt sits low on her waist. She's cut her hair short and her features look fuller. Her skin is healthy and glowing, but her eyes are dull with grief.

I wonder how long it is until she has her baby. What month is it now? September? No, October. I try to catch her eye, but she either refuses to meet my gaze or doesn't register that I'm there. She stares out the back window as the community disappears behind us. Bitumen wavers in the heat. The sides of the road are chalky pink dust. The bush is parched khaki, waiting for the rain.

I look back at Nona. Her feet are stretched out in front of her, the soles dry and dusty, heels cracked. Along the edge of her left foot I can see a scar. A long black welt.

We pull into the hospital grounds and park the car. Follow the drift of people around the back to the morgue. There's got to be over a hundred people. Our passengers melt into the throng of mourners. I lose sight of Nona.

Men are singing, thrusting spears at the morgue entrance. The women stand back. Clapsticks pound like the thump of a wooden heart brought to life. An old man plays the *yiḏaki* to one side. He looks like the old man from the Arnhem Club, but I might be imagining it.

Mum moves to stand in the shade of a nearby shrub, and I follow. Behind us, some preschool-aged kids are playing, climbing trees. They seem oblivious to the ceremony in front of them. A little boy laughs loudly.

I search the crowd with my eyes. Aiden is standing slightly to one side with a few of the guys from his band. His eyes meet mine, then quickly drop away. I can't see his parents or Mattie anywhere. I wonder who his adopted Yolŋu family is. I realise I've never asked him.

The huddle of women moves forward. Their hands are in loose fists above their heads. Elbows bent, they shake their hands back and forth as if rattling a cage. One of Nona's aunties leans into Mum and whispers, "They are the rock. It's a dance of water. The tide comes in and gets the body. The tide goes out and takes it back into the ocean, the car."

The morgue doors open and the men flood in. An orderly appears. He doesn't seem at all perturbed by the spears around him. I suppose he's seen all this before. He looks almost bored as he latches the door open and disappears again.

The women start crying-singing, soft and mournful, as the men move in to get the body. I can see Nona now, pounding on the wall as the men reappear. They are carrying a stretcher. The body is strapped to it, bound in a white bandage like a mummy. I'm relieved we can't see the actual body. It is just the shape of Lomu, laid out, small and thin. A frail sliver of human life.

The men lift the body into a waiting troopie loaded with colourful blankets and plastic flowers. The clapping and wailing continue as the car inches down the side driveway. Then, suddenly, by some silent agreement, the singing stops. People start to walk to their cars, or wait for a lift in the shade of nearby trees.

Rripipi and her relatives materialise from the crowd. I see Nona and Gulwirri go past in another vehicle with some aunties as we climb back into the troopie. Mum pulls out of the car park, just one in a long line of snaking white four-wheel-drives. The vehicles drive slowly, one behind the other, hazard lights flashing.

We arrive at the airstrip as they're carrying the body from the troopie to one of two small planes parked on the tarmac. The swell of singing, *bilma* and *yidaki* surrounds us. Rripipi leaves Mum's side, making her way to the front of the crowd. She starts to wail, letting the tears run freely down her face. Gulwirri and the smalls are beside her. I catch sight of Nona again. She is holding a little girl in her arms, trying to restrain her. It's Lomu's daughter, Kaneisha. She lunges forward, breaking from Nona's grasp, running towards the body. She's screaming as she paws at the bandages.

I have to know. I ask Mum, "What's she doing? What's she saying?"

"My daddy can't breathe … Let my daddy out …" Mum's words melt into sobs. She clutches my arm, holding me close.

A young man hurries forward and grabs Kaneisha. She buries her face in his shoulder, still crying. He looks too young to be Nona's husband. His clothes are shabby, his face gaunt but familiar. I see a glimmer of a boy I once knew, proud and strutting. "Is that Jimmy?"

Mum nods.

The body is on the plane now.

The pilot closes his cockpit door, preparing for take-off. He starts the engine and taxis down the runway.

I see Nona and Gulwirri climb into the second plane with the smalls.

32.

2001

I watch from the chain-link fence.

Nona pushes her Aunty Tina aside so she can sit next to the window, closer to me.

She's leaving. Leaving Yirrkala. Our shared bedroom. Me.

And she's not planning on coming back.

What will life be like without her?

I feel a sob rise in my chest.

The pilot starts the engine.

Mum puts a gentle hand on my shoulder and says, "I'm going to miss her too."

33.

2007

I can see Nona's tear-stained face through the plane window.

But she doesn't look at us.

She doesn't look at anything. Not her mother and sisters in the cabin. Not the crowds outside. Not the plane holding the body, disappearing into the clear blue sky.

She just stares blankly ahead.

She looks empty.

Despairing.

34.

2001

Nona presses her hand against the plane window.

I see the pale brown of her palm, five fingers outstretched.

I hold up my hand in a mirror of hers, wide open against the fence.

My tears are flowing now.

I can't hold them back.

I feel a huge, gaping emptiness. A void.

35.

2007

Kaneisha is still sobbing in her uncle's arms, her small body heaving, arms flailing, cheeks wet.

The engines grow louder, building to an urgent hum.

I look back at Nona, framed by the plane window.

My breath is shallow, hardly there.

I keep my eyes on her face as it shrinks into a small dot then disappears.

The plane shuttles down the runway.

The wheels lift.

And then they're gone.

36.

2007

I make my way to the mango tree at recess. Miniature green fruit has started to appear, tiny and taut at the end of red-brown stems.

Selena and Nick are already there, with Benny, Reggie and Matt. The boys are getting ready to play basketball, changing into runners as they talk.

"Did you hear? They're talking about banning us from the lookout."

"Who – you specifically, Benny? I wouldn't blame them," quips Nick.

I sling my school bag onto the grass as Reggie and Matt laugh.

Benny blushes. "Us as in everyone. As in white guys."

"Why?" asks Matt.

"Too much graffiti up there, they reckon."

Selena is sarcastic. "Gee, whose fault is that?"

Reggie scoffs, "It's a joke. They can't tell us where we can and can't go. Dad said all those permit things have been scrapped for months now. We can go wherever we want."

I've never liked Reggie. He's the kind of guy who pushes

in at the front of the canteen line just because he's in Year 12.

"It's traditional land. It's sacred." I hear the voice loud in my ears. It takes a second before I realise it's mine. The guys are all looking at me now, surprised.

Reggie laughs. "Everything that sticks out of the ground here is sacred, isn't it?"

I keep my voice calm and strong. "It's Yolŋu land. They're letting us be here. It's not that hard to show respect."

"The mine signed a deal. They're leasing this place."

Reggie nods, backing Matt up. "Yeah, it's like if I rent a house from you and then you tell me, 'Oh, but now you can't use the dunny.'"

A hee-haw of laughter. A slap on the back.

Nick looks uneasy, caught in the middle. He stays quiet.

I'm fuming inside. I can't do this now. Not with Mum teary every hour. Not with Lomu waiting to be buried. Not with Nona in Darwin, and that voice still whispering, *What was he thinking?* I pick up my bag. "I'm going to the library."

Reggie makes a face at Nick, as if to say, *What's up with her?*

Nick hurries to catch up as I start to walk away. "Hey, you alright? Sorry about your mum's friend."

I say it blunt and to his face, like a test. "It wasn't her friend. It was my *wäwa*. My brother."

"That's rough."

"He was your age. Eighteen."

I think of Aiden. *Another One Bites the Dust.*

I can't do this now.

But Nick isn't giving up. "Are you mad at me for some reason?"

I keep walking.

"I know Reggie can be a dickhead but he's harmless. He was just joking."

"I don't find it funny."

"Maybe you just took it the wrong way. You're upset about

this death. I get that. It's full on." He reaches out and grabs my shoulder. "Rosie. Stop." His bright blue eyes search my face. "Do you want to talk about this?"

I can't do this now.

I shake my head. "I really do have to go to the library. I'll catch you later."

"Okay." He lets go of my shoulder.

I keep walking.

★

Dad calls and I start crying. I'm sobbing into the phone.

I hear his voice from the other end, strong and firm. "Just let yourself feel it, blossom. I know it hurts. It should hurt. He shouldn't be dead."

I blow my nose. It's loud, wet and messy.

He says, "I wish I was there to give you a hug."

"Me too."

"I'll come up for the funeral, once they know when it will be."

I'm heartened by the thought of him being close, present, here.

I wipe my tear-stained face and blow my nose again. "I can't wait to see you."

★

I make Mum an Earl Grey tea and sit with her on the lounge. I haven't let myself cry in front of her: she cries enough for both of us. She talks about how Nona's family are coping and the likely funeral arrangements. They think it will be held in Yirrkala, but they'll have to wait until the body comes back from Darwin. I listen in silence, nodding every now and then.

She says, "You're quiet."

I shrug.

"I heard you on the phone to your dad before."

Usually, if one of us has the phone in our bedroom, the other at least pretends they can't hear. I wonder why Mum has broken this unspoken rule. "Yeah? And?"

"I wish you'd talk to me, Rosie."

Silence.

She tries again. "I do understand you, know."

"Understand what?"

My tone is deliberately harsh. I'm hoping she'll drop it, but she's determined. "I know you think I see life in black and white …"

We've never talked about what I said in the car that day.

"Mum, please, can we not get into this now?"

She is starting to get teary again. "Of course. I just … I know you talk to your dad more than me … and I don't really understand why that is … what I've done wrong …"

I feel a wall go up inside me. I snap, "Not everyone feels the need to discuss every little detail of their lives."

"You really think I do that?"

It's such an understatement that I laugh.

Mum looks devastated. "I just try to be open. Honest. I'm human, Rosie. If I'm hurting or worried I say so. I treat you like an adult. But maybe you'd prefer it if I was like your dad. If I never told you anything at all."

"He tells me stuff."

She shakes her head, disbelieving.

I arc up. "He does. And he listens, too. Which is more than you do."

"I see." I can tell it's taking every fibre of Mum's being to stay calm and under control.

She picks up her mug of tea and takes it to her bedroom.

I feel even worse than before.

I start spending lunchtimes in the art room. Ms Naylor gives me special permission.

Nick tries to be understanding but can't help grumbling that he feels like a third wheel when it's just him, Benny and Selena. I tell him I'm behind with my major artwork, which is true. He makes two-on-two basketball with Reggie and Matt an every-lunchtime event to fill the Rosie-sized hole. Selena is relegated to playing cheerleader and watching from the sidelines. She moans to me about it in class.

I say, "Come and hang out in the art room if you're so bored." Sometimes she does.

Nick sends me short but sweet texts.

Missing U. Draw faster.

My triptych starts to take shape.

I sketch a shadowy background of trees. Hidden amongst them are ghostly, partly obscured versions of Lomu. Lomu in the bush, holding *guku*. Lomu sitting at our kitchen bench. Lomu in his old job, collecting garbage.

Selena asks, "Is that meant to be the guy who died? It's kind of creepy."

I ignore her. I smudge the charcoal together, blurring the lines.

I draw Lomu not in black, but grey.

He is a ghost, a memory. He is a spirit.

I feel a bit better knowing he isn't forgotten.

★

Nick is teaching lessons four afternoons a week now. The

build-up has started and the pool is crowded with little kids and their parents trying to escape the relentless humidity.

I go back to catching the bus. I don't mind.

I get on, say hi to Tony and make my way down the air-conditioned aisle. Most days I pass Aiden with a polite nod. We haven't sat together since his outburst about Nick. But today he looks up at me and pats the seat beside him.

I hesitate, then sit.

He doesn't say anything, just scrolls through his iPod and chooses a song. He holds out an earbud. "This was one of your *wäwa*'s favourites."

He doesn't have to tell me who he's talking about.

I put the earbud in my ear.

Aiden pumps up the volume and Yothu Yindi's "Treaty" swells into life. It fills the bus with raw emotion, optimism and hope.

> *This land was never given up*
> *This land was never bought and sold*
> *The planting of the union jack*
> *Never changed our law at all*
> *Now two rivers run their course*
> *Separated for so long*
> *I'm dreaming of a brighter day*
> *When the waters will be one*
> *Treaty yeah treaty now…*

We sit together and listen.

★

I cradle the phone and speak as quietly as I can. I can hear Mum rattling around, washing dishes in the kitchen.

"Dad … can I come and visit you some time? In Yilpara?"

There's silence on the other end. Not the reaction I was expecting – or needing.

I prompt, "I was thinking ... maybe when you fly back after the funeral."

"Won't you still have school?"

"Well, in the summer holidays, then."

His voice sounds strained. "That's not the best time of year to come."

"I know that but –"

"We don't have air con."

"We don't have air con here either."

"The build-up in Yilpara is stinking hot. And then if the wet starts there are heaps of mosquitos."

"I know what the weather's like in December, Dad."

"It's not that I don't want you to come ..."

But that's what it sounds like, and it hurts. I'm confused. Why doesn't he want me to visit? I stayed with him in Gapuwiyak, but I've never been to Yilpara. He only transferred there a few years ago. I thought he'd be pleased I want to come. I catch sight of my reflection in the bedroom window. I look thin and pale.

"Rosie, I know you've been having arguments with your mum."

"What ...? I think I liked it better when you guys didn't talk."

"Look, it's normal. You're a teenager. But if you're trying to run away from that –"

"I'm not. I just want to visit my dad."

"It's not a definite no. Just let me discuss it with your mum."

"It's your decision, not hers."

"I know that. And ... I'll think about it, okay?"

My eyes are hot and prickly. I blink, hard, to keep the thunderstorm of tears at bay.

★

I draw the trunk first, curving up and around the hollow in the centre. Then the branches, reaching up like arms to touch the sky. Then the roots, long and dripping, thick and sinewy enough to swing on. I don't need to go and look at the banyan tree to know its shape, its form. Nona and I used to play there all the time, near the *buŋgul* ground, where they do ceremony and bury people. We would climb as high as we dared, or until an adult told us to come down.

I use charcoals in ten different shades of brown, and blur them into grey and green. The roots become hair, wiry like her afro. And under that, the earth becomes her face. Not as it is now, etched with worry and years of grief, but as it was when Nona and I were young. Round. Plump. Vibrant, with an open smile and browning teeth.

It is Rripipi. My *momu*. It is what her name means: the place in the hollow of the banyan tree, amongst the roots. A place of safety.

★

Nick catches up with me as I'm heading to the bus. "Hey, I was thinking, I've got work this arvo, but maybe you could come and do laps. I finish at four. We could hang out after."

His expression is sweet and hopeful. I've been distant lately and we both know it. He thinks it's about the death. I know it's about more. But I don't want to get into it now, so I say, "I've got lots of homework."

I see a flicker of hurt in his face. His joke comes out as a snap. "Hey, *I'm* the one in Year 12. Exams start next week, remember?"

I try to keep things light. "Then maybe you should study too. In case you change your mind about uni."

"That's not going to happen." Nick kicks at the concrete.

"When am I actually going to get to see you, Rosie?"

I feel bad. "It's not that I don't want to hang out, it's just … the funeral starts tomorrow."

"Where is it?"

"In Yirrkala."

"What time?"

I realise he's picturing a Western ceremony, with people dressed up in suits, and a priest. The kind where people stand around and cry for a few hours, then go home.

I say, "These things can go on for weeks, sometimes months."

"Well, which bits are you going to?"

"All of it."

"You serious? So you're going to be missing school?"

I nod. He looks disappointed and annoyed and confused all at the same time. I can see him searching for the words, wondering what to say. Eventually, he comes out with, "Well, tell them not to take too long, okay?"

"Nick …"

"I'm joking. I just … I'll miss you, Rosie. I already do."

He moves closer and kisses me oh-so-gently on the lips. Something inside me starts to melt, then I hear a car honk from across the road. I look over and see my dad grinning at us from the driver's seat of mum's troopie. What is he doing here?

I start to blush as he jumps out and makes his way towards us. "You must be Nick. Great to meet you, mate."

He pumps his hand enthusiastically. Nick looks bemused. He's probably wondering where this mad bushman came from. Dad is dressed in khaki shorts and a Garma T-shirt from 2001. His chin is covered in stubble and his hair is greying, pulled back in a thin twist of ponytail. His nose is sunburnt red: the dusty Akubra on his head can't be too effectual.

He sees Nick's confusion. "Oh, sorry. I should've said. I'm Rosie's dad, Pete."

"Um, right … Nice to meet you."

"Just up for the funeral."

Nick nods. He's taking this pretty well. I'm gaping like a goldfish.

Dad grins. "Thought I'd surprise you, pick you up from school … Surprise!"

I force a laugh, wishing he or Mum had warned me.

Dad says, "Why don't we all go and grab a coffee? I've heard so much about you, Nick, and I only come up here now and then."

I jump in quickly. "Nick's got work."

It's not that I mind them meeting, and Dad seeing me kiss Nick is embarrassing but hardly a disaster, but I know if we sit down and talk, the three of us, it won't be pretty. Dad will work out I lied; he and Nick have nothing in common. He'll think all the crap Mum's no doubt told him is true, and maybe some of it is. I don't know how I feel about Nick right now. I mean, I love him. I understand him. But I don't always like what comes out of his mouth.

Nick smiles at Dad, eager to please. "I finish at four."

Dad's grin widens, as he turns back to me. "Great. We can go for a swim, I'll buy you an ice-cream, then we'll grab that coffee – and be home in time for dinner with your mum."

"I have homework, Dad –"

"Stuff homework. You're outvoted. Nick and I agree, don't we, mate?"

"We do."

★

The Irish waitress at the Walkabout brings our order over. We're at the cafe out the back of the motel. "Two cappuccinos and an iced coffee?"

The iced one is for me. I'm happy with my choice. Dad insisted on sitting outside, where there's an undercover area with tables and chairs. The fans aren't working and we're all coated in a thin sheen of sweat. I'm so on edge I'd be sweating even if we were sitting in ice-cold air conditioning. I feel like I'm picking my way through a minefield, trying to keep the conversation on safe ground. So far it's been okay. We've stayed in neutral territory, polite questions like what Nick's planning on doing after school (teaching swimming) and how long Dad's been a teacher (about fifteen years).

The waitress looks hot, her pale skin flushed red. She shoves the drinks onto the table. Chocolatey foam spills onto saucers. She ignores it and stalks towards the motel pool.

There's a Yolŋu mum there with three kids, about to go for a swim.

The waitress leans over the metal fence. "You lot eating here?"

"Bought some chips."

"You need to have a meal to swim." Not even her beautiful lilting accent is enough to make it sound friendly.

She moves back inside, scowling. The family start to gather their things. No arguments. No fuss. Dad shakes his head and mutters, "Shame job."

I brace myself, and sure enough it comes.

"They've got to have rules."

Dad looks at Nick, unsurprised. In that moment, I know Mum has told him everything. All her thoughts and fears about Nick. Her attempts to get us to spend less time together. Dad says, "Do you think if *we* wanted to swim, they'd let us?"

Nick shrugs. "That's different."

"How?"

Nick knows how much I admire my dad, but I've never heard him lie about his opinions, and he doesn't start now. He says, "Well, *they're* different, for a start."

"How are they different?"

I hate Dad at this moment. It seems like a carefully laid trap. I try to interject. "Can we talk about something else?"

"In a sec, Rosie."

Nick meets Dad's gaze, head on. "I know what you're thinking, and it's not 'cause they're black. I'm not racist." He struggles to find the words. "It's just their culture ... it's totally different to ours."

"Everyone's different – the Tongans, Africans, Iraqis ..."

"Yeah, but they still live like us, in normal houses in town. Their kids all go to school. They want to learn English and get jobs."

Like the true teacher he is, Dad says, "Well, let's deconstruct that –"

I'm mortified. "Dad!"

But he ignores me. "The housing thing for a start. I admit, most of the houses in Yirrkala ..." He shrugs. "They're awful. They are. But there's twenty people living in some of them. And they're old. They were built when I was a kid. I grew up out there, did Rosie tell you that?"

"No."

"It was a mission. My parents were with the church. They taught English."

Nick shifts in his seat. "Well, I think that's good. They should learn English."

"I agree. Yolŋu elders do too. But they also want to be strong in their own culture. Their own language."

I can tell Nick's out of his depth. He retreats to more familiar ground. "Dad says the council fix those houses all the time, and they just get trashed again. They don't look after things. Like their cars. I always see them on the side of the road, broken down or out of petrol."

"Because people aren't used to handling money –"

"Yeah, and they waste it on booze."

My inhalation is so short and sharp it's audible. I expect Dad to explode, but he keeps his voice low and quiet. "And why do they do that? I mean, it's a massive generalisation but let's run with it. People who drink that much are trying to escape reality, or create a new one in their heads."

I think of me at the lookout party. Before I realise what I'm doing, I nod. Nick sees this and gives me a look, as if to say, *Whose side are you on?* I stop nodding.

Dad continues. "They've had their whole way of living dismantled in three generations. They got lumped with a mine they didn't want –"

Nick seizes on this. "But they get money for that. Heaps of money. And special treatment, too. Like the kids at our school. They get so much help, a special room, different home-work … and they all drop out by Year 10."

"If you tried to learn in German, you'd probably struggle too." Nick shakes his head, but Dad continues. "Those kids have real knowledge – it's just not reflected in the classroom. Take them out bush, and it's a whole other story."

I think of our childhood trips to Bawaka and say, "It *is* pretty amazing how well they know the land, how it's all con-nected, the plants and animals, the seasons …"

Dad nods, "And kinship. That's a complex mathematical concept."

Nick's face is a frown. He drains his cappuccino. It has to be cold by now. "I'm not saying they don't know stuff, or they can't be nice people … just that they're different … you know, underneath …"

"We're all fundamentally human. We all feel, bleed, hurt, love."

I know Nick's thinking of Shaniquwa when he says, "It's not the same. Rosie understands."

Dad looks at me, not comprehending, as Nick continues, "She told me – it's Yol-noo and Na-paki – them and everyone else."

Dad looks at Nick, then back at me again.

There's a heavy disappointment in his eyes, but he nods and lets it drop.

★

Dad is silent as he drives Mum's troopie back to Yirrkala. It's the first time he's driven me home from school since I was little. It should feel great. My dad is here and he's acting like a real dad. It's a shame it comes with parental disapproval.

I stare out the window. The dirt at the side of the road blurs from deep cocoa to bright apricot to white and back again. I see white *dhaŋarra* flowers in the bush. I think of Lomu and his family. Our family too.

I feel like I need to explain. "Dad …?"

He grunts an acknowledgement that he's heard.

"I know you didn't like what Nick said … but some of it is true … at least, it's true as far as he's seen in school or town. He's only been here two years … and he had a bad experience in Sydney. I think it really affected him …"

Dad's expression is impassive. Blank. At least he's listening.

"But if you just got to know him better you'd see he's pretty amazing … he's fun and funny, and caring and sweet … You saw how patient he was with the kids he's teaching at the pool. He tries to come across as tough but he's not … inside, he's not … inside, he's just like you and me …"

I realise the irony of what I've said too late.

Dad scoffs. "Fundamentally human, eh?"

I don't know what else to say, so I fall quiet.

The air thickens and greys as we approach a tract of bush

that's being burnt off. Eagles circle and swoop above it, searching for prey. The smell of smoke fills the car. I wind my window up and look out. We pass the edge of the fire. Ribbons of flame dance into green-brown bush, leaving scorched black grass and white ash behind.

As we near the community, Dad says, "I'm not going to lecture you, Rosie. It's your choice who you go out with. Do what feels right for you."

The problem is, I don't know what that is anymore.

★

I walk with Mum and Dad to the *buŋgul* ground next to the old banyan tree. It seems eerily appropriate that the grandmother clan decided to hold Lomu's funeral here. The place where we once played. Where Lomu's life started and ended.

The tree is roped off and the lower branches are covered in shadecloth now. It has become a place of mourning. No-one is allowed to sit or walk under it, or play amongst its dripping roots. I look up at the majestic branches and shudder.

Dad tells me it has already been smoked, *Momu*'s house too. He heads off to find the men. I follow Mum to a nearby shelter to sit with the ladies. It is just metal poles and a roof of branches and leaves, but it provides shade and relief from the afternoon heat.

Rripipi is sitting on a woven plastic mat, in front of a two-room tent. She's surrounded by sisters, daughters and grandchildren playing. Gulwirri sits to one side, staring numbly at the fine orange sand. She looks devastated. Mum sits beside her. I do too.

I see two young women adding water to a cut-off plastic milk container. It is filled with *gapan̲*, white clay paste. I watch them mixing it, checking the consistency, and realise it's the smalls, Yumalil and Lilaba. They must be twelve and thirteen now. Women already. They start to smear the *gapan* on each other's faces. A thick white line across the forehead, then a thinner one back over the centre of the skull. Black hair turned white, a stripe like a skunk. Most of the other ladies are already similarly marked.

The smalls make their way towards us. "Hi, *Yapa. Ŋamala*."
"Hi."

They look at us, *gapan* in hand, their faces a question. Mum nods and Yumalil kneels next to her. Lilaba squats by my side. She is a miniature Nona, just skinnier and shorter. I tilt my face to the sky and close my eyes. Light dances through my eyelids. I feel four bony fingers smear cold, chalky paste on my skin. Across my forehead. Over the top of my head. Hair pulled taut.

I open my eyes as she adds another layer, her eyes full of gentle concentration. She catches me watching her and grins. "Looks good."

I smile back at her, then look around. Mum and I blend in with the group now, apart from our pale white skin. Despite this difference, I feel part of something.

The sound of a *yidaki* hums from a cluster of men nearby. And suddenly there's movement. The men walk forward, then dance towards the structure that holds the body. It is a small room, made of black cloth walls pinned to a frame of branches. Flags line the approach, fluttering gently in the breeze. They are the colours of the clans: red, yellow, rainbow, black, white. The men stomp and flick their way towards it, in time with the *yidaki*, clouds of sand erupting at their feet. Their shrieks pierce the evening air, cries of war and grief. Three young boys, each no more than four years old, follow, mimicking the men's steps.

I catch sight of Aiden, doing his best to keep up. He's slightly back from the group, copying another young guy. He knows the basic steps, though. His body moves in unselfconscious

215

angular jabs and thrusts. I feel almost jealous. He looks so at ease. The way I used to be.

Just behind him, a group of women are dancing. They twitch their hands and feet in small, precise motions, as if dusting or picking leaves.

Time passes, in a blur of *buŋgul* and *manikay*, dance and song. The fabric of the funeral is, of course, death. Grief hangs in the air. Grief at losing someone so young. A brother, a father, a son, a nephew, a cousin. But as I sit there, watching, listening, I realise there are threads of life woven in too. It is a gathering, a celebration, a sending-off. A ceremony to ensure Lomu's spirit reaches the next world.

People approach and fold me into their open arms. Some I know, or recognise vaguely from childhood. Some I haven't seen since Bolu's funeral. Those I don't know introduce themselves as my aunty, mother, uncle or child. They call me Mätjala, or my skin name, Ŋarritjan. I relearn to respond to these names. They say sorry about my *wäwa*. I can't help feeling I haven't earned their condolences. I haven't been here. And I wasn't there for him. He had become a stranger. Like Nona.

I constantly look around for her, but I don't see her anywhere.

I start to pick out words from the low chatter around me. *Gapu. Ŋatha. Marrkap'mi.*

Rripipi hands Mum a small blue plastic jar. Mum opens it and massages the soft folds of skin on my *momu*'s upper back. The smell of Dencorub fills the air.

I finally catch sight of my *yapa* as night starts to fall. Dark mingles with the smell of smoke. The tents around the *buŋgul* ground glow, illuminated by the crackle of campfires. Lilaba lights one in front of where we are sitting. Nona moves in beside it and sits cross-legged, hands resting on her swollen belly. I try to catch her eye, but she is always doing something – talking to people, texting on her phone or watching the dancing.

She doesn't look at me once.

★

The days settle into a pattern of migration, up and down the hill. From home to the *buŋgul* ground and back again.

Dad is staying in our spare room. I love having him around. I help him cook, making big batches, enough to feed us and our Yolŋu family. Our house swells and ebbs with bodies and shy smiles. People come to help us carry meals, or rest on the couch, or sleep.

We make endless cups of tea. Guḻwirri teases Mum for her "tea that tastes like dishwater". Dad and I drive into town and stock up on black tea bags, powdered milk and sugar. We buy in bulk.

Sometimes, during the heat of day when there's no cere-mony on, we play cards or watch TV or I do homework to the sound of Dad strumming softly on his guitar. We fall into the habit of eating dinner in front of the ABC news. We watch it together, Mum, Dad and I, before walking back up to watch the *buŋgul* in the cool of evening.

For the first time I can remember, we feel like a real family.

Mum doesn't cry on my shoulder or confide about how she feels having Dad around. I can tell she's making an effort to be stronger. It makes me both sad and relieved.

Sometimes Dad sees me texting. I'm sure he must know it's Nick, but he keeps his word and doesn't comment. I'm grateful for the reprieve. I don't tell Nick much about what happens each day. Just enough to let him know the funeral is still going, and that everything's okay. That we're okay. And I'll be back at school as soon as this finishes.

Nick returns every text, but never calls. When I ask him about it he jokes that he doesn't want my "Gold Digger" Kanye

West ringtone going off in the middle of something important. It's like he knows there's stuff going on that he can't or won't understand.

I miss him. I miss his arms around me. But it wouldn't feel right to invite him out here, or to go and see him in town. So I call and he texts. And I text and he doesn't call. At first it bothers me, but then it starts to feel okay.

Dad takes over making Mum her morning Earl Grey tea. They seem comfortable together, like old friends. We get home late from the funeral and they talk deep into the night. I lie awake in bed, straining to hear their soft murmurs from the lounge. I'm worried they'll discuss me and Nick, but they don't. They talk about politics and the community, mutual acquaintances and their families.

I sift through their words, looking for clues about who they were when they were young, together and in love. I realise I don't know much about them, as people, pre-me.

I hear them laughing together and wonder why Dad left.

*

I sit on mats in the dirt, watching the *buŋgul*. I sit with Gul̲wirri, R̲ripipi and Mum. The smalls, and other relatives, come and go. Sometimes Nona sits with us too. I'm so aware of her presence my skin tingles when she's nearby.

There's a constant flow of people coming to ask things, like who's going shopping, or how they can get transport, or what comes next in the ceremony cycle. Sometimes R̲ripipi answers, but other times it's Nona. She answers with cool and calm. Authority, even.

I wait for her to acknowledge me, and eventually she does. She leans over, her eyes on the dancing, and says, "These are the red flag dancers from Numbulwar."

It's not much, but it gives me hope.

Another day, she performs with a group of girls doing a flowing modern Christian dance. The music is a cross between soft tribal rock and gospel. I watch her small, rounded belly sway gently from side to side in time with the beat. Even pregnant, she's more coordinated and graceful than I've ever been.

After the dance, she takes a seat in the empty space beside me. A Yolŋu minister takes the microphone and starts to preach. His sermon is in Yolŋu Matha, peppered with confused English phrases. "Glory God." "Our Lord Jesus be praised." "Rising on the earth." The young people don't pay much attention, but *Momu* drinks it all in, her face earnest.

Nona looks over at me, proud. She indicates the minister. "My husband's father."

I avoid the strangeness of the word *husband* and ask, "Is he here? Stretch, I mean."

She points at a group of men standing on the far side of the *buŋgul* ground. I make out his figure, at least a head above the others.

I say, "No doubt about it. Your baby's going to be tall."

Amusement dances on her lips. "Could've been Stretch Junior ... but it's a girl."

"A girl?"

"Lucky, hey?"

I borrow her words from so many years ago. "Not trouble like boys."

A small, shy smile passes between us.

★

My phone is ringing. The caller ID says Nick. My heart starts pounding. Why is he suddenly calling? I thought we agreed ...

I thought he said ... I force myself to answer before my mind can run riot.

I try to sound casual. "Hey. What's up?"

"Hey, yourself, funeral girl."

"What kind of name is that?" I laugh.

He sounds sheepish. "It sounded better in my head."

"Is everything okay?"

"Is now an okay time to talk?"

"I'm in bed, about to crash."

"If you're tired ..."

"No, it's fine. Now's good."

There's an awkward silence, then Nick says, "So ... my formal's on Saturday night."

I've already missed muck-up day and Nick's last day of school. I thought the funeral might end in time, that I might be able to go. But Nona says it's only halfway through and, to my surprise, I don't want to leave. I just want to be here, soaking it in.

Still, I feel bad for Nick, so I say, "I'm so bummed I'm going to miss it."

"Yeah. Me too."

There's something he's not telling me. I can sense it.

I wait, and finally he says, "Rosie, I was thinking ... no-one else is going solo. Seriously, even the losers have dates. And the other day I was talking to Tiffany – you know Tiffany in my year?"

I have a vague mental image of long brown hair and freckles. One of Nick's exes.

"Her date has pulled out. He was supposed to fly up from Perth. They've been doing the whole long-distance thing and, anyway, he can't come. So she asked if I want to go with her."

The last bit comes out in a rush, like if he rips the bandaid off quickly it will hurt me less. I'm silent, taking it all in.

Nick says, "Rosie? You still there?"

"Yeah, I'm here. And it's fine. If you want to take someone else ..."

"Hey, I want to take you. But you're out there doing whatever you're doing and you won't come."

For a moment he sounds annoyed. I'm annoyed too. "Nick, it's a funeral, remember? I can't control how long it goes for."

He quickly backs off. "I know. I'm sorry. I just ... wish you could be there."

There's a pause. Then I say, "Me too."

★

I try to avoid dancing, but family keep asking me to join in the *buŋgul*. They remember me taking part when I was young.

I say, "I don't remember how to do it."

They say, "It'll come back. We'll show you."

I politely decline.

Eventually, Lilaba tries to pull me to my feet. I say, "*Yapa*, please, don't make me. Have you seen me dancing?"

She shrugs. "Don't remember."

Nona's voice cuts across the group. "I do. At our *bäpa*'s funeral."

Pain flickers across her face at the mention of her dad. A cut exposed.

Gulwirri picks up the story, explaining to Lilaba. "Rosie would've been – what? Six or seven?"

Nona says, "Eight. We were eight." The memory is still firm in her mind. "I'd been trying to teach our *yapa* the cockatoo dance. I told her – just stand back there in the dark. No-one will see you. You can practise. She started behind me, but when we finished she'd disappeared."

I say, "I was concentrating!"

221

Nona shakes her head. "She was dancing backwards, trying to run away."

The women smile, teasing me with kind eyes.

I smile back at them. "We can't all be good dancers like Nona."

★

Lomu's daughter, Kaneisha, becomes my small shadow. She follows me around and sleeps curled in my lap. I'm reminded of her arms slung softly around her dad's neck in our lounge room. Grief washes through me all over again. It comes and goes like the tides, sometimes barely there, other times enough to drown you.

Our *momu* watches, with sad but approving eyes. "You're her *mukul bäpa*. Her aunty."

I play quietly with Kaneisha, games I remember from being a kid. Round and round the garden. This little piggy. I recite nursery rhymes I thought I'd forgotten. I ask *Momu* where Kaneisha will live. She tells me Tina is living at Bawaka now; she's going to take her. I'm relieved to know she'll have a stable home.

One afternoon, Kaneisha reaches out and touches my hair. She pulls something from it, then repeats the action. Her fingers are gentle and probing.

Mum looks over and says, "You must have nits."

"I couldn't."

She parts my hair gently. "You do."

I can hardly believe it. "I haven't had nits since primary school." I take a risk. I look at Nona, and add, teasing, "I used to get them from you, didn't I?"

Nona hesitates. Then, to my relief, she smiles. "Thought I got them from you."

222

★

I sit as still as I can. Mum combs conditioner through my wet hair. She's using a fine-toothed nit comb she found at the back of the bathroom cupboard.

It's Saturday night. Nick will be at his formal. With Tiffany. I feel so confused. Part of me is jealous as hell, and part of me thinks I wouldn't want to be there anyway.

Mum's touch is gentle. Careful. Loving. She teases out knots and searches for eggs and the tiny creepy-crawlies. I can feel her warm breath on my neck. I feel suddenly emotional.

I say, "You used to do this every week, remember?"

Mum nods. "Sunday night. Nit night. Before the craziness of the school week."

We both smile.

She rinses the comb at the bathroom sink. "It was kind of nice, wasn't it? In a weird way. A chance to just sit down together and talk. No agenda ... no logistics ... no big emotions ..."

She gives a small self-deprecating laugh. I know she's giving me a chance to talk, to make things good between us.

I hesitate, then say, "It's Nick's formal tonight."

My voice sounds strained. It's been so long since I offered her even a scrap of information about my life. She opens her mouth to say something, stops herself, then says, "If you want to go, I could drive you in."

"It's okay. I don't want to."

"Are you sure?"

I nod. I don't dare say any more. If I do I'll start crying and it will all tumble out and she'll say she knew Nick wasn't for me all along, and I'm not ready to hear that. I haven't made up my own mind yet.

So I stay quiet.

And she keeps combing.

I feel the sting of tears in my eyes.

But I stay quiet.

✦

I make pancakes. We haven't had time to shop again. The pantry is almost bare, but there's flour, eggs, long-life milk. I whisk and fry, then carry the flat golden circles up to the *buŋgul* ground with a container of golden syrup. They're an instant hit, gobbled down amidst smiles, drips and dribbles.

I hear Nona say, "Mätjala."

I look up in surprise. It's the first time she's addressed me like that since we were kids.

"Do you remember when we were little? The Queen's Birthday?"

I catch on. "We made pancakes …"

She nods. "Every year. And we'd get all dressed up, in tiaras and pretty dresses."

Mum smiles. "I'm sure I've got a photo of that somewhere."

I add, "And we'd eat jelly. Mum never let me have jelly. Only on special occasions."

Mum is still adamant. "Too much sugar isn't good for your teeth!"

Guḻwirri grins, then pulls back the left side of her mouth to reveal brown edges and cavities. She jokes, "See?"

The memories are flowing back now. A whole cascade of them. "And remember when we stole Barbies?"

"That was your idea!"

"It was definitely yours."

Rripipi says, "I believe Rosie. Nona always did everything first."

It was a family joke when I was little. I arrived in the world five days before Nona, but she beat me in everything else. She smiled first, laughed first, took her first steps months before me. She learned multiple languages while I struggled with one.

Nona smiles, "Hey, I didn't know it was stealing. We were only three or something."

Yumalil is listening with big eyes. "What happened?"

Mum says, "I remember that. Your ŋamaḻa and I went shopping at IGA. You girls were cruising around. Then we all climbed in the car. You were playing happily in the back seat. We were almost home, and you'd been so quiet. We thought, *What's going on?* We looked around and there were half a dozen Barbies back there! You must've just walked out with them because you were so short!"

Kaneisha has been listening from my lap. She pipes up, "You got Barbies?"

Guḻwirri shakes her head. "Kaneisha, don't get any ideas!"

We all laugh. We laugh together.

★

Nona looks exhausted. Heat shimmers over the *buŋgul* ground.

Mum says, "Why don't you go to our house for a bit? Have something to eat, some cold water and a lie down."

Nona nods, appreciative.

"Rosie will take you."

Mum drops us down the hill, then drives back up. We're left alone. Nona climbs the stairs and enters our house. She looks around. I try to guess what she's thinking. "Been a long time since you were here."

She nods.

"Does it feel strange?"

"*Yaka.* It feels … happy. Lot of memories."

She smiles.

I turn the fan on and get the cold water from the fridge. We sit, nursing glasses of cool liquid on our knees. She is in the same armchair her brother sat in.

I say, "He came here, you know. Your *wäwa*. A couple of months ago. He had Kaneisha with him. He seemed happy ... well, maybe not happy, but fine. I never thought ..." My voice breaks. I start again. "Do you know why? Did he give any signs?"

"Don't know. I've been at Gikal."

There is the longest silence. It is steeped in loss and regret. I'm comfortable enough to sit with it, and let it linger.

Eventually, I move back to the kitchen to make us lunch. By the time I finish, my *yapa* is dozing, her head slumped back on the chair. I sit opposite her and eat my cheese and tomato sandwich. Her face is soft and unguarded. She looks exactly like she did when we were kids, apart from the protruding belly that rises and falls with each breath. In, out. In, out. She's so lean it looks like she has swallowed a basketball.

I can hardly believe it's real.

Nona wakes and eats lunch. We walk slowly back up to the *buŋgul* ground. The heat clings like a second skin. We pass frangipani trees with fragrant white flowers that smell of honey in clumps as big as my head.

I say, "I think I saw your baby kick, while you were sleeping. Your stomach moved, kind of like a little person jabbing from the inside. Is it possible I saw that?"

"Maybe. I feel it ... but from outside I'm not sure."

"When are you due, again?"

"February."

"I can't believe you're going to be a mother."

A confusion of emotions flits across her face. "*Ŋamala* says she'll look after it for me ..."

I'm surprised to hear this. "Do you think she will?"

I don't want to admit it, but the idea makes me anxious.

Nona says, "She's drinking less. And she's come to all the appointments."

Her voice is hopeful, like she's searching for a way out. But I sense she knows it's not a long-term solution.

We cross Balnguma Road. A flock of black cockatoos rises screeching from a nearby tamarind tree. The *buŋgul* ground is in sight. A collection of dusty parked cars and tents. People bunched in the shade of quickly made shelters. The enormous banyan tree draped in shadecloth, like mourning clothes, stretching its arms high and wide. Camp dogs strut around. Two race past us, snarling. Nona's hands subconsciously move to protect her stomach, as she shoos them away. "Tsa! Tsa!"

After a few more steps, she says, "I like going to the hospital, seeing those nurses. I started thinking maybe I could do that. Be a nurse. It would help, you know. Help me look after this baby. And help *Momu*. She's getting old, too old to look after the smalls. If I had a job I could do that."

I hear the weight of responsibility in her voice. I feel for her. Ache for her. I say, "Nurse Nona. It makes sense. You always said … when you came back from Darwin …"

She looks down, embarrassed. "I haven't even finished school."

And suddenly there's a wall between us again. A deep, gaping wound. A festering silence. Something inside me screams, *Just tell her you're sorry!*

But I don't get the chance. Lilaba races towards us. "*Go.* We're going to *Momu*'s house."

"Why?"

"Women's dance."

I'm suddenly nervous. "I'll just watch."

Lilaba shakes her head, firm and decided. "*Momu* said to bring you too."

We sit outside Rripipi's house in her newly fenced yard. I watch as the smalls skip away to line the side of the road with wreaths and flowers. We sit for ages. One of my knees is touching Nona's. I want to say something, but the moment has passed. There are too many people here now. Too many ears listening. I don't want to embarrass her. I don't want to embarrass myself.

The afternoon greys into evening, then glows into dusk.

Finally, the men approach, playing *yiḏaki* and *biḻma* and singing. Nerves kick in as the ladies stand and start to dance. My hands are shaking. Nona gestures, indicating for me to follow. I try to copy her movements, flicking my feet in the warm red dirt. My hands make small dusting motions as we walk down the street. Before I know it, we're back at the *buŋgul* ground, but this time I'm on the stage. Me and the ladies. Fluorescent lights illuminate our every move. They're so bright that I can't see beyond them, but I know there are hundreds of people watching from the darkness.

My stomach is churning. I've never been a performer. When we were little, Nona used to make up dances with Sheree and Minhala and other girls after school. Sometimes they'd perform them before the football games. I was given the job of operating the CD player. I'd stand back, happy to watch Nona shine. Her choreography was passionate and fun. She could do an incredible Michael Jackson impression. Her performances drew small crowds.

And now here I am on the *buŋgul* ground beside her. Someone shoves a wreath into my hands, and the clapsticks change from slow beats to a frantic hammering, faster and faster. The smalls and Nona take off, running, crouched low, their hands twisted in front of their faces. I have no idea what's going on. I try to shrink back, hiding behind the old ladies. I spot my mum, but she's over on the other side of the huddle of dancers.

Nona darts back in next to me, indicating the shelter with her lips. I realise she's telling me I have to put the wreath out there. It suddenly looks miles away. I start to panic. Nona's eyes are kind but amused. She gestures again. I tell myself it's okay. I'll just go quickly. I dart forward and hear Rripipi yell, "Wait! It's not your turn!"

I blush, embarrassed, before realising she's yelling at the other girls too. I've been concentrating so hard I hadn't noticed. From the outside, these dances look harmonious and calm. But here, in the middle of things, it is busy, chaotic and loud. Instructions fly, crashing into each other mid-air.

Rripipi yells at me again, "Mätjala! Now!"

I rush forwards and hear her holler, "Dance properly!"

I try to mimic the other girls as I dance to the shelter and deposit my wreath. Some of Nona's cousins are there to receive it. I spot Nona and hurry back to her side. She gives me a small smile of approval. I feel warm inside.

The music changes. The beat slows. The *yidaki* sends out mournful vibrations. I realise the older ladies have rocks in their hands. They must've picked them up while we were dancing. I can't help staring as they start bashing the rocks on their heads in time with the *bilma*. I see blood. I look over at Nona, alarmed, but she's in her own world now, hitting her bowed head with a closed fist. It's the same action as the old ladies but not as brutal. I start to copy her, and we sink down to the ground. We sit cross-legged, thumping our skulls.

And then I hear it: the sound of a soul tearing into the night. A cry pierced with grief. I don't need to look to know it's Gulwirri. From beside me, I hear Nona join in. The sound is terrible and primal. An aching, keening question to the world: *Why?*

I feel their pain inside me. I feel it exploding. Out of the corner of my eye, I see Rripipi throw herself forward onto the ground. It is like when Bolu died, but worse. Her body hits with a sickening thud. Women help her up, but she throws herself forward again and again and again. Her body lies, looking soft and broken on the earth.

And then the music stops.

★

Sand thumps onto the coffin. The minister, Stretch's dad, says soft prayers in a blend of Yolŋu Matha and English. Song pierces the still evening air. The men's voices are thundering and deep; the women's, high and warbly. I remember what Nona told me when we were kids. They are singing Lomu home. Home to heaven, or his homeland, or both.

Nona sits beside me, her voice blending in and out of the others. Tears stream down her cheeks, dark rivers of sorrow.

I murmur softly. "Wherever he is, I hope he's found your dad."

A small, sad flicker of memory crosses her face. "Maybe they're fishing together in Bawaka."

Our eyes meet and, in that moment, we are so close we are breathing together.

The singing trails off. People rise slowly to their feet.

Nona holds my gaze. "See you tomorrow?"

I hesitate, confused. I thought the funeral was over.

She says, "*Bukuḻup*, you know? Where they wet you?"

Hazy memories resurface. "Am I supposed to come? Is it for everyone?"

"It's for family."

Her voice is laden with meaning. She's giving me a chance to start over.

Rripipi has heard us. "It's not just for family. It's for people who've handled the body. Or anyone who's felt grief or wants to be cleansed."

I hold Nona's eyes with mine, like two small hands clenched together in the dark.

"I'll be there. What time?"

★

I stand in a row of people, behind Dad, in front of Mum. Jimmy is at the front, holding a long green garden hose. He hollers to Yumalil, who turns it on at the tap. A weak stream trickles out, pooling in the red dirt at his feet.

He yells again. *"Bulu!"*

She gives the copper tap a few more twists. The stream becomes a small fountain. The line starts to move slowly forward. One by one, faces and bodies are drenched. Cleansed. The men are first, the pallbearers and dancers. Aiden is amongst them. I watch as water soaks his blond curls. He raises his face to the spray and steps forward, before emerging out the other side, dripping and smiling.

I see Lilaba scamper past and wave her to my side. "Where's Nona?"

"Went back to Gikal."

"When?"

"Last night."

I feel myself deflate. I wanted to do this with her, side by side. "But ... she said she was going to be here – just yesterday ..."

"Her *mukul* is really sick. Too sick to come to the funeral, even. Last night she called. Nona went with Stretch and his dad."

"What about the cleansing?"

"*Momu* says she'll just have to smoke any meat she eats until she can do another *bukulup*."

231

In front of me, Dad shakes his wet head like a dog, spraying a shower of drops over everyone nearby. Mum laughs, but I can't bring myself to smile.

A voice says, *"Yapa."* But it's not the voice I want to hear. It's Jimmy, gesturing me forward. I step towards him and feel the beat of water hit my skin. It's warm from the sun. He raises the hose and lets the water thunder down on my head. It drenches everything, from my eyelashes to my thongs. I feel small rivulets trickle down my body, seeping into every crevice and pore.

I thought I would feel released and whole.

I thought it would feel like I was starting again.

But Nona's not here, and I don't and it doesn't.

37.

2007

Selena's voice sounds tinny on the phone. "You coming to Nick's party on Saturday?"

"I don't know."

She tries to wheedle me into it. "You have to. Everyone's going." She takes a guess at my hesitation. "You're not mad at Nick for taking Tiffany to the formal, are you?"

I think about it for a moment and realise I'm not. I'm really not.

Selena continues, "I swear, they hardly hung out at all. Nick was with his mates all night."

I say, "It's not that. I'm just not sure I'm ready for a party, you know, because of the funeral."

I feel like I've been living in another world. The dancing. The stories. The sense of family. The contrast of life and death. It makes this party seem frivolous. Of course I can't say that to Selena.

She says, "I thought Nick said you were coming back to school."

"I am. On Monday."

"So that's perfect. You can ease back into things on Friday night. Catch up on the goss."

I'm silent.

"Come on, Rosie. This is a big deal, Nick finishing Year 12. He really wants you to be at this party. I mean, he hasn't wanted to pressure you, but it means a lot to him, I can tell."

I know she's right. Nick has been amazing. He hasn't pushed me at all about coming, just let me know the option is there. I want to go, for him, but I'm scared. Scared of what, I don't know. My mind flip-flops between yes and no, stay home or go. I say, "I'll think about it."

★

Mum leans against my bedroom door. I'm brushing my hair, starting to get ready.

She says, "You look beautiful."

"I don't feel beautiful."

She hesitates, then says, "I'm sure Nick would understand if you didn't feel up to going."

"I know. This is my decision." For the first time ever, I add, "Pick me up at eleven?"

Mum laughs. "Someone scrape my jaw off the floor! No arguments, then? No negotiating?"

"Nope."

She fiddles with some flaking paint on my doorframe, trying to look disinterested. "I didn't know if you and Nick were still together …"

Irritation flares. "Well, we are, Mum. And tonight is a big deal. He's finished school forever. And I've already missed so much. The least I can do is go to his party."

Mum raises her hands in surrender. "Okay. Fair enough. I just thought −"

"Well, don't."

She reaches out to hand me something she's had clenched in one fist. I take it and hold it up. It's a dress of plain calico, adorned with bells and colourful tassles. I try not to gag or laugh. "When did you get time to make this?"

"I didn't make it. It used to be mine, when I was young. Can you believe it?"

I pretend to admire it, as she continues: "Talking to your Dad about the old times reminded me I still had it. I don't have much from those days, but I kept this for you. Try it on."

I slip the dress on, over the top of my singlet top and shorts. It fits perfectly.

"Wow. If your dad could see you now …"

He flew out this morning.

Mum is beaming. "Lucky the '70s are back in."

"Are they?"

Her face falls. "Oh, you don't have to wear it. I mean, if you don't like it. I just thought … I know you love it when I make you clothes. You have ever since I made those matching pants for you and Nona when you were little … but, as you know, I haven't had time. It's been so exhausting with the funeral and your dad staying and work …" She looks suddenly self-conscious. "Sorry, you don't need to hear all this." She starts again. "I thought you might want something special to wear."

She's trying so hard I can't bear to say no.

I say, "Thanks, Mum."

I hug her.

She hugs me back, squeezing like she doesn't want to let go.

★

I arrive at the party feeling conspicuous, and not just because of what I'm wearing.

Mrs Bell ushers me in, exclaiming loudly, "Wow, would you look at that dress! It reminds me of when I was a girl."

I try to sound upbeat. "Yep, it's original '70s."

She looks impressed and thrusts a party pie into my hand as I follow her through the lounge room and out to the back garden. They've gone to a lot of effort. The trees are smothered in fairy lights and citronella torches smoulder, keeping mosquitos at bay. The pool glows translucent blue. Girls wearing bikinis splash in and out. Most of the boys are near the bar. The line for drinks looks about three bodies deep. Daft Punk is pumping from speakers strategically placed around the yard.

Mrs Bell weaves through the crowd, to where Nick and his dad are setting up a keg in the back corner. "Nick. Look who's here!"

His face lights up. "Hello, stranger." He kisses me on the lips.

Selena appears from nowhere. "Oh my God. Do you want to come to my room and get changed? You should've texted. I could've met you out the front." She drags me off to her room before too many people see me. "I can't believe your mum made that ..."

I don't bother correcting her.

She opens her wardrobe, and designer dresses bulge out. She indicates for me to have a look, but my heart's not in it. What I wear doesn't seem important. I'm waiting for her to ask me about the funeral or how I've been or what I'm feeling. But she doesn't. She just asks, "Do you want sexy or sophisticated?"

"You choose something." I feel numb, as if I'm not really here.

She claps her hands like an excited kid. "Oh good. I love it when you let me choose."

She selects a low-cut dress in pale pink. It's something out of a David Jones catalogue, something I would never usually wear, but I can't be bothered arguing. I slip it on.

Selena says, "Did you see who's behind the bar?"

"I didn't get a chance —"

"The Elites."

I don't get it. Selena's hated the Elites ever since they kicked her out.

"Steph was hinting that they wanted to come. Like, major big fat hints. She even offered to be in charge of making cocktails. So I relented and invited them."

"Since when is it 'Steph'?"

Selena shrugs and grabs my hand. "Come on. You look wicked. Let's get us a margarita." She drags me back outside into the crowd.

I feel myself swallowed up by the music and noisy chatter.

★

I drink. Selena's right. The margaritas are good. I stand sipping as she giggles and gossips with the Elites by the bar. "Steph" and her followers are all dressed immaculately in short skirts, singlet tops and fake tans. They flirt with the Year 12 boys and laugh a bit too loudly.

I look around for Nick and spot him near the now-set-up keg. He told me a few nights ago that his dad was buying this especially for the occasion, like some kind of strange male peace offering. A sign that he's proud, despite Nick not going to uni.

I make my way over, hoping we'll get a moment alone, but Nick is mid-conversation with Reggie and Matt. Some Year 11 girls stand next to them, hanging off their every word. I think they're the same ones from Libby's party, so long ago.

Reggie is smirking. "Some dickhead broke into our house today."

"Yeah? What'd they take?"

"Petrol from the mower and a pair of thongs." Laughter from the girls as Reggie says, "Yolŋu for sure. Left my iPod just sitting there."

Matt chuckles. "Too funny."

Nick throws me a nervous glance. "Guys ..."

Reggie just looks at him. "What? It was sniffers. They cut the hose too – right in the middle. That's the part that gave Dad the shits. You should've heard him. 'Why couldn't they take it from the end so I could still use the damn hose? Fifty-dollar hose, that.'"

Nick says, "It's not like he can't afford a new one." He's trying to move the conversation on, but Reggie doesn't take the hint.

He looks straight at Nick. "It's like you were saying about the lookout – they just do whatever the hell they want, like they have some supreme right. Someone should tell them how the world really works."

Nick looks frozen to the spot. He doesn't meet my eyes. I want to feel surprised that he said this, but I don't. I just feel sad. I pull on his hand. "You got a moment?"

He lets me lead him away from the group, looking guilty as he asks, "What's up?"

I don't want to get into an argument, so I try to keep it simple. "My head's not in party mode. Sorry. I might call Mum, ask her to pick me up."

His body sags. "You can't be serious."

"I just ... with the funeral ..."

"I told you, you didn't have to come."

"I wanted to be here. It's just that, now that I am ... I don't know."

His face softens. He pulls me into his arms. "At least let me drive you home. I've barely seen you."

"It's your party. You can't leave."

"It won't take long."

"Are you okay to drive?"

"I'm fine. Let's go."

I hesitate, then nod. I want to tell him everything that's happened. I want to make him understand. I want to feel his arms around me, hear him say everything's okay.

I follow him back into the house to get his keys.

Reggie is stuffing his face with chips from the snack table. He sees us pass. "Nicko, where you going?"

"Just a quick drive out to Yirrkala."

Reggie looks interested. "Yeah? Maybe we'll come." He calls across the room. "Matty boy, you up for that little mission?"

"What – now?"

"Why not?"

"I'm a bit pissed to drive."

"Nick's giving us a lift, aren't you, mate?"

I shoot Nick an uneasy look. What are they talking about? Why do they want to come? I just want to be with him. I want to block the world out. I want to block us in.

We're on the front lawn now. Nick turns back to them. "Fellas. Another time. I've got to drop Rosie home."

"So drop her, then we'll do it."

I ask, "Do what?"

There's steel in Nick's voice. "Not now. We want to be alone. Rosie's been away –"

"For the two-week funeral? What a bludge. I might need to go to one of those."

"Shut up, Reggie."

Reggie sees he's serious and stops walking. "Bloody lovebirds."

Matt says, "Piker."

"Later, then, okay?"

Nick ignores them, and presses the central-locking button on his key. The Hilux doors snap open. I climb in. The boys are still beside the ute, watching us leave. Through my closed window, I hear Reggie start singing. "Bah, bah, bah." I recognise the tune to "Another One Bites the Dust".

My body tenses up. Nick pulls away from the kerb. We leave them behind us.

"Why was he singing that?"

Nick shrugs. "I don't know. They're morons."

"I know they're morons, but why that song?"

"Probably some reference to me being pussy-whipped or something."

"Have you ever sung it?"

"I don't know."

We're on the main road now. It's a sixty zone but he picks up speed.

"Did you sing it when that guy died? You know, the one in the car crash?"

He looks at me, not understanding. I say, "We had a meeting about it at school. Do you remember? A young guy – died a few months ago. Did you sing that song after the meeting?"

I see a glimmer of recognition in his eyes. "I don't know. If I did it was just to get a laugh."

"Are you sure about that?"

"I wouldn't have meant it, Rosie."

I stare ahead of me, silent. We turn left towards Yirrkala and the street lights of town disappear behind us. Nick speeds up to one hundred, flicking his high beams on. The red and white reflectors either side of the road glare back at us. Behind them, the scrub is dark and shadowy. I see Lomu swinging from a branch. Nona keening as he's lowered into the ground. Kaneisha screaming, *My daddy can't breathe.*

Nick mutters, "I knew this would happen."

My voice is sharp. "What?"

"Your bloody dad."

"This has nothing to do with him."

"Doesn't it?"

"He didn't say anything about you —"

"Bullshit. He hated me, Rosie. And if you want the truth, I didn't like him either. He's so 'save the world', 'be politically correct'."

"And you think there's something wrong with that?"

Nick shakes his head. "He can say whatever the hell he wants. He's out there living that. At least he's not a hypocrite —"

I can't believe what I'm hearing. "You think I'm a hypocrite?"

"You act like you're so connected to 'the community' but you're not. Selena told me what you said about that girl, your so-called sister ... that it meant nothing. You haven't hung out with that family in years. But then someone dies and you're all involved. And your dad shows up and you start talking about how great the culture is, and how much they know about nature ... so yeah, I'd say that's hypocritical."

We're hurtling along now. Margaritas swirl in my stomach. I lean against the window, propping myself up. The glass is cold from the air con. It forces me to focus. I am here. This is real. I'm really hearing this. What Nick thinks. What I haven't wanted to hear.

We pass through a section of bush illuminated by flames. More burning off. I smell smoke and see Nick's face in the dim orange glow. His lips are set in a grimace. His eyes are hard. I suddenly feel like I don't know him at all. I'm breathing heavily. I try to stay in control. "Nick ... maybe you're a bit drunk —"

"I'm not."

"You're obviously angry —"

"Well, seriously, Rosie ... I've tried to understand ... but don't lecture me about it when, underneath it all, you think what I do. You just don't say it. At least I'm honest about it!"

I'm crying now. "If you hadn't met Shaniquwa …"

"I regret telling you that." He almost spits out the words. "You always thought you were too good for me."

"That's not true."

A smouldering silence. It seems to last forever. I see the first of the signs flash past us. No grog. No porn. And the stencilled *No racism. No intervention.* I'm struck by the bizarre thought that I still haven't pointed it out to Nick. It seems ludicrous now.

Nick swings left into the community, turning his high beams off. I check the lit-up dash. He's going seventy in a forty zone. "Slow down."

He does. Just a little. We pass two dark figures walking by the side of the road. Nick swerves to miss them. "Shit! How are you s'posed to see these people at night?"

We speed past a group of young kids playing tip in the glow of a streetlight near the shop. He pulls into the driveway of my house. I'm relieved as we crunch to a stop. Our newly installed sensor light clicks on. I almost laugh. Thanks, Intervention. Just what I need right now.

My cheeks are wet and hot. I barely look at Nick as I get out and slam the door. His tyres churn on the gravel as he takes off. I watch the Hilux round the corner and head up the hill. It disappears into the night.

I'm standing so still, so stunned, so frozen, that the sensor light clicks off.

I look up at the stars. They're spinning. Thousands of them. Spinning out of control.

★

I sit down on our driveway. The sensor light clicks on again, then off. The air is so humid it seems to hold me. I feel gravel digging into my bum. Mosquitos whine around my head. I slap at them. Somewhere up the hill, a man and woman are fighting. I don't know what they're saying, but it sounds ugly. A few camp dogs join in.

The sensor light clicks on again and I see Mum on the stairs in her pyjamas. She takes a step down towards me. "Rosie?"

"Yeah." My voice sounds haggard, thick and heavy as the night. She walks down the steps and over to my side. I either look terrible or I stink, because she says, "You've been drinking."

"Just a bit."

"Come inside." She squats down beside me. I see her register my pink dress, but she simply says, "What's wrong? Did something happen?"

I shake my head. I can't bring myself to talk.

Mum puts her arms around me and I cry.

And cry.

And cry.

And weep.

Eventually, she helps me up and we walk towards the house. "Let's get you into bed. We can talk about this tomorrow."

★

Morning burns through my curtains. I open my eyes. I have a thumping headache and a shredded heart.

Mum sits on the edge of my bed and offers me a glass of water. It's not Berocca, but it helps.

I tell her everything and she just listens.

She doesn't tut-tut or judge or try to relate it to her life.

She just listens.

I realise I've underestimated her.

★

I get off the bus and drag myself into the school grounds. I feel like a dead girl walking. Everyone will stare. Everyone will know. *Did you hear? Nick and Rosie broke up.*

But it's all in my head. I look around and everything is normal. I spot Selena standing near the library with Stephanie and two of the Elites. They're looking at something on Stephanie's phone.

I try to walk past them, towards the lockers, but Selena calls out. "Rosie ... have you seen this? Come here."

I walk towards them, slowly. Reluctant. Stephanie holds out her phone so I can see. "My older sister works at the mine. She took this photo this morning."

It is a photo of a bitumen road. On it, in enormous white spray-painted capital letters, are the words *THIS IS NOT YOUR LAND.*

I look up at Selena. She meets my eyes. I know she recognises the writing, the style, because I do too.

The bell rings, and we start to move to class. Selena falls in beside me as we walk to English. She hands me a plastic Woolworths bag.

"Your dress. You left it at my place."

"Thanks." I stuff it into my backpack.

"It actually wasn't that bad when I looked at it in daylight. Kind of cool. Vintage, you know?"

My voice is dull. "It used to be Mum's."

"No way. It was a great party. Pity you left early."

I look at her, wondering. Did Nick tell her about our fight?

I get my answer as she adds, "Sorry to hear you and Nick broke up."

I don't know what to say. My chest tightens. My eyes are hot.

"He got completely busted, if it makes you feel any better. Dad found him passed out on the couch with bits of white

paint on his hands on Saturday morning. He was already suss –
you know, with Nick's history? But then he went to work,
heard all about it there. When he got home he was furious.
Said if the cops found out …"

She's watching me closely now. I realise she's sussing me
out, seeing if I'm going to tell. I wonder if Nick asked her to
do this. The hot feeling in my gut seethes and burns. I want
to say, "I'm going to the police. I'm going to report this." But
I don't. Even now, I don't have the guts.

I say, "I'm not going to tell, Selena."

"Oh. Good. I told Nick you wouldn't, but you know …
break-ups can get messy, can't they?"

She smiles and flicks her hair as we walk on.

She's right next to me but we feel miles apart.

★

No-one else knows who wrote it. The photo is forwarded from
phone to phone, then posted online. Some kids think it was
written by a Yolŋu person. Others argue it was Ŋäpaki. Or
some kind of protest about the Intervention.

THIS IS NOT YOUR LAND.

Then whose land is it?

★

I enter the pool, sidestepping mangoes ripe and rotting on the
ground. I've come a bit early. I know the hours he works. I
want to swim some laps. The water is like velvet, warm and
smooth. I feel my body calm as I swim back and forth.

I rehearse the words I want to say. *You have issues, Nick.
Issues from your past. You've got to deal with them or they'll swallow
you.* It all sounds clichéd and corny.

I'm about to turn at the wall when his body slips into the water next to mine. It still takes my breath away. I have touched almost every beautiful muscle of his tanned body. Almost. I long to reach out now.

I force myself to surface and stand up. Feet on pebblecrete. Back straight. I push my goggles up so I can look him in the eye. "I know you did it."

"Yeah, I did. And you know what? It felt fucking great. Bloody Abos, think they can tell us what to do."

His words are violent and ugly. They aim to hurt, and they do.

"This isn't you, Nick."

"What would you know? Frigid bitch."

I feel my heart crack into a million pieces. There is nothing I can say. I put my goggles back on and push off the wall. They fill with tears before I reach the other end.

One, two, three, breathe.

One, two, three, breathe.

Don't think about Nick. Or what he said. Just swim.

One, two, three, breathe.

One, two, three, breathe.

Don't think about Nick. Or what he said. Just swim.

★

I finish the second part of my triptych. Each panel is small, just thirty centimetres square. It is lunchtime, but Ms Naylor is buzzing around, preparing for her next class. She comes to look over my shoulder. "Hey, that's starting to take shape."

I step back and stand next to her. To see what she sees. The first panel is adapted from my sketches of Lomu after he died. It is his spirit walking down Shady Beach, bleeding into the landscape. The second is Rripipi on her verandah. Her face is squashed into the bottom-left corner. Her hair is an upside-down banyan tree. Its branches meld into her scalp, but the roots are torn and ragged, flailing in the air, an unruly afro.

Ms Naylor says, "You've really captured an atmosphere. It feels ... sad. Melancholy. Like something's been lost."

I say, "I guess it has."

She seems about to say something, but changes her mind. She looks at the work one final time before moving back to her desk.

I start on the third panel. Smudging charcoal. Darkening the lines. Blurring greens into blues and greys and whites. I draw a face swirling into water, the ocean or a pool. The features are nothing remarkable, the expression blank. I don't know if it's smiling or frowning, swimming or drowning.

Time seems to disappear.

I'm startled out of my trance by the school bell, marking the end of lunch. It is only when I finish that I realise what I have drawn. It is me. Mätjala. Driftwood. Smooth and shaped by the ocean. Pushed around by the tides. Washed onto a shore somewhere and lying unnoticed.

Broken.

38.

2007

"He's going to win, Rosie. Kevin-oh-seven!"

Mum's face beams with excitement. It's election night and we're home, watching the coverage on the ABC. "How great would it be to get rid of Howard?"

I shrug. "Does it really matter? You and Dad are always saying politicians are all the same."

I take a sip from the tiny flute of champagne she's poured me. It tastes fizzy and cold and much better than beer.

Mum says, "Yeah, but Rudd might end the Intervention."

"So what?"

She looks at me in disbelief. "I'm going to let that one through to the keeper. But only because I know you've got break-up blues and, of course, 'cause it's your birthday."

I turned sweet sixteen today. I always thought I'd have a big party, but nothing feels sweet since Nick and I broke up. I keep crying at awkward moments, like when we watched *Ratatouille* at school. It's a cartoon about a mouse who cooks, for goodness sake. I had to make a quick dash for the toilets so no-one would see me bawling.

Mum said, "Okay, so no party – what about dinner at the Walkabout or the Arnhem Club instead? You could just invite a few close friends." But things have been weird lately. Selena's spending more time with the Elites, and I've realised I let friendships slide. The people I used to chat to in the breezeways or at the canteen, the ones I ignored while I was in Nick Land, have moved on. They've formed new groups. They have new people to talk to before assembly. I feel totally alone.

And in the back of my mind, as always, is Nona. Her birthday is five days after mine. She'll be sixteen soon too. Sixteen and six months pregnant. I've thought about asking Mum for her number but something stops me. I content myself with updates. Mum says her pregnancy is going well. Her mother-in-law is getting better. Stretch has been offered a job as a Dhimurru ranger. They're thinking of moving back from Gikal to live with Stretch's brother's family at Ski Beach. I'm torn about whether I want her to or not. There's been another suicide there recently and, according to Mum's friend Sadie, many more attempted. The mood in the community is grim.

Labor gains another seat on the ABC's big electoral map of Australia. The seat turns from blue to red. Mum grins. "I think they're really going to do this!"

Something small and mean inside me wants to provoke a fight. I want her to feel as miserable and guilty and angry and let down as I do. So I say, "It's not like the Intervention's been that bad, anyway. I mean, people made such a big fuss. 'The army's coming. They're going to take our kids.' And what? Nothing. A few extra government people walking round. Signs. Sensor lights. Fences."

"You know it's about more than that."

"The whole thing is a joke."

"It's psychological, Rosie. This kind of stuff affects people deeply. Look at what's been going on around here."

"Same old shit, isn't it? People dying every other week."

Mum stares. "You're really pushing me now. That's insensitive."

The small, mean thing inside me whispers, *Good*. But before I can say it out loud, Mum is distracted by another electorate on the TV map changing to red.

She grins. "Rudd's almost got it. I better call your dad."

She picks up the phone and dials. As soon as he answers, they launch into a dissection of who has what seats and what's still needed for Labor to win. Mum seems animated and alive.

I think how different our lives might've been if Dad hadn't left her. Left us.

She's looking at me now, holding out the phone. "Someone wants to say happy birthday."

I take the phone. "Hi, Dad."

"Mum says you're being a grump."

He's so direct that, despite myself, I smile. "Thanks a lot, Mum!"

She looks at me, confused, as Dad continues. "That's not allowed on your birthday, okay?"

"It's not like I've got heaps to celebrate."

"Excuse me? Excuse me? You're healthy and able. You have two parents who love you and ... drum roll ... we might even get a semi-decent government in tonight."

"Trust you to throw that in."

"Wait – I've saved the best 'til last. Mum and I both chipped in and bought you a return ticket to Yilpara for your birthday. You fly down the day after you finish school."

"Are you serious?"

"I can't wait to see you down here, blossom."

And I'm crying. Again.

At least this time the tears are happy.

★

Dad meets me at the dirt airstrip in a bomby old four-wheel drive. It's a silver Toyota Land Cruiser that looks as old as he is. It has two dark grey stripes and about a hundred tree scrapes down the side. Both the back-seat windows are missing. I try to yank the passenger door open, but he stops me.

"Just wait. I need to open it from the inside."

He does something fiddly with the handle and the door swings open. I climb in beside him and put my seatbelt on. Dad doesn't bother. The sun glares down at us, as the engine rattles to life and Dad starts to drive. He seems nervous, peppering the silence with questions.

"Flight okay?"

"Small plane, hey?"

"First time in a single-engine?"

"Were you nervous?"

"This what you expected?"

The community is right next to the airstrip, but Dad wants to show me around first. We veer onto a dirt track, heading for the ocean. I look out, drinking in my surroundings. The land is flat, scribbled with scrub which flares into bush then shrinks back again. Everything has a crisp brown edge, curled and panting in anticipation of the wet season. I'm grateful for the salty breeze whipping in through the open windows.

We emerge onto the beach and drive along the hard wet sand. Blue Mud Bay lies sprawled to our right, its calm aqua waters hazy with heat. It is breathtakingly beautiful. A brahminy kite drops and dives, emerging with a fish in its beak. I suddenly understand why Dad and the community have been fighting so hard. This place is as much about the ocean as the land: to not have sea rights would be to give so much away.

Dad is uncharacteristically on edge. "So, Rosie ..."

"Yeah?"

"I'm glad you came. There's a lot I want to show you here. People I want you to meet."

I cut him off, pointing to a small shelter set back in the dunes. "What's that?"

It is little more than a corrugated iron sheet propped up on dead tree trunks.

Dad follows my gaze. "A men's shelter. They send sniffers down here to dry out. There are three there at the moment. You remember Nona's brother? Jimmy?"

I remember him from the funeral – gaunt and shabbily dressed.

"He's using his Yolŋu name now, Batjula. Anyway, he's one of them. Got caught breaking and entering last month. High, of course. Did your mum tell you about this?"

If she did, I don't remember. "Maybe."

Dad misinterprets the Nick-sized gap in my memory, and nods. "Batjula *has* been in a bit of trouble lately. It was lucky your *momu* was there to argue on his behalf. The court agreed to let the community bring him down here. It was either that or jail."

I look back at the shelter as we drive past. I can see the black smudge of an old campfire in the sand, but there's no trace of anyone there now.

Dad guesses at my thoughts. "Probably gone out hunting."

He drums his fingers anxiously on the steering wheel.

★

As we drive into the community Dad points out the sights. The shop. The art centre. The women's resource centre. The school demountable. It's bigger than I imagined. There appear to be three streets. The houses are low grey brick and corrugated iron, like the ones in Yirrkala. I wonder if they were all built by the same people at the same time. They are worn and old, but there's a touch of pride about them here. Most have well-kept gardens. One is immaculate, with frangipani and pawpaw trees, and a carefully trimmed green lawn. I point to it. "Who lives there?"

"The traditional owner."

"Nice garden."

"His son works on it all the time. He's had to put a sprinkler on the grass lately, but it'll go nuts once the wet sets in. Bloody build-up feels like it's going forever this year."

He pulls into the street closest to the beach, and stops outside a newer-looking house. I get out, grabbing my bag from the back seat. "Is this your place?"

"Yep." But he just stands there, fiddling with his keys.

"We going in?"

He nods, then slowly leads the way up the path. He pushes the unlocked front door open to reveal a lounge room looking straight onto the bay. I gaze out at it. "Wow. Great view."

"Not bad, huh? This house was built just before I moved in."

I look around. There are two Education-Department-issued couches, a coffee table and a TV. The room is neat but sparse.

Dad sees the fine beads of sweat on my face. "I did warn you we don't have air con."

"It's fine."

An open bedroom door reveals a jumble of colourful blankets and a pile of mattresses, both doubles and singles. The other bedroom door is only slightly ajar. I peer through the crack and see a carefully made double bed with a blue floral blanket. In the back yard there's a washing line, hung with Dad's shorts and T-shirts, mixed in with bright cotton skirts and singlet tops, a kaleidoscope of patterns and colours.

I'm confused. "Do you live here by yourself, or …?"

He seems nervous. "Well, it's my house. As a teacher I get a house. But I choose to share it. Rosie … I've been seeing someone down here. A woman."

My mind goes into freefall. "Who? Is she Ŋäpaki?"

"Yolŋu. She's not here at the moment. She's in Darwin doing some language work with the university."

"What's her name?"

"Muthali."

"Does Mum know?"

"Yeah. She does."

I feel like screaming. How could she not tell me? Or make Dad tell me? Then I remember our fight. Mum hurt and angry, saying Dad wasn't honest or open like her. That he didn't tell me things. Is this what she meant?

Dad guesses at my thoughts. "Your Mum wanted me to tell you before you came, but … I didn't want to say it on the phone and … I thought it'd be better in person."

"Why didn't you tell me when you were up for the funeral?"

The look in his eyes is pathetic. Weak. He can't even answer. We both know there's no excuse.

I ask, "Is it serious?"

"We've been together a few years, since I moved here from Gapuwiyak, really —"

"A few years?!"

"I didn't want to say anything until I knew if it would last."

"And when was that going to be?"

He shrugs lamely, and stares out at the bay. Disappointment wells deep inside as I realise what this means. All our catch-up coffees when he's come to Nhulunbuy, the times I've poured my heart out to him on the phone, and he's said nothing.

I am suddenly struck with a thought. I feel like vomiting. "Have you got any other kids?"

"I had the snip when you were six. Rosie, where are you going?"

I realise my legs are in motion. I walk through the kitchen and out the back door. I find myself on a deck, and trip down the steps, into the sandy backyard. There are no fences here, so I make straight for the beach.

Dad is following me. I snap back at him. "I'm going for a walk. By myself."

"It's the middle of the day. Can't we talk about this?"

"No."

I can feel the sun burning me. My T-shirt clings to my body. I remember the pilot telling me it was ninety-six percent humidity today. Was that just this morning?

Dad calls from behind me. "Rosie. At least take some sunscreen. Or water. What about water?"

I ignore him and keep walking. I can't go back there now. How can I stay in that house? The house they share. I can't tell if it's sweat or tears coursing down my face.

When Dad finally catches up with me, he's a panting mess of red cross-hatched cheeks and bulging eyes. "Rosie, please. Come back. It's too hot out here."

I turn to face him. "Get me on a plane out of here. Today."

"I can't. You know that."

"You planned this, didn't you? So I couldn't leave?"

Guilt flickers in his eyes. Even if that wasn't his plan, it must've crossed his mind. He holds his hands out as if calming a skittish horse. "Don't get hysterical."

"I'm stuck here."

I look down the flat white-sand beach. The sun glances off the water, searing my eyes. There's nowhere else to go.

"Come back. Come on. This doesn't change anything."

"Are you kidding? All my life I thought you were out here for some big ideal. Indigenous education, the whole Blue Mud

Bay thing, sea rights, blah blah blah. I sat and listened to you have a go at Nick –"

"I believe everything I told him. Just because I have a partner here –"

"– and all the time you were shacked up with some woman."

"– she's not just some woman. I love her, Rosie."

His words stop me short. I can hear myself breathing, loud and ragged. And then I'm sobbing. Sobbing for my dad and some woman I've never met. For my mum and her boyfriends who've left. For me and Nick and his hurtful words. For Lomu and his tiny daughter. Nona and her unborn baby. For love and hate and all the confusion in between.

Dad pulls me into his arms and holds me in a sweaty embrace. I let myself cry salty tears.

★

As we walk back up from the beach, Dad says, "I thought you'd want some privacy, so I set you up a tent outside."

He points to a two-man tent pitched in the shade of a tree to the side of his house. It's angled towards the bay to catch the breeze. There's a swag in there, and a clean sheet folded neatly on the end. He's made a real effort.

He says, "Of course, you can stay inside if you want –"

"This is fine." I suddenly feel exhausted. "I might have a rest."

"Is there anything I can get you?"

"I'm right."

Dad looks like he's about to say more, but he closes his mouth and takes a step back towards the house. "I'll be around if you need me."

He heads inside. I crawl into the tent and lie down. It feels like an oven. I don't know if I sleep or pass out. Whatever it is, it's sweaty and dreamless.

★

I feel like I have been clubbed over the head. I can hardly move. My body is on fire. I force myself to sit up in the tent and notice that Dad has left some cool water near my feet. At least, it used to be cool, now it's lukewarm. I gratefully take a sip and wipe my face on my damp T-shirt.

Outside, I can hear voices singing what sounds like gospel songs. I wonder if I'm hallucinating. I crawl out of my small oven and stand up. Dizziness hits me, then passes. The singing peters out. I look across the yard and see four Yolŋu women and a straggle of kids watching me from the shade of a tree. They smile shyly, but don't say anything. I take a step towards them as my mind grasps for the words.

I manage, *"Nhämirri nhe?"* How are you? Then I revert to English. "I'm Rosie, Pete's daughter. You know the teacher? He lives here."

They nod and smile amidst a flurry of words I don't understand. I catch the word *ŋatha* – food – and realise I am hungry.

The lady closest to me indicates the little girl on her lap. "This is Nyiknyik, small mouse. She's your *ŋamala*, your little mother. She'll take you down to the beach, look for mud mussels and crabs."

Nyiknyik stands with a shy smile. Her hair is cut short and curls around her face.

I hesitate. "Have you seen my dad?"

"He's *ŋorra ŋurra*." When she sees I don't understand, she explains, "Having a rest. You go. We'll tell him."

I quickly walk back to my tent, grab the bottle of water and follow Nyiknyik down to the beach. It's a pretty arc of white sand with a small estuary and mangroves to one side. Ideal croc territory. The other kids follow us in a ragtag procession. I ask their names as we go. I start to remember basic phrases in Yolŋu Matha. *"Yol nhe yäku?"* What's your name?

Muthimuthi, Djeṯ and Bandawi help me look for mud mussels near the mangroves. It's low tide and the mudflats are exposed. I remember doing this with Nona, competing to see who could find the most. Today, we pile them into a communal Woolworths bag. Nyiknyik comes back with a crab she's found somewhere deeper in the tangle of roots and branches. She flashes me a wide, white-toothed smile.

I slap at my legs and ankles, feeling something biting. Djeṯ laughs. *"Yakaay! Mintjirri.* Sandflies."

The kids don't seem to be affected, but I'm getting massacred so I retreat. I sit in the dappled shade of what they tell me is a *luŋiny* tree. The sun is lower now. I realise hours must've passed. Whole hours without thinking about Nick. It's a welcome relief.

Bandawi comes back and starts to make a small fire. The others tumble out of the mangroves and roast our haul amongst the flames. They hand me things to eat, telling me what they're called. Mud mussels, oysters and crab.

Dhän'pala. Maypal. Djinydjalma.

The flavours explode in my mouth, transporting me back to a time when I ate these every other day, to the point that I'd gone to Sydney with Mum and insisted on ordering oysters, then refused to eat them because they weren't milky enough, not fresh from the rocks.

I repeat the words back to them and consign them to memory.

Dhän'pala. Maypal. Djinydjalma.

I chant them over and over, imprinting them on my brain. This time I won't forget.

★

Dinner is fresh fish cooked over a campfire. The kids and ladies eat with us too. A few Yolŋu boys join us, their dark, laughing faces illuminated by the flames. They joke around with Dad, sometimes in English, mostly in Yolŋu Matha. They clearly like him. He fits here. I watch silently, taking it all in.

Once the food is gone, the boys drift away, and the ladies and kids start singing a gospel song, the same one I heard this morning.

I help Dad carry some cups and plates inside. I wash them and he dries up. Dad looks over at me and smiles. A peace has been made, but it's still tentative between us.

I make an effort. "Are those boys related to Muthali too?"

"I think everyone's related down here. One way or another."

"Do they live in this house?"

"No, they're students. It's just me and Muthali and her sisters who live here – the ladies you met this morning? Them and their kids – the ones who took you to the beach."

I'm curious. "Doesn't it bother you, having all these people coming and going?"

He shrugs. "Everyone shares everything here. It's *gurruṯu* – you know, kinship. The best and worst thing about Yolŋu life. You can always ask for things, but you're always being asked for them too. It drove your mum crazy when we first moved to Yirrkala."

I look up at him, curious. He hardly ever talks about Mum.

"I was constantly loaning things out or giving things away – money, lifts, kitchen utensils. She'd be cooking dinner and I'd hear this 'Pete! Where's the small sharp knife?'"

"She used to cook?"

Dad laughs. "Don't tell her I said this, but she was never very good. I did most of the cooking, but she still tried to do dinner every now and then, so I didn't feel like a neglected husband."

I smile in recognition. "That's exactly what she says when she sews me dresses. Except it's 'neglected only child'."

Dad smiles too. I feel warm in the glow of our shared history. I was only seven when he left. I don't have many memories of the three of us together, but now I realise our memories are linked across time and space by my mother.

Dad says, "She's a good woman, your mum."

I force myself to ask. "Why'd you leave us?"

He looks at me in surprise. "Your mum asked me to move out."

I'm stunned. I'd always assumed it was the other way around. "Why?"

He knows he owes it to me to be honest, and forces himself to meet the question head on. "When I think back now, I see there were hundreds of reasons. I knew and loved this place. She was from Sydney. It took a while to adjust. Me being away teaching every week probably didn't help. I knew she felt isolated but I didn't really understand. I blamed her for being negative, for not making the most of it here. We found out later she had post-natal depression. If it wasn't for Guḻwirri and Rripipi …" He shakes his head. "They helped her through the worst of it. Made sure she was never alone."

★

I spend my days with the kids. We collect bush foods and berries. We go fishing, and hunt with spears for stingrays in the shallows. Knee deep in water, I'm nervous at first. "Are you sure this is safe? Aren't there crocodiles in here?"

Nyiknyik smiles, unconcerned. "We've got Tiger."

Tiger is a ratty little camp dog, who the kids adore.

"If *bäru* come, he take Tiger." The thought of Tiger being devoured doesn't seem to bother her. She shrugs. "Anyway, *bäru* don't live here. They live over there."

She waves towards an inlet just around a sandy corner. I feel a bit safer, but not much.

I let my hair get greasy. My legs are covered in bites – fleas, sandflies and mosquitos. At night, I scratch in my sleep. But I don't care. I feel alive and free. I feel like a kid again. The only thing missing is Nona. I think about her a lot. I wonder when I'll see her again, and what she'll remember most: dancing the *buŋgul* together, or my words at the school. They are seared into my memory. I'm sure they're etched into hers. *The whole sister thing, it doesn't mean anything ... I don't even know her anymore.*

Dad is happy I have company during the days. It's school holidays, but he always seems to be busy. There's someone to drive here or there, or something to fix, or someone to talk to about school or politics. I don't mind. I know I'll see him in the quiet of evening. That's when we talk. Our conversations span generations and cultures.

He tells me what Yirrkala was like when he was growing up. There was a market garden on the oval, and people lived in humpies on the beach. They grew sugar cane and peanuts where the mine is now. People had to work and send their kids to school for rations. He tells me how confused it made him feel. On one side, he had Grandpa and Nan trying to "let the natives maintain their language and culture". Yolŋu Matha wasn't allowed in the classroom, but beyond the desk it was fine. Unlike other missionaries, my grandparents even learned to speak it. But on the other side, he had his *wäwa*, Nona's dad. Bolu hated school, even from a young age, and said he "felt like he was being taught to live like a white man". Dad was caught between two worlds. He escaped to boarding school and university, where he studied teaching, but the red dirt was in his veins.

"I couldn't wait to get back here. I convinced your mum to come too. It's such a great life for kids here. I loved seeing you and Nona grow up together …"

"Yeah?"

"You were inseparable. Like me and Nona's dad when we were small. We were always at each other's houses or out bush together, hunting and mucking around."

"Did you stay close?"

"Not as teenagers. I went away for most of high school. He stayed here. When I came back to visit he was drinking, smoking pot. It was only as adults that we found a common ground again. Once we both had kids. And then I lost him all over again, for good …"

There are tears in his voice and in the corners of his eyes.

Maybe everyone who grows up here has their Nona.

★

It is my last night in Yilpara. The campfire is a smash of burning embers and our stomachs are full of stingray and roast potatoes. I sit next to Dad under the wide open sky. He picks gentle melodies on his guitar; they float from us out into the ether. The fading evening light makes the sand glow in pale pinks and mauves. A translucent moon hangs low, kissing the ocean. Along the beach, I can see the glint of other fires, and huddles of families cooking whatever they caught that day.

I lean back on my elbows. "I can see why you like it here."

Dad puts his guitar down. "Yeah? What do you like about it?"

"You can forget the world exists. When you're here, it's all there is. You're just … being."

I know Dad understands.

I ask, "Think you'll stay here forever?"

"Maybe."

I search for the words. "Dad ... how do you know you're doing the right thing?"

He sounds surprised. "I don't."

"But you always seem so sure ..."

I'm thinking of Nick, of course. It's a bad habit that's hard to quit. Sometimes a few hours pass, then a memory slaps me across the face. Or my thoughts drift back to his grin, his eyes, his laugh. I miss that Nick. I miss him so much it hurts.

I tune back in as Dad says, "I don't *feel* sure. Some days I wake up and think we should all just leave. All the Ŋäpaki. Just get out of here and leave the Yolŋu to sort things out. But I know, realistically, that's never going to happen. So I stay and I teach even though I'm full of questions ... Hell, sometimes I think even me teaching English is damaging the culture. But I don't have any easy answers, Rosie. All I know is the answer is not to do nothing ..."

I wonder if that's where I went wrong. If I'd done something, said something, earlier, would Nick and I still be together? Would Nona and I still be friends? I realise I've been paralysed by indecision and fear.

We sit in silence. He is completely at ease with it. He's been living and working with Yolŋu people for almost twenty years now. I suppose it makes sense that he's taken on some of their ways. I gaze into the embers until their orange glow is imprinted on my eyeballs. Brightness dances across the darkness wherever I look.

Eventually, he says, "I hope you'll come down again and meet Muthali."

"I'd like that."

Dad looks relieved.

We look up at the stars.

He points out the Milky Way and the Southern Cross. I think of Nick and his tattoo, and Nona and her unborn baby.

I see the red blink of a plane flying over.

★

I wake before sunrise and walk down to the beach. It stretches out in front of me, a gleaming white curve of sand. The ocean is still and quiet. Deep marine blue. I walk just below the dunes. My footprints leave a solitary track.

In the distance, I can see three black figures walking along the water's edge. They have spears in hand, and a small white dog trails behind them. One of the guys has a familiar strut. As they get closer, I see it is Jimmy. I don't know the other two. They are all just wearing shorts. No shirts. Their smooth black muscles ripple in the soft light of early morning.

As they approach, Jimmy gives me a nod. I remember Dad telling me he uses the name Batjula now, so I use it and he smiles. He says something to the other guys that includes my name, Mätjala, and the word *yapa*. The guys nod hello and keep walking. They're intent on their fishing, but Jimmy walks up the beach and plants his spear in the sand next to me. He squats down, looking out at the ocean. "Dolphins out there this morning."

"Yeah?"

"Milkie was playing with 'em. Swimming out and diving."

He indicates the little white dog, who has taken a grateful seat beside him. I smile, using the excuse to look at Jimmy's face, his eyes. They seem clear. Focused. Healthy.

As if he can read my thoughts, Jimmy says, "Police sent me down here. Too much sniffing. I'm not doing that anymore.

Don't want that."

"That's good."

"Think I might stay down here. There's good hunting. Good fishing."

"You mean live down here?"

He nods. "Too much trouble in town."

I think of the healthy kids here in Yilpara. Their glowing black skin and full white smiles. "Maybe it's better for you."

Even as I say it, I think of Nona.

Jimmy says, *"Miḏiku*'s out at Gikal now."

It takes me a moment to remember that *Miḏiku* is what brothers call their sisters. He's thinking of Nona too.

I say, "She told me. At *Wäwa*'s funeral."

I can feel his eyes on me. On my face. "She was happy, you know. To come back from Elcho. To go to school again and see you. When she come back, some of the boys was teasing her, 'Why you want to go to school? Are you woman or a girl? Only little girls go to school.' But *Miḏiku* didn't listen. She said, 'My friend Rosie goes there. She the same age as me. She gonna help me.' And the boys say, 'Who this Rosie? Yolŋu *yäku?*' She told them, '*Yäku* Mätjala but she Ŋäpaki one.' And they laugh, saying Ŋäpaki is different. But the next day she go anyway."

I can't meet his gaze. His story is new to me but I know how it ends. It ends with Nona walking out of a science lab and never coming back. It ends with graffiti on the road near the airport. Nona unable to meet my eyes. Us dancing together, but worlds apart.

I look up at Jimmy and know someone must have told him everything. Nona or Rripipi, probably. I force myself to meet his eyes. "If you see her ... can you say ... if she wants to study again, I'd like to help. I don't know how but ... if I can ..."

Jimmy returns my gaze. "You prob'ly see her before me."

★

Mum picks me up at Gove airport. I can see the questions in her eyes, but she holds herself back, simply asking, "How was it?"

"Good."

"How's your father?"

"Good."

"Just good?"

I don't know where to start. I say, "How about we go home and you make me a cup of tea and I'll tell you all about it?"

She smiles. "Sounds like a good trade."

Mum peers out at the darkening sky. A front of smouldering dark grey is rolling towards us. There's a flash of lightning in the distance, and mist on the road ahead. As we drive towards it, a few droplets spit onto the front windscreen. "Looks like the wet's about to begin."

By the time we reach home it's pouring. The rain buckets down, hard and urgent, grateful for the release.

I climb out of the troopie and let it soak into me, my face, my body, my legs and arms. Fat drops explode in the dirt at my feet. I smell earth.

I stand there, getting drenched. Cleansed.

Mum gets out and does the same.

She raises her arms to the sky.

39.

2008

I lay low. Mum and I have a quiet Christmas and New Year's Eve. The wet season gives me a good excuse to hide. I spend lots of time inside, either online or watching DVDs.

Outside, the days build to a humid crescendo. I'm reminded of an experiment Ms Bamkin told us about once. They put a frog in hot water and slowly turned the temperature up. It went up so gradually the frog didn't notice when it was boiling. Luckily for me I am saved from a similar fate by daily downpours of driving rain. They cool the whole place, and then the cycle starts again.

Some days, I feel lonely. I think about calling someone, but Selena's on a family holiday in Bali and, anyway, things are awkward between us now. And I don't feel comfortable calling anyone else because I haven't called them in ages. Mum becomes a kind of surrogate friend.

One morning, over yoghurt and muesli, I say, "Hey, Mum … I was thinking …"

"Yeah?"

"Do you still need help at work? Or did you just need someone before Garma?"

She looks pleased and surprised. "I'm sure we could find you something to do."

We wait for a break in the rain, then walk across to the art centre together. The grass by the side of our path is waist-high and luminescent green.

She says, faux-casually, "Oh, by the way ... I meant to mention, I bumped into Anya's mum at the post office yesterday. I thanked her for having you to stay last year, and she said you and Anya haven't hung out in ages. Well, not at her house, anyway."

I should've known I'd never get away with lying in a place as small as this. I consider making up another cover story but it doesn't feel right. "I stayed at Nick's. It was his eighteenth. Nothing happened. I mean, nothing ... you know. I'm sorry. I shouldn't have lied."

"I guess you know I'm going to have to punish you, right?"

"Do your worst."

I mentally file through her options: grounding, housework, no lifts to town, no internet, no mobile phone.

"No more seeing Nick. I think that's appropriate, don't you?"

I look over at her. She winks. I double-take. She's actually smiling.

I smile back at her and say, "I don't think that will be a problem."

"Good."

I guess, sometimes, Mum can be kind of cool. In her own weird way, of course.

★

I help Mum with a linocut workshop she's running for seven sisters. Rripipi is one of them. I'm guessing my *momu* got control of the stereo this morning: Elvis plays softly as they work, making prints for a special exhibition.

As I hand my *momu* a piece of lino, I ask, "What's this exhibition about?"

"It's the story of seven sisters who went out in their *djulpan*. Their canoe. They gathered all the different foods: turtles, fish, yams, berries. You can see them in the sky at night. Seven stars together."

One of her sisters leans over, grinning. "Actually we have eleven sisters, but that didn't fit with the story."

I have to laugh. "What, so four of them just didn't make the cut? How did they feel about that?"

Rripipi shrugs, grinning. Her sister cackles and says something in Yolŋu Matha. They both laugh, deep and hearty.

Rripipi translates. "She said we voted them out – like Yolŋu *Survivor*."

"You watch *Survivor*?"

Rripipi grins. "She does. Not me. I like *Law & Order*."

She chuckles again. They're good company, these ladies. The cackling sister says, "You call me *Momu*. Like your *momu* here, okay?"

I nod. Rripipi sees her sister's blade slip a little, and quickly admonishes her in Yolŋu Matha. She catches me watching and explains, "This is *Yirritja* – our mother's clan art. We're the *djuŋaya*. We can't make mistakes."

The sister pushes the ruined piece of lino to one side. I hand her a new one from a nearby pile. Rripipi sticks out her bottom lip, using it to indicate the ground beside her. "Sit there. Make a print. Use one of those spare ones."

Mum has heard. She nods from a few ladies over. "It's fine.

As long as you still jump up and grab things if the ladies need them."

"Sure."

"I'm not paying you to slack off here."

"Five bucks an hour. That's got to be below minimum wage, doesn't it?"

"You complaining?"

"Hell no."

We're both grinning.

"What are you going to do with the money, anyway?" she asks.

"I don't know."

"Maybe you could start saving for uni."

I look up at her sharply. She's never mentioned uni before. I didn't think it figured in her mind.

Rripipi mutters, "*Nhä ... uni, eh? Manymak.*" She's already deep in concentration, drawing her design in pencil on the lino. I make out a stingray and a turtle.

Mum nods at Rripipi. "There's an art school in Sydney that would be perfect for Rosie. COFA. But Sydney's so expensive, she'd have to start saving now."

She looks at me, as if to say, *What do you think?*

I'm stunned. Has she known all along? Something inside me soars. I try to play it cool. "I've still got a few years, Mum. But, yeah, I guess it can't hurt."

I am smiling as I look back at my blank grey square of lino.

I begin sketching.

★

My print starts to take shape. It is the outline of two girls, lying one in front of the other on the side of a swimming pool. They are in identical positions – bodies long and flat on the tiles, one hand trailing in the water. One is wearing a one-piece swimming costume, the other a wet T-shirt and shorts. For the first I carve thick, deep lines, so her body will come out white. For the other I leave solid lino and carve around it, knowing it will come out black. Their faces are turned away. They could be anyone. But they're not.

Rripipi looks over at my work. I can see understanding in her face.

She says, *"Yapas, ŋi'?"*

Sisters. I nod. She looks approving. "I'll take a print of that. When you're finished. Send it out to Gikal for your *yapa*."

I like that idea. I hope Nona will see it like I do: a reminder of how things were before they got complicated.

Rripipi turns back to her own work. She's almost done now. Her panel is awash with sea creatures and a boat floating on reflected stars.

She feels me looking, and points to one corner. "See that? Mätjala. Driftwood, like you."

I hesitate, then ask, "Why did you call me that?"

She looks up at me, not understanding. I try again. "I mean, driftwood is a funny name, isn't it? It just kind of floats around, like it's lost on the ocean ..."

She shakes her head. *"Yaka*, 'float around'. It's a strong name. The wood is strong."

I've never thought about it like that before.

She adds, "Anyway, everything has its place. Like my sister Ritjilili here. Her name means muddy water, like waves. Muddy water's important too."

The cackling sister raises her eyebrows at me, indicating her agreement. They do that a lot, these ladies. I'd almost forgotten how much is conveyed by their bodies.

Mum indicates for me to help her clean up the printing area. As I stand, I hear a familiar voice. "Rosie."

Mrs Bell is hovering by the door to the print space. She looks uneasy and out of place. "I was hoping you might be here."

"I work here now, actually. At least, for the holidays."

"Oh, that's great. We just got back from Bali."

She looks so nervous that I say, "It's good you came out."

She smiles, grateful but flustered. "Oh, you know, I've been meaning to ever since we moved up here. And I remembered you saying last year … that it was fine …"

"More than fine. The art's here to be seen."

She shifts from one to foot to the other. I wonder what she wants. "I'd show you around but we're just about to print."

"Oh no, that's fine. I can look around myself. I just wanted to say … I'm sorry about you and Nick." She lowers her voice. "I was really disappointed when we found out about that … thing near the airport. I thought he'd gotten over that stuff. I mean, the graffiti stuff, but also what's behind it. I'm sure he told you about that girl in Sydney … the Aborigine?"

I nod.

"That whole experience really shook him up. It shook us all up, actually. It's why I was scared to move up here, why I was worried when he started going out with you. Not that it's an excuse. I mean, I know there are still lots of good Aborigines around. Like, I'm sure, these ladies here. Creating this beautiful art."

I look over, praying Rripipi and her sisters haven't heard. Luckily, they're engrossed in putting the final touches on their work.

Mrs Bell puts a gentle hand on my arm. "Anyway, I'll look around. Who knows … might even buy something."

She gives me a smile and moves back into the main part of the art centre.

I watch her go.

★

The breezeways and corridors are filled with chatter. Students huddle in the undercover areas to keep dry. The trees are dripping from an early downpour, their trunks painted dark by the rain. The grass is texta green. It's the first day back at school. Everyone wants to know who went where. Who hooked up with who. Who broke up. Who did what. Who said what. Who likes who. The past couple of years, this has been one of my favourite days. But today I feel outside the gossip.

The only thing that catches my interest is Selena telling me that Nick stayed in Bali. He started a dive instructor's course while they were there on holidays. His parents paid for him to stay and finish it. Now he's working over there. Despite everything that's happened, I'm happy for him.

I say, "He'll be good at that — after all his swimming teaching."

Selena nods. "That's what I thought too."

We talk like it was an amiable break-up, like Nick and I are still friends. Pretending makes things easier somehow. I still sit with Selena in class, but at recess she has other plans. She doesn't go to the mango tree. There's no point, now that Benny and Nick have left school. Instead, she starts towards the metal seats in front of the computer lab. She looks back at me. "You coming?"

I hesitate, unsure.

"Steph invited us to sit with them."

I've never sat with the Elites before — I've never been asked — but I've heard them talking in class. It's always inane gossip and bitching about other people.

I say, "I might go to the library. There's a book I wanted to get."

Selena doesn't seem surprised. "Suit yourself."

She turns and walks away. I stand there for a moment, feeling lost. How have things changed so much since last year?

Have I changed? Has she? Or is it the whole world that's shifted?

I hear a flurry of wings in the sky above me. I look up to see a blue-winged kookaburra come to rest on the metal fence near the library. It perches for a moment, then opens its beak and, to my surprise, starts to laugh.

★

I pass Anya in the library. She gives me a shy smile and indicates the book I'm holding. It's *An Intruder's Guide to Arnhem Land*.

She says, "That's a good book."

"My dad recommended it."

"Some of it is kind of dense, but other bits are great. Like the history of Yirrkala. You should definitely read it. I mean, since you live out there."

She seems nervous. I am too. We haven't spoken in ages.

I ask, "How was your summer?"

She blushes. "I'd love to say I went to heaps of parties or on some exotic holiday … but we just stayed around here. Mum and Dad had to work. It was pretty quiet."

I smile at her. "Sounds like my holidays too."

★

"Give me the run-down, blossom."

It's Wednesday night. Dad's on the phone.

"How's your first week back at school? Year 11 this year. That's the start of the HSC, right?"

"Yeah, kind of. I don't know. They say the work we're doing now will sort of count."

"Kind of. Sort of. I can tell you've really been listening."

"Whatever. How are you? How's Muthali?"

We've reached a good equilibrium, Dad and I.

He says, "She's in Canberra, actually. They flew a bunch of people down there. For the Apology, you know?"

"Dad, I'm not a total ignoramus. I do watch the ABC news."

"Thank God, or I'd have to disown you. I think your mother would too."

"I'd rather watch *Home and Away* but we still can't get reception for Channel Seven."

"Blasphemy! I'm blocking my ears!" He laughs at his own joke, like the true dag he is. "So, are you going to watch it? Want to see Kevin-oh-seven say sorry?"

"They're showing it at school tomorrow."

"Yeah? So they should. It's a big deal. Although actions speak louder than words."

"What do you mean?"

"Well, it's all very well to say sorry, we stuffed up, but what are they doing now? Are they really trying to make things better? Have they repealed the Intervention? No."

His words fill me with a strange kind of hope. "So you don't think the words are important?"

"Sure, they're important – they're symbolic. But it's what you do that counts. That's what people will remember."

I think of Nona and pray that he's right.

★

I sneak in a few minutes late and stand up the back, feeling conspicuously alone. Mrs Reid calls for silence, then turns up the volume on the big screen. I look around the hall. The whole school is crammed in here together. I see Jennifer "The Asian". Ali from Iraq. Luke and Charlie Mack. Mattie and Dhatam' and a group of junior Yolŋu girls. One of them catches my eye and waves. I wave back. It takes me a second to realise it's Lilaba. There's a smile on my face as I keep looking around

275

the room. There's Aiden with his friends. Selena and the Elites. John Lane sitting near them, trying to catch Selena's eye. Anya and Anita White. Anya indicates the empty spot beside her and I goose-step into it, grateful for her invitation.

The Apology is just starting. The Leader of the Opposition comes on first. He sounds halting and insincere. Kids start talking, mucking around.

Mrs Reid yells, "Quiet! Listen, please!" but I can tell her heart's not in it.

Then the Prime Minister comes on. This time she's louder. "Listen! This is it, guys!"

Kevin Rudd's voice fills the room. He speaks from the heart, and apologises for the suffering of Indigenous Australians. He apologises for the removal of kids from their families. Acknowledges the impact on their communities. I hear Selena and Stephanie giggling. Mrs Reid shooshes them and, after a bit of muttering, they fall quiet.

A few of the teachers look moved. A couple of the Indigenous kids too — not the ones from here, but from other places. Most of the Year 12s' faces are solemn, like they're trying to prove how mature they are. The other students whisper, giggle, gaze blankly or listen, trying to understand.

I catch sight of a face that stands out. His hazel eyes are fixed, staring at the screen. His face is stony and set. I watch Aiden as Rudd continues. "For the pain, suffering and hurt of these Stolen Generations, their descendants and for their families left behind, we say sorry. To the mothers and the fathers, the brothers and the sisters, for the breaking up of families and communities, we say sorry. And for the indignity and degradation thus inflicted on a proud people and a proud culture, we say sorry."

The word sorry punctures the air like the beat of a drum. Aiden's lips contort, like he's trying not to cry. The coverage ends, and they cut to shots of crowds watching around Australia.

Martin Place in Sydney is full. Alice Springs Mall is packed. There's a group of Yolŋu ladies in Canberra wearing *Sorry* T-shirts. I wonder if one of them is Dad's girlfriend. There are shots of Indigenous women in Brisbane openly weeping. Even the men look affected. Their faces are a collage of joy, loss, pride and triumph.

Sorry. A little word that means so much.

Sorry. A simple word, but so hard to say.

★

On the school bus, I come straight out with it. I'm surprised by my own guts. But I've tried ignoring things before and I know where that got me.

"I saw you during the Apology. You looked pretty cut up."

Aiden shrugs. He's not embarrassed or defensive. "It was emotional."

"You know anyone who was taken? My dad said it didn't really affect people round here. Well, not the way it did down south."

He packs his iPod away, carefully coiling the headphone lead and tucking it neatly into the front of his school bag. He does it gently, as if packing away the memory of the music along with the equipment. His voice is quiet as he says, "My nan was taken. From the desert."

"Your grandma?"

"She was Luritja. She got rounded up near Alice. They took her to Melbourne, but she moved back to Papunya when she was older. That's where we lived before we moved up here."

I am stunned. I look at Aiden's curly blond hair, hazel eyes. "I didn't know."

"Well, now you do." His tone is friendly. His eyes invite more questions. I accept the invitation. "So you grew up there?"

277

"Mattie and I were two of three white-skinned kids in the whole community. I was convinced that when we turned five we'd all turn black. Don't ask me about the logic of that. My parents were obviously fair."

I grin. "Hey, don't worry. I was so confused when I was little I thought Nona's black might wash off!"

He laughs, and I know he's laughing with me.

I know he understands.

★

I push the cultural centre's door open. The room is empty, apart from Mrs Reid, who is working at her desk. She's so absorbed in whatever's on her computer that she doesn't hear me enter. I knock lightly on the door.

She looks up. "Rosie. You don't have to knock to come in."

"You were working ..."

"Pfft."

She pushes her keyboard to one side and indicates for me to take a seat in front of her. "What can I do you for?"

"I was thinking about that girl ... the one with the baby? Who graduated last year?"

"Marcy."

"Yeah."

"What about her?"

I'm strangely nervous. "Well, I heard that you helped her a lot. Organising child care, being flexible with her studies."

Mrs Reid's eyes flick to my stomach. "Are you ...?"

"No." I'm blushing. "Not me. I was thinking of Nona. She came here last year? Briefly? From Elcho?"

Mrs Reid nods her recognition.

"She's a friend of mine. Well, more than that actually. She's

278

my sister. She wants to be a nurse. Not that she'd come right out and tell you that straight off. But she's wanted to since we were kids. And now with this baby she's started thinking about it again."

"When's she due?"

"I'm not sure. Soon. She's living out at a homeland at the moment, but her grandma said she'll probably move to Ski Beach once the baby's born."

"Have you got her number?" Her eyes are smiling.

I smile back at her. "No, but I can get it."

★

Mum reads out the numbers and I plug them into my phone. New Contact. Nona.

She looks up at me, curious. "Are you going to call her?"

"I don't know."

"You should."

I shrug. I want to but, as always, something holds me back. That familiar puree of shyness, guilt and nerves. What if she doesn't want to talk? What if the whole thing is just awkward? I feel like I've come a long way, but I'm still me. I still hesitate to reach out.

I look at New Contact Nona every few days.

I pass on the number to Mrs Reid, but never dial it myself.

★

Anya and I sit together in the library. At first Selena is an out-of-bounds topic, a bruise that we don't touch. But, gradually, Anya opens up. "It really hurt, you know. I couldn't understand it. I mean, you knew what it was like to lose a friend. All those girls we hung out with in primary school, the ones who moved away. And Nona, you'd lost Nona …"

"That's a bit different."

"It wasn't to me. Years 7 and 8 it was just us. We sat with other people at lunch, but you're the only one I spent time with out of school. And then Selena came and things got weird."

I nod. "It felt like we were competing for her friendship."

Anya looks disbelieving. "Is that what you thought was happening?"

"Well, yeah. You guys were always hanging out, buying clothes together and stuff."

"I only did that because of you … 'cause you seemed to like her so much, I thought maybe if I was more like that …"

I can't believe it. I feel touched and confused. And guilty.

"… but then the whole thing with Nona happened. It was so wrong, that stuff she said in science. I had to tell Mrs Reid …"

I'm stunned. "That was you?"

She nods. "I felt so bad for telling and not owning up. But by then you two were so wrapped up in the boys anyway, you didn't care if I was there or not."

She looks miserable even thinking about it.

I know there is only one thing I can say. "I'm sorry."

She nods her acceptance, seems suddenly nervous. "Hey … do you want to stay over Friday night?"

"At yours?" I'm surprised.

She back-pedals quickly. "Yeah. Just if you want to. I mean, no pressure."

"I'd love to … but I'm busy."

"Oh, that's cool. Doesn't matter."

I can tell she thinks I'm lying. I explain, "Aiden's band's playing. You know East Journey? They're doing a gig on the basketball courts in Yirrkala. You could come, if you want?"

She looks up at me, shy and hopeful. "Yeah?"

"Come to my place first and we'll walk down there together."
Her eyes are shining.

★

Anya's mum drops her at our house. The East Journey concert starts at seven. We stroll across to the basketball court in fading light. The *djäpana* glows red as the sun sinks beneath the horizon. We can hear the jangle of mixed chords and riffs as the band warms up.

As we get closer, I see a small crowd of young kids forming a miniature arc in front of the speakers. A few adults hang back towards the oval. Apart from that, the courts are empty. Still, I have lived here long enough to know they will come.

The band begins to play, the music swelling up into the night. A full moon splits the sky. We sit in darkness: the court and oval lights are still broken. Luckily, someone's rigged up a few makeshift spotlights to illuminate the band.

Aiden squints out towards us. I wave but I don't think he sees.

They're really getting into it now. The sound is louder, fuller, bigger, more embracing. I look around. Sure enough, more people have gathered. By the third song, there are hundreds of dark eyes gleaming, watching alongside us. I can feel their pride. The whole community must be here. A few of the kids grin at me. One tugs on my clothes.

"Hey, Mätjala."

"Mätjala!"

"Ŋarritjan!"

"Hello!"

I see a group of ladies and recognise Rripipi's laughing sister.

I say, *"Nhämirri nhe, Momu?"*

Her eyes smile back at me from the dark. *"Manymak, gaminyarr. Latju, ŋi'?"* Great, no? The music.

I nod agreement and echo the word back at her. *"Latju."*

Anya says, "You know everyone here." Unlike Nick, so long ago now, she sounds impressed. Wistful. Almost jealous. "It must be amazing to be part of this. To be part of a community."

I say, "Yeah. It is."

I realise that I mean it.

The bass is pounding now. I can feel it throbbing through the concrete into the soles of my feet. It reverberates in the base of my ribcage, shaking my heart and everything inside me. I feel linked to these people and this place and these stories.

I look up at the moon and feel its shimmer on my face.

I feel home.

★

Mrs Reid spots me at my locker and approaches, a grin on her face. "Did you hear? Nona's had her baby."

I nod. "Mum called me. But how did you …?"

"We've been in touch, a few times now. I tried to phone her again this morning and – what do you know – she was in hospital. A little girl. Isn't that gorgeous?"

I say, "We're going to see her this afternoon." I don't admit I'm nervous as hell or that I haven't seen her in months.

Mrs Reid smiles. "Say hello from me."

I smile back, trying to look confident. "Will do."

★

I haul myself up onto the grubby vinyl front seat of Mum's troopie and slam the door behind me. Metal grates on metal.

Mum is beaming. "Ready to meet your little *waku*?"

My stomach twists and churns. There are beads of sweat on my forehead. "Mum, are you sure she wants us there? I mean, she's only just given birth and … we go rushing in … Isn't that kind of intrusive?"

"We're family, Rosie."

"I haven't seen her in ages."

"You saw her at the funeral."

"I know but …"

I let the sentence dwindle into silence. I don't think I could articulate the clash of emotions inside me even if I tried.

Mum speaks gently, as if comforting an upset toddler. "She wants you there. Rripipi said for you to come."

★

We park in the hospital car park and enter through the back doors. They swish open automatically at our approach. We climb the blue lino stairs to Ward Two. As we pass the nurses' desk, we see Rripipi up ahead on her phone. She waves us towards a nearby room. "This one."

One, two, three steps, and we're there. No time to back out. The room is full. Three of the beds are occupied by Yolŋu ladies who look like they're in their twenties. One is quietly breastfeeding, another is holding her baby as it sleeps. The third angles past us and walks out the door.

I can't see Nona for the huddle around her bed. Guḻwirri, the smalls, Sheree and Tina and various other aunties are there, all talking animatedly in Yolŋu Matha. I catch sight of the baby in Guḻwirri's arms. She's wearing a miniature pink suit covered in butterflies. Her face is dark brown and squashed, eyes closed, tiny hands bunched in fists. A wisp of new life.

Guḻwirri holds out the precious bundle. I look around and spot Nona perched on the side of her bed, drained but glowing. My eyes ask, *Is this okay?* She nods.

There is so much I want to say. So much I want to tell her.

But I don't get the chance.

The baby is thrust into my arms. I hold her tiny body, gentle and awkward.

I say, "She's beautiful," and I mean it.

I ask, "Does she have a name yet?"

"Ritjilili."

It sounds familiar. "What does it mean?"

Rripipi grins at me. "Muddy water – after my sister."

I start to laugh, then stop quickly as the baby's eyes flick open. Two big brown all-encompassing globes stare up at me. I could swear she's looking into my soul. The world stops.

I hear Mum ask, "Does she have an English name too?"

Nona says, "I called her Rosie."

40.

2001

I see her through the water, bubbles rising from her mouth, lips curved in a smile.

She raises a hand and makes a peace sign, like she's posing for an underwater photo. Her long legs push up and off the bottom of the pool. She jets towards the light above us and surfaces laughing. I come up for air beside her.

She is gasping for breath as she jokes, "When in doubt, peace and pout."

It's her golden rule for photos lately. I think one of her cousins made it up. I grin as I tread water beside her.

She holds out a skinny, brown arm. "Look. Goosebumps."

"Want to get out?"

"Ma'." She hauls herself up and flops onto the edge of the pool. She is wearing a wet black T-shirt and shorts. I pull myself up behind her, tugging at my red one-piece, making sure it covers my bum. Her feet are so close they dance in my face.

I close my eyes, feeling happy. Whole.

Then I hear her voice. "Your mum booked the plane. I leave tomorrow."

I plummet back to earth. "Why do you have to go?"

Her hand traces imaginary patterns on the surface of the water. "I miss my family."

I can't hide my hurt. "I thought I was your *yapa*."

"You are. Always will be. That will never change."

I want to believe her, but things are already changing and I know they'll change more. The thought frightens me. I search for reasons to make her stay. "But ... what about school?"

"They have a school over there too, silly."

"Are you going to go?"

Nona's shrug ripples from her shoulders to her toes.

"I thought you were going to be a nurse. You can't do that if you don't go to school."

"Maybe I'll be rockstar instead."

I lift my head and see her grin. It stretches from ear to ear. I smile and rest my cheek back against the warm tiles.

We lie there, one behind the other.

Two bodies rendered colourless, silhouetted by the sun.

We could be anyone, anywhere.

We are just two girls.

Sisters.

Nona and me.

Acknowledgements

It would not have been possible to write this book without the help of Merrkiyawuy Ganambarr-Stubbs, who shared her knowledge, expertise and time. She was among the first to hear the idea for the novel, and the last to proofread the finished manuscript. *Wirrki ŋarra marr-ŋamathina.*

For anyone who wants to learn more about Yolŋu culture, I recommend the book *Welcome to My Country* by Laklak Burarrwanga and her family. Thank you to Laklak for permission to adapt material for one of my chapters, and for allowing me to use Bawaka as Bolu's homeland.

Heartfelt gratitude to Dhängaḻ Gurruwiwi, Djalu Gurruwiwi and Dopiya Yunupiŋu, my *wäwa* Yotjiŋ and their family for adopting me and inviting me and my family to share many amazing experiences. Their friendship and generosity has been, in many ways, the inspiration for this story. They also allowed me to use Gikal as Stretch's homeland.

Many people shared their stories of living in Yirrkala and Nhulunbuy, helping to bring Rosie and Nona and their families to life. Thanks to Abigail White, Scott Beverstock,

Yalmay Yunupiŋu, Tara Canobie, Kate Smith, Andrea Campbell, Stuart Kellaway, Will Stubbs, Annie Studd, Beŋgitj Ŋurruwuthun, Barbara Taylor, Melissa Kennedy, Andrea Kingston, Kathryn McMahon, Claire Rafferty, Mark Tanner, Imogen Louise and Sherri Hedges, Katrina Hudson and Leila Dunn, Rarriwuy Marika and Robyn Beecham.

Those who read drafts of the novel made it stronger, and more rounded and real. Samanti Desilva, Ros Wheatley, Abigail White, Melanie Herdman, Annabel Davis, Kaneana May, Jarvis Ryan, David Curzon and Pip Atkins – this book would not be what it is today without your thoughts, suggestions and encouragement.

Thank you to the women at Yirrkala childcare – Lisita Taulani, Fatai Fainga'a, Karishma Patel, Kristina Ateli Miorin and Margie Saukuru – for looking after my children so lovingly, giving me time to write.

Yalmay Yunupiŋu, Mushroom Records and Sony generously allowed me to use the lyrics from the Yothu Yindi song "Treaty", and the members of East Journey let me borrow the name of their group for Aiden's band.

My agent, Elizabeth Troyeur, and Jeanne Ryckmans from Black Inc. believed in this book even when it was still a work in progress. It was a pleasure to work with Nikola Lusk, who guided me through the editing process with skill and sensitivity.

Thank you to my mum and dad for always encouraging me to follow my passions. To my wonderful husband, Jarvis, for sharing the crazy ride that is life, and always being on my team. And finally to my children, Louis, Rosa and Nina, for their love and laughter, and for making me wonder, *What would your lives be like if you grew up in Yirrkala?*